WAYNE STINNETT

MAN
OVERBOARD

A JESSE MCDERMITT NOVEL

Caribbean Adventure Series
Volume 23

DOWN ISLAND PRESS

Library of Congress cataloging-in-publication Data
Stinnett, Wayne
Man Overboard/Wayne Stinnett
p. cm. - (A Jesse McDermitt novel)
ISBN: 978-1-956026-59-7
Cover and graphics by Aurora Publicity
Edited by Marsha Zinberg, The Write Touch
Final Proofreading by Donna Rich
Interior Design by Aurora Publicity
Down Island Press, LLC

If you'd like to receive my newsletter, please sign up on my website.

WWW.WAYNESTINNETT.COM.

Once a month, I'll bring you insights into my private life and writing habits, with updates on what I'm working on, special deals I hear about, and new books by other authors that I'm reading.

The Jerry Snyder Caribbean Mystery Series

Wayward Sons

The Charity Styles Caribbean Thriller Series

Merciless Charity	Enduring Charity
Ruthless Charity	Vigilant Charity
Reckless Charity	Lost Charity
Enduring Charity	Elusive Charity
	Forced Charity

The Jesse McDermitt Caribbean Adventure Series

Fallen Out	Rising Force
Fallen Palm	Rising Charity
Fallen Hunter	Rising Water
Fallen Pride	Rising Spirit
Fallen Mangrove	Rising Thunder
Fallen King	Rising Warrior
Fallen Honor	Rising Moon
Fallen Tide	Rising Tide
Fallen Angel	Steady As She Goes
Fallen Hero	All Ahead Full
Rising Storm	Man Overboard
Rising Fury	Cast Off

The Gaspar's Revenge Ship's Store is open.

There, you can purchase all kinds of swag related to my books. You can find it at

WWW.GASPARS-REVENGE.COM

To all my friends, cohorts, and associates at Tropical Authors. We have only each other to blame. I'm looking forward to some great things coming out of our motley band of miscreants, boat bums, and bubble heads. Always remember, when life's events conspire to toss you overboard, you're not alone.

"I wanna take your boat as far as it goes
Feel Jamaican sand between my toes
I wanna ride on the wind just as far as I can
I won't be any trouble at all
I can sleep anywhere at all
And I don't eat very much
For a Hollow Man"
– The Boat Drunks

Jesse's island in the Content Keys

Everglades

To Miami

Gulf of Mexico

Flamingo

Key Largo

FLORIDA KEYS

Jesse's Island

Islamorada

Florida Straits

Marathon

Big Pine Key

Rusty Anchor Bar and Grill

Key West

The Florida Keys

CHAPTER ONE

May 5, 2022
Coco Plum, Marathon, Florida Keys

From his living room window, using a pair of powerful binoculars, Robert Grant could see boats out on the water over fifteen miles away. He knew this because he'd looked it up when the Realtor who'd sold him the property had told him the building could be seen for over ten miles.

Robert was a numbers guy—had been since he was a child. Where artists could see subtle variations in shape, color, and hue, he could visualize digits and how they related to and interacted with one another. He'd excelled in math when he was in school, so much so that he often found the lessons tedious and boring. Frequently, when his fourth-grade teacher demonstrated how to do a multiplication problem on the chalk board, Robert had spouted the answer as soon as she'd drawn the line under the pair of stacked integers.

So, instead of taking the Realtor's claim at face value, he'd asked what the building's height was and how high above sea level the ground was on which it had been built. Then he'd looked up the actual geometric formula and found that the distance to the horizon

in miles was equal to the square root of one-and-a-half times the viewer's height in feet.

Bonefish Tower Condo was 170 feet tall, the tallest building in the Florida Keys, and the land it was built on was ten feet above sea level, putting the roof a staggering 180 feet above the water. That was extremely high for the hurricane-prone stretch of islands at the southern tip of the state, but the building had already weathered a number of them.

Grant had bought the penthouse suite, though he'd found the Realtor to be an imbecile. The floor of his new condo was about twelve feet below the roof and at six feet tall, standing in his living room, his eyes were roughly 174 feet above sea level, meaning the horizon was just over sixteen miles away.

Artists knew color, Realtors knew curb appeal, but Robert Grant knew numbers.

It was his fascination with mathematics that had led him to how he earned his living. Having graduated from Clemson University with a bachelor's degree in finance, he'd set his sights on retiring by age fifty. To that end, he'd worked hard, ignoring all the social norms for a young man right out of college.

He'd graduated just before the turn of the century, about the time computer engineers were starting to realize there was a huge problem looming on the horizon—Y2K.

By then, personal computers, or PCs, had been in widespread use for over ten years, and large companies and organizations like NASA had been using computers since Robert's father was a child. But computer manufacturers had overlooked one small detail during all that time. Dates were entered with a two-digit format for the year. Society had simply dropped the nineteen from any given year. Robert had been born in '75 and had graduated college in '97.

His final report card had been dated 4/24/97, one week before commencement.

During his final year of college, Robert's roommate had been a computer engineering major. During their last semester as seniors, Robert was inputting data on his computer, creating a thirty-year amortization table, when he looked up and asked Bill how a computer could tell the difference between the years 1927 and 2027.

His roommate looked up with a knowing grin, ready to school the finance whiz on the world of computers. Then his mouth had slowly fallen open.

Now, at forty-seven, Robert Grant had amassed a large fortune, mostly through stock trading and investments. He drove a German-engineered car and lived and worked higher than anyone for almost a hundred miles. He also owned an estate in the U.S. Virgin Islands, a mountain retreat in North Carolina, and several office buildings in California, where property values rose higher than the buildings. Many of his properties were leveraged to the hilt, waiting on financing from a South American company which at first had seemed keen to invest. So, he'd made the investment for them, certain the deal was golden.

Robert looked up from his desk in his home office. He stared out the window for a moment, marveling at the varying shades of blue stretched out before him. The sea was calm and changed from a turquoise color close to shore to dark indigo farther out. The sky likewise moved from pale blue near the horizon to brilliant cerulean high above.

The investors would come through. The prospectus he'd sent them was simply too compelling not to. Once it was over, he'd have no further dealings with them. But today wasn't about business. Several months ago, Grant had decided he needed a change in his

personal life.

He had everything he'd ever wanted. Or he would have. Once the South American businessmen he'd brokered—and actually financed—the deal for, came through with the promised investment, his assets would be free and clear again, and his coffers replenished.

He could easily retire then and live an extremely comfortable life on the interest from his investments.

But Robert had nobody to share it with. He'd never married and had no children. He'd considered such things a distraction from his ultimate goal. He'd overshot his mark, forsaking all else to become wealthy, without considering what would come after.

So, he'd done the logical thing. He'd turned to his computer to find someone to share his lifestyle with—or what he considered his new lifestyle would be once he stopped working from dawn to dusk, seven days a week. And once the South American investors wired him the money, he needed to keep from losing a huge chunk of his holdings. He knew the investment was good—beyond good, in fact. He couldn't understand why they were dragging their collective heels. So, he'd gone ahead and made the investment for them, leveraging his own assets and severely over-extending his ability to pay.

It was a leap of faith.

The prospect of not working had frightened him at first. He'd worked all his life. The hope of finding someone to show him how to live the rest of it seemed daunting. He'd approached it in the same way he did everything—analytically. He'd joined a few dating sites on the Internet and interviewed potential mates as he would a new secretary, by inviting them to his office first, just to see if there was any common ground. His latest guest was due any minute.

The phone on his desk buzzed and he picked it up. "Grant

Holdings."

"Um, hello," a woman's voice said, in slightly accented English. "I am Katya Popova. I am to meet Robert Grant."

"Go to the last elevator," Robert directed. "I'll open the door for you."

He hung up the phone and pushed a button on a small box next to it. A yellow light came on, indicating the elevator door was opening. A moment later, the light turned red, letting him know the private elevator car was in motion. On the ground floor, a key was needed to open the door and there were no buttons for individual floors. His elevator stopped only on the ground floor and his living room.

Closing a ledger book and his laptop, Robert rose from his desk and walked around it into his living room. The young woman he was about to meet for the first time would be the seventh such candidate.

He'd dismissed the first six within a few appointments, each having some flaw or another—too tall, too short, too heavy, too skinny, but mostly they'd been after money. Robert could have a $1000-a-visit call girl every night if that was all he wanted. Nearly half were like the woman coming up in the elevator, foreign women looking for a husband so they could remain in the country. Robert couldn't find fault with that, but they had to bring a lot more to the table than just a desire for citizenship.

When the elevator door whisked open, Robert found himself looking at an exceptionally attractive blonde almost as tall as he was. She wore an expensive-looking blue silk blouse, open at the neck, but not too revealing, and navy slacks with a razor-sharp crease. Her height was mostly natural, but the two-inch heels on her feet helped. Her hair framed an exquisite face, with full lips, an aquiline nose, and eyes the color of Arctic ice.

Her bio on the dating site had said that Katya Popova was born in the Czech Republic in 1990, making her thirty-two years old—fifteen years younger than himself. She'd immigrated to the United States with her parents at the age of fourteen and moved from Connecticut to South Florida just three years ago.

"Good afternoon," he said, stepping forward and extending his hand. "I'm Robert Grant."

The fingers that took his were long and slender, her grip firm and sure. The nails were long, but not excessively so, and well-manicured with a neutral-colored polish.

"I am pleased to meet you," she said, stepping out of the elevator. "I am Katya."

They'd exchanged a few messages through the website, which soon became private emails, and then a couple of lengthy phone calls. She'd cleared the last bar during the most recent call, when she'd told him that she had been an American citizen since the age of twenty-one, seven years after arriving in the country. He didn't have to worry about her being someone just looking for an easy ticket to citizenship.

"Please come in," Robert said, waving a hand toward the seating area in his expansive living room.

"Thank you," she said, moving toward the floor-to-ceiling sliding glass doors, which opened onto a well-appointed terrace. "Your view is magnificent. I do not see how you can do any work here."

Robert stared at her from behind. She moved with the grace of a gazelle, a slower version of a runway model's catwalk. She was obviously comfortable in heels. She was slim but curvy in all the right places.

She turned and faced him, clasping her hands together. "May I

speak openly, Robert?"

He smiled. "I hope that you will."

"I have my own money," she said bluntly. "I am not looking for dates or a sugar daddy. Nor am I interested in sex with just anyone."

"I'll be equally frank," he responded, smiling. He liked her open, straight-forward attitude. "I am only interested in finding someone who is looking for a lifetime commitment and children. If either of those is off the table, we can say goodbye here and not waste each other's time."

A slow smile spread across her face, revealing perfect teeth. "I like a man who knows what he wants. These are things I too want, and I have met a string of men before you, Robert Grant."

CHAPTER TWO

July 5, 2022
Yucatan Strait

It was a dark and stormy night. Sure, that sounded clichéd and corny as all hell, but it was the only way to describe *this* one. It was always dark at night, so yeah, I guess maybe that part was redundant, but in the middle of a tropical depression, with low-scudding clouds blotting out sky and driving rain hiding everything behind a silvery veil, it was especially dark; the kind of night when a person could marvel at the awesome power of nature.

The wind howled at thirty knots, with gusts up to fifty, seas were running upward of fifteen feet, and lightning was flashing all across the sky. The storm raged, trying to get its act together enough to warrant getting a name.

It wasn't a good night to be out in a boat but that's just where I was.

Not just any boat, mind you, but a 199-foot custom-built yacht converted for oceanographic research. And *Ambrosia* was far from an ordinary yacht; she was way faster than most any yacht her size. With her work platform at the stern lowered to water level and locked, she was 215 feet, overall. But no amount of speed could've helped us

avoid the storm.

The night bridge crew consisted of Axel Troutman at the helm, straining his eyes to see ahead, Ross Mosely at navigation, who mostly watched the instruments and electronics, and Giselle Lopez, assistant yeoman, who watched us and tried to anticipate our needs.

Being barely five feet tall, Giselle couldn't quite reach the overhead grab rails, one of which I kept a firm grip on. Instead, she held onto the back of the helm and nav seats, which were locked into position.

The deck wasn't pitching wildly, but there was no rhythm to the waves as the storm intensified, sending towering walls of water in all directions like a washing machine.

We'd been heading north at twenty knots in the Yucatan Channel, having transited the Panama Canal two days earlier, when the storm blew up out of nowhere, the low forming right on top of us. We had to slow to ten knots as the storm moved slowly eastward, and we pressed on to the north.

I knew eventually we'd escape the wind and the waves it was kicking up. But first we had to ride it out.

There were many ways to ride out a storm. The best would be in a protected harbor, the boat tied securely to a dock, while you watched the reports on a hotel TV. Caught at sea, a powerboat could turn into the wind to take the brunt of the waves on the bow. A sailboat would have to reduce sails or dowse them altogether and switch to engine power to turn into the wind and waves. A sea anchor could be deployed, which was like a small, heavy-duty parachute that is dragged in the water from the bow. It could keep a boat heading into the wind without any power.

But *Ambrosia* was large enough that we could fairly ignore the storm and continue as we were, just at a slower speed. It'd have to get

a lot worse before we'd be forced to heave to.

Wipers cleared the windshield, but with the rain falling so hard, and the darkness so complete, the foredeck was only visible when lightning flashed very near.

Just then, it did, followed almost instantly by a loud boom.

Ross's head jerked up from his console. "Whoa! That was close."

The flash of lightning revealed a large rogue wave rising up ahead of us. They were called rogues because they were rare: actually, two or more waves, combining or colliding to create one short-lived wave that was much bigger than either contributor. This one was twenty feet if it was an inch.

"Hang on," I said, calmly but loudly, as the bow sprang up and the wave crested over it.

The sudden pitch of the bow caused Giselle to lose her grip on the seats, throwing her backward. I caught her around the waist as she stumbled and pulled her close to steady us both. I grimaced at the added weight, trying to remain upright, while holding onto the overhead grabrail with one hand.

The bow pierced the wave near its crest and seawater washed back over the sun pad area, rolling off the foredeck through scuppers. The forward part of the ship hung out over the trough for a moment, then the bow came back down as the wave lifted the ship and passed beneath. We slid into the trough, only to rise again to meet the next wave.

I shifted my grip forward on the overhead monkey bar, pulling Giselle back to where she could reach the chairs again.

She looked up at me, her expression communicating both thrill and concern.

"We'll be fine," I assured her. "*Ambrosia's* been through worse."

She smiled and returned to her position. The rest of the crew

had been restricted to quarters when the storm started, so the only ones I had to concern myself with were the three with me on the bridge. Had anyone been out on the foredeck, they'd have been swept away and probably lost at sea. Trying to find a person's head bobbing in waves as tall as a house would be nearly impossible.

We continued northward for another twenty minutes when suddenly, the rain stopped, and I could see whitecaps stretching far ahead of us.

They no longer looked quite so tall.

I stepped over to the port hatch and looked up through the window. It was a new moon night, so the sky was dark, but I could see thousands of stars among a smattering of trailing clouds.

"Don't like the weather in the tropics?" I asked rhetorically. "Just wait an hour."

My voice sounded loud without the pelting rain accompanying it.

"That was one heck of a storm," Axel said. "Reckon it'll get a name? They've already used Alex and Bonnie."

I grinned. Though it'd been seventeen years since my third wife was killed on our wedding night, hearing her name always brought back fond memories. Memories that I should have felt guilty about since I was now married for a fourth time. But I allowed myself that vice.

Over the next hour, the waves started to diminish, and we increased speed to twenty knots, *Ambrosia's* most economical speed. It took a lot of energy to move the vessel through the water. At twenty knots the two main diesel engines each burned more than a hundred gallons of fuel every hour, ten gallons per nautical mile. They burned less at a slower speed, but at a higher rate per mile. With thirty thousand gallons on board, *Ambrosia* had a range of over twenty-five hundred nautical miles, keeping a twenty percent fuel

reserve.

Finally, the sea state settled as we moved farther away from the storm, and I was able to end crew restrictions. Not that it mattered—it was nearly midnight, and few of the crew would be up. Everyone on board knew if they were restricted to quarters, they should try to sleep.

I heard footsteps on the spiral staircase and looked over to see my first mate, Matt Brand, coming up.

"Hope you were able to get some sleep," I said.

"Oye, was a bit rolly there for a bit," he replied in his piratical Cornish accent. "Was fine once I drifted off, mind. Reminded me when I was a lad on me granfer's crab boat."

"We're clear of any foul weather," I said. "The storm's moving off to the east to bother Cuba. Not much else to report—we haven't seen a ship in hours."

"Go get some rest then, yeah? I'll see ya at sunup."

Since Matt was now also a sea captain of unlimited tonnage, and would soon command *Ambrosia*, we'd relaxed our watches, taking six hours each night, with Val, Axel, or Ross in control for most of the day.

"You have the conn," I said, letting the others on the bridge know that Matt was now in control of the vessel.

I went through the hatch in the aft corner of the bridge, next to the operations center, and strode down the long interior passageway to my quarters.

When I entered, Finn was waiting to greet me. I squatted to his level and wrapped an arm over his shoulder, patting him on his chest and flank as he squirmed excitedly in my bear hug.

"How you doing, old buddy?" I asked as we tussled a little. "Did you take care of things while I was gone?"

Finn replied by lifting his head and licking the side of my face.

"He wouldn't go to sleep," Savannah said, standing by our stateroom hatch in a thin, white T-shirt that barely covered her hips. "I think he was worried about you being outside in the storm."

As I stood, Finn rolled onto his side, atop my feet, his thick tail beating the deck. "Completely dry," I said, and bent to rub his belly for a second before pulling my feet out from under his side and stepping over him.

"That was quite a storm," Savannah said, coming toward me. "Or are we in the eye?"

"No, it's moving off to the east," I replied, tossing my cover on the table. "Seas are diminishing. How's Alberto?"

"He stayed up late and watched the storm through the sliding door," she replied, stepping into my arms.

Glancing at my watch, I saw that it was after midnight. "Happy birthday," I said burying my face in her neck and hair as we swayed together with the *Ambrosia's* movements. There was a faint smell of coconut there, one of my favorite scents.

"When do you go back on duty?" she asked.

Our watch schedule was posted on the Metis tablet, and I saw one on the table by my hat. She knew our routine.

"Not until zero nine," I replied. "Got something in mind?"

She stepped out of my embrace, then took my hand, leading me toward the stateroom. "Nine hours? It's my birthday. I think I can come up with an idea or two."

CHAPTER THREE

I could hear Alberto laughing when I woke up. The door to our stateroom was closed and I was alone. Then I heard Savannah shush him. Getting up, I went over to the small dresser and got a pair of clean boxers from my drawer. Then I went into our private head for a quick shower. Ten minutes after waking, I was dressed and stepping out of the door into our living area.

"Oh, good, you're up," Savannah said.

"Most of me is," I offered as a reply, as I crossed the little galley to the coffee maker.

I poured a mug, took a sip, and turned around. Savannah and Alberto were at the dinette and Finn was sitting on the floor beside them.

"So, what are we doing this morning?" I asked.

"It's only an hour before you have to take over on the bridge," Savannah replied.

I looked at my watch and confirmed that it was 0800. I'm usually an early riser, up before the sun. Savannah and Alberto were also. I hadn't even heard her when she got up.

"We've been up for two hours," Alberto said. "But Mom said we had to be quiet because you had a really hard night."

Savannah blushed slightly. "It was a terrible storm. I'm sure it must have drained him."

"Yeah," I replied with a conspiratorial grin. "Drained and sore. All that bouncing around just about did me in."

"It's Mom's birthday and she's fifty-one!"

"Yes, she is," I replied, bending over and kissing her cheek. "But she still looks the same as the day we met."

"When was that?" he asked.

"Almost twenty-one years ago," Savannah replied.

He studied her face for a moment, then turned to me. "You're wrong," he stated flatly. "She doesn't even look close to thirty."

"Why, thank you," she said, hugging him tightly.

I noticed the Metis tablet in front of him. "Where are we right now?"

He looked up at me and smiled. "Two hundred and thirty nautical miles west-southwest of Key West."

I looked up and pretended to think. "Hmm, I think that's just about where we turn and make our run through Cuban waters."

"The waypoint's ten miles ahead," he announced proudly.

"Then we'd best get a move on," I said. "We don't want to be late for your mom's party. Want to go up to the bridge with me?"

"Yeah!" he exclaimed, then looked over at Savannah.

She smiled at him. "For an hour or two. But once we're in U.S. waters, I want you back here for your lessons."

Alberto had just turned ten two weeks earlier. His birthday, like mine, usually falls on a celestial date—his on the summer solstice, the longest day of the year, and mine on the vernal equinox, the day in the spring when day and night are equal. He was an unusually smart kid and often surprised us with his sharp wit and keen knowledge of the world around him. He was like a sponge, soaking up information at an alarmingly fast rate.

Savannah and I had adopted Alberto just over a year ago, after

his mother had been killed in a gang-related incident up in Fort Myers and he'd been set adrift in a small boat. Since then, he'd learned a lot from the two of us, as well as from Mayra Santiago, a former schoolteacher and the wife of the ship's chef. She tutored her own grandson, Fernando, as well as helping with Alberto. The boys were the only kids on the boat.

"Go get some shoes on," I told him.

He hurried into his room as I finished my coffee.

"Make sure he comes back by ten o'clock," Savannah said. "Mayra and Fernando are coming up for math lessons."

"That should be just enough time," I said, as Alberto rejoined us. "You ready?"

"Oye, Cap'n," he replied, trying to mimic Matt's Cornish accent, but his voice cracked just a little, something I'd noticed a couple of times in the past week. He was reaching that awkward adolescent stage, so it was to be expected.

Savannah and I both laughed.

"Give the admiral a hug, Swab," I told him.

He dutifully hugged her and then we left for the bridge, Finn trotting along ahead of us. When we reached the hatch, Finn stopped and looked back, waiting.

"No opposable thumbs, huh?" Alberto asked him, a line I'm afraid he picked up from me.

He pushed the lever down and shoved the hatch open.

"*Mytten da*, Cap'n," Matt said. "Weren't expectin' ya for another hour, yeah?"

"*Mytten da*," I replied, returning the Cornish morning greeting. "What're you still doing here?"

"Such a lovely morn," he said, giving me a knowing look. "I called down and told Val to take her time. She's below bringing up

17

some lunch."

"We had nothing better to do," I said, knowing why he'd stayed on past his six-hour watch. "I figured we'd start the day early."

"We're comin' up on our easterly turn," he said. "If you've still a mind to cross this far south."

"It's four hours up to the northern tip of Cuba's claim," I said. "Then another four back to where we'd be in just half an hour by crossing that spur at fifty knots."

"We're three hundred miles from port and a hundred from Cuba."

I knew what he was saying. Cuba claimed a slice of the southern Gulf of Mexico, an area of water about thirty miles wide, extending north-northwest from the western tip of the island nation for over a hundred miles. There were a few small fishing villages along that part of Cuba's coast, but nothing that warranted a maritime claim on that much water.

By cutting across the spur, we'd be in waters they claimed for only about half an hour, but after that, we'd still be twelve hours from Marathon, our destination.

"Make the turn, Matt," I said, knowing this was the reason he was still on duty.

Alberto headed over beside Bernie Knight at the nav station and Finn followed dutifully.

"Aye, Cap'n," Matt said. Then he turned to Kris Carter. "Make your course zero-seven-zero degrees, helm."

"Seventy degrees, aye," Kris repeated, turning the big destroyer wheel a quarter turn to the right. He held it there for a moment as the bow came around and the rising sun moved directly in front of us, then brought the wheel back to center and said, "Zero-seven-zero degrees."

MAN OVERBOARD

Matt pushed the button on the intercom for the engine room. "Bridge to engineering. Bring the turbines online, Mister Silva."

"Give me a couple minutes and I'll pass the controls to the helm," came Heitor Silva's reply.

"As soon as you get the green light," Matt said to Kris, "engage the turbines and bring our speed up to fifty knots."

To starboard, Alberto had donned a headset and was listening to the surrounding water intently. He often spent time with Bernie or Ross, listening for whale sounds. He'd become quite adept at identifying them.

Finn sat just behind them, looking out the port hatch. Of everyone on board, I think he was most anxious to reach dry land.

We'd been at sea in the area of the Galapagos Islands for two weeks before coming through the Panama Canal. Finn had a little grass patch on the stern, but it was nothing compared to running from palm tree to palm tree on our island.

I wanted to get home, as well. I wanted to take my little flats skiff out into the backcountry with just Savannah and Alberto. I wanted the quiet and solitude. I was looking forward to being home for a while.

We'd be in Marathon for a week, but *Ambrosia* was only scheduled to be there for a couple of days. Then Matt would take her on to Bimini, where she'd be put in dry dock for a month, undergoing some minor retrofitting and electronics upgrades.

Savannah, Alberto, and I would fly to Bimini the following week, then spend the rest of July and most of August flying crew, technicians, and parts in and out as we readied *Phoenix* for her first sea trial.

It was hard to believe, but in just a few weeks, I'd be in command of a long-range, nuclear-powered research vessel.

CHAPTER FOUR

Two men sat at a table in the back room of an upscale downtown Miami restaurant, both clean shaven and dressed in expensive tailored suits. One man was about sixty, his dark hair flecked with gray, and the other was still in his thirties, with sandy, shoulder-length hair just covering his ears.

At such an early hour, there were no other diners in the restaurant and a server stood off to the side, hands clasped in front of her, waiting to be beckoned for anything the two men might desire.

"You're promising a lot," the younger of the two men said. "How do I know you can deliver?"

"My people can do anything," Mike Spencer replied. "You want to disappear, it can happen. A whole new identity awaits you."

"There are...certain people trying to find me. The kind of people who won't stop just because I disappeared."

"Would they stop if you were dead?" Spencer asked, his voice low. "That would be the ultimate vanishing act, and one I have arranged several other times."

"How do you—?"

The elder man raised a hand to head off the question. "That's something you don't want to know anything about. Rest assured,

there will be no doubt that you met an untimely end."

The younger man thought for a moment as he chewed his food. Finally, he put his fork down. "Then there's the whole 'where does my money go' thing. It's one thing to start over and a whole different thing to start over with nothing."

"That's actually the easy part," Spencer said, tenting his fingers and leaning forward. "You have access to it and my company has a numbered account in the Caymans. We will help you liquidate all your assets and holdings, then transfer it all into the numbered account in Grand Cayman. That's when my technicians go to work. They will break it up, move it around to hundreds of different numbered accounts in Switzerland, Singapore, Luxembourg, Ireland, Monaco, Hong Kong, and Lebanon. This all takes place in a matter of seconds. Then it all goes back together, in hundreds of small deposits, into a bank account under your new name. As I've said before, the amount is always equal to your initial transfer, down to the penny. Minus ten percent, of course."

"And you say you've done this before?"

A woman with sun-streaked blond hair came into the back area, walking straight toward the two men's table. Spencer rose and took both her hands, kissing her lightly on the cheek.

"Katya, allow me to introduce you to Mr. Smythe," Spencer said, then turned to his guest. "This is my wife, Katya Popova."

Smythe rose and shook hands with one of the most beautiful women he'd ever laid eyes on. "A pleasure," he said.

"I trust that Mike has given you all the answers you wanted?" Katya asked.

She had a trace of some East European accent Smythe couldn't quite place. He looked over at Spencer, who pulled a chair out for his wife and smiled as she slid seductively onto the chair, smoothing the

back of her skirt as she sat down.

"Katya is an integral part of my organization," Spencer said, then turned to her.

She smiled at her husband, then turned an appraising eye on Smythe. "I have read over your bio and psychological evaluation. I do not think that name suits you at all. You look like a two-syllable man to me, something rugged to complement your look. Mason, perhaps. Or Lockwood?"

Smythe looked back at Spencer. "I still don't get why I had to talk to a psychologist."

"You have had many years to become the man you are today," Spencer said.

"Your old name suits you," Katya added. "You have grown into it. A new identity must be aligned with the new man you will become."

"Katya will accompany you on your journey," Spencer said. "She will be your 'mail-order bride' in this new life we will create. A single man of thirty-eight would draw attention. Why is he still single? What's wrong with him?"

"My wife?"

"For a short time—a month or two, until you are settled and established. Then you will have a terrible fight and she will fly home to Czechia. People will forget the mysterious part of your arrival and gossip only about how they think you were...what's the word?"

"Catfished," Katya said, smiling. "I love that word. I will be your Internet wife, who swindles you into marriage to get to America. It is all over television, *90-Day* this and *90-Day* that. My actions with your new friends in your new community will be talked about for years and you will be viewed as an unfortunate sucker. Then you will be killed in a horrible accident, where your body is left

unrecognizable."

She pointed at the expensive Rolex on his wrist. "The body will be wearing your watch and in your car. The height and weight will be correct, and dental records substituted electronically. It is foolproof, no?"

"Where's the body come from?" Smythe asked, thinking the whole thing a bit more gruesome than he'd planned.

"Do not worry," Katya said. "The morgue here is full of unclaimed bodies."

"What about an autopsy? Any body in the morgue has probably been embalmed or something."

"An autopsy on a car wreck victim is very rare," Spencer said. "Trust me, we know what we're doing. This will work."

Smythe looked over at the perfect blonde. "You've done this kind of thing before."

"Several times," she said, reassuring him by putting her hand on his. "We will make a good couple, I think."

Spencer wiped his mouth with a linen napkin and rose. "I really must go," he said. "I have a meeting with another client across town. So, I will leave you in Katya's capable hands. She will provide you with the rest of the details."

Smythe stood and shook hands with him, then sat back down as Spencer walked out. He glanced at Katya, and she smiled, making him feel even more uncomfortable.

"Do not worry," she said. "Mike knows what he is doing. You are in good hands with us."

"You pretend to be another man's wife," Smythe said, choosing his words carefully. "And your husband is okay with that?"

She pulled her hair around the left side of her face and let it dangle over her shoulder, looking him straight in the eyes. "How old

do you think my husband is?"

"I don't know. Sixty, maybe?"

"Very close," she said, her smile radiant. "He is sixty-one and I am nearly half that."

"What's your point?" Smythe asked.

"A man reaches his prime, sexually, in his early twenties," she replied. "Did you know that?"

"I've heard that mentioned," he replied, becoming even more uncomfortable.

She leaned closer and put a warm hand on his thigh. "Women, on the other hand, do not reach their peak until forty. I still have many years to go. So, my husband and I...well...we have an understanding. A lucrative understanding."

CHAPTER FIVE

The light on the engine controls changed from red to green. Kris moved the turbine's impeller controls to forward, then moved all four engine controls together up to about three-quarter throttle.

There was a noticeable increase in speed and *Ambrosia* quickly accelerated past thirty knots. A moment later, the imaginary line on the chart plotter appeared ahead of the icon representing our location.

"Forty knots, SOG," Kris said just a minute later, checking the chart plotter and its speed-over-ground display. Then a moment after that, "forty-five," he announced.

As the ship approached fifty knots, he pulled back slightly on the throttle controls. We had at least a two-knot current at our stern, as the Yucatan Current helped carry us northward to join the much larger Gulf Stream.

"Fifty knots, SOG," Kris reported.

"All eyes forward," Matt said, as Val McLarin came up the steps with a tray of breakfast and lunch sandwiches.

She put the tray on the counter and silently joined us, looking ahead.

"Nothing on radar for thirty nautical miles," Bernie advised.

"Let's hope it stays that way," I said, noting that we'd crossed the

line and were now in Cuban waters.

Alberto listened on the headphones and watched the radar screen, occasionally lifting his chin and standing on his toes to see out the windshield.

Giselle would be going off duty soon. Val had arranged the younger woman's schedule, so she'd be on the bridge with her during the morning watch and then spend part of the night watch with me. But for now, the more eyes looking forward, the better.

At fifty knots, *Ambrosia* traveled the length of a football field in three seconds. Most boats *would* appear on our radar, but the Florida Strait was notorious for small rafts—Cuban people trying to escape to America. Even the best radar wouldn't pick up some of the smaller ones.

Our transit across Cuban waters lasted twenty-eight anxious minutes.

"Still nothing on radar," Bernie said. "And we just crossed into American waters!"

"Make your speed twenty knots, helm," Matt told Kris.

Alberto pulled his headphones down and let them hang around his neck. "We're home already?"

"Home waters," I replied. "But we won't be in Vaca Key Bight for about eleven more hours."

"It'll be dark when we get there?"

"Just about," I replied. "We should drop anchor just in time for sunset. You have work to do, don't you?"

He hung up his headset without question or debate, said goodbye to everyone, then went back through the interior hatch toward our quarters with Finn.

As Axel came up the spiral staircase, *Ambrosia* began to slow until Kris adjusted the throttles and announced, "Twenty knots, Mr.

Brand."

"Steady on course zero-seven-zero."

"Ahead steady," Kris replied, then got up from the helm seat and turned to Axel. "She's all yours."

As Axel took the helm seat, a loud, ripping sound suddenly split the air, and a jet fighter streaked past our bow, then climbed almost vertically.

"*Aree faa!*" Matt shouted in surprise, ducking instinctively.

The dual tails with twin jet engines between them told me all I needed to know. "I have the conn, Matt," I said loudly. "Flank speed, helm."

I pushed the ship-wide intercom button. "All hands, this is the captain. Aside from those on the bridge, please move quickly to your cabins and stay there."

I didn't explain why—everyone on board heard the MiG-29 as it screeched past, not more than thirty feet off the surface of the water.

Ross hurried up the steps and moved over behind Bernie.

"Maximum radar," I said to Bernie. "Ross, get Homestead on the horn and let them know we were just buzzed by a MiG-29M, armed with air-to-air and air-to-surface missiles. Give them our location, heading and speed, and request assistance."

Both men responded and got to work.

"Where'd that bugger go?" Matt said, staring up into the sky in the direction the jet had disappeared.

The VHF crackled with static as *Ambrosia* gathered speed. I could just make out a man speaking Spanish but couldn't tell what he was saying. The radio was on Channel Sixteen, the international hailing and distress frequency.

"Surface contact," Bernie said. "Twenty-two nautical miles, bearing one-eight-five. It's a powerboat, heading toward us at thirty-

one knots."

"Can you tell what kind of boat?" I asked.

He put on his headset and activated the passive sonar, turning the mic toward the ship approaching from more than twenty miles away.

I knew that hearing it would be a long shot.

"Forty knots," Ross said, watching the speed-over-ground indicator on the chart plotter while Bernie tried to locate the approaching boat.

"Had him for a second," Bernie said. "Then I lost him in the cavitation when we went over forty." He pulled his headphones off and handed them to Ross. "Have a listen to the playback. It sounded to me like a Pauk-class corvette."

Ross listened intently, playing the sound bite back a couple of times.

"That's what it is, Skipper," he finally said, looking over at me. "Top speed of thirty-four knots."

I did the geometry in my head. If the patrol boat turned due north to try to intercept us, he'd be about twelve miles from our lay line as we passed and by the time he got there, we'd be eight miles past him.

"Weaponry?" I asked.

"Usually armed with a seventy-six-millimeter gun," Matt replied. "It 'as a range of ten miles."

"They'll be lucky to get within that range," I replied, then turned to Ross. "What did Homestead say?"

"Two jet jockeys are six minutes out."

"How accurate are those seventy-sixes?" I asked Matt.

He grinned. "From over eight miles, they'd be lucky to hit their own bleddy island."

"Sixty-one knots, SOG," Axel reported.

I didn't think this was going to last long enough for Florida Air National Guard to even get to us. But FANG's response was always necessary.

Most encounters with Cuba's military were just muscle-flexing games. The patrol boat wasn't a concern—it'd never get close enough to use its gun effectively.

The MiG was a different story. The M variant was as a multi-role fighter. It was armed with a lot of missiles as well as a thirty-millimeter cannon.

The plane's problem was fuel. It was hard to come by in Cuba and the regime wasn't inclined to use it frivolously. The MiG was probably out of San Juan in the southwestern part of the country, more than 150 miles away. It'd burned a lot of fuel just getting here, and by now the pilot was realizing the patrol boat wasn't going to be able to stop or harass us. I hadn't seen a belly tank under the MiG, so getting way up here and then getting back to its base would easily burn through nearly a third of a tank of fuel. And that was if it had taken off with full tanks.

We all heard the shriek before we saw the plane. It blasted past on the port side from behind us, then banked right while climbing away. I felt quite certain he was heading home. It was a no-win situation. The MiG pilot had to know American fighter planes were on the way. The F15 Eagles out of Homestead were a better than even match for the MiG, and there'd be two of them, where the Cuban pilot was apparently flying solo.

"It's headed south-southeast," Ross reported. "Climbing slow and steady."

"Motor vessel *Ambrosia*, motor vessel *Ambrosia*, this is Captain Belson, Florida Air National Guard, out of Homestead. Both the

MiG and the patrol boat are bugging out."

Without a sound, a pair of F-15s in a staggered formation streaked past on the port side. We only heard them once they were gone. I leaned out the hatch and watched as the two American fighters climbed vertically and separated, making sure any Cuban radar screens would show not one but two planes.

"Bleddy busy air space, innit?" Matt said, as I pulled my head back.

I picked up the mic and spoke into it. "This is Captain McDermitt of the research vessel *Ambrosia*. Thanks for the assist, Captain Belson."

"They were just harassing you," he said. "They do it now and then but lack the gas or guts to play the long game."

There was a pause before he added, "You *do* know you crossed into their territorial waters a few miles back, don't you, Captain?"

"I wasn't aware," I lied, knowing he'd probably heard the same thing from every sea captain he'd had to assist in these waters. So, I embellished some more. "We're at least a hundred miles from Cuba, headed to the Florida Keys from Mexico."

"They claim a long, skinny stretch between U.S. and Mexican waters" Belson said. "We'll hang around way up high for a little while as you make your way to Florida."

"Thanks again," I said into the mic, then hung it up.

"Resume twenty knots," I told Axel.

"Twenty knots, aye," he replied, pulling back on the throttles.

I pushed the button for the intercom. "Bridge to engineering. You can shut down the turbines, Heitor."

"What was that?" he asked.

"A Russian fighter plane with Cuban markings," I replied. "A couple of F-15s out of Homestead chased it away."

"Are you sure you won't be needing the turbines?" Heitor asked.

"They won't come back," I assured him. "Go ahead and shut them down."

"Aye, Captain," the ship's engineer replied.

I nodded at Matt. "Go and get some rest," I said, then turned to the others. "That goes for the rest of you, too. If you don't have the 0900 watch, clear the bridge."

One by one, Kris, Giselle, Bernie, and Matt headed down the steps.

"That was certainly exciting," Val said. "But is it worth the risk just to save a few hours?"

"He was never going to fire on us," I said. "The MiG was just to slow us down so the patrol boat could bully us. As soon as they knew we were in U.S. waters and could outrun their boat, the pilot was at a stalemate at best. Let the crew know to secure from restrictions."

We soon settled down to a more routine passage. But Val had been right in her assessment—it had been a risk. Sure, it wouldn't have been in the pilot's best interest to come around a third time and put a missile through our hull. Not with the F-15s so close. But that didn't take into account human nature.

What if the guy had lost his wife and kids in an accident and didn't feel like he had anything left to live for? What if he hated Americans? I needed to weigh risk more carefully. In a game like that, it was more than just a fighter plane and patrol boat. People were involved, and sometimes people did stupid stuff.

All too often, it was a permanent solution to a temporary problem.

.

CHAPTER SIX

The guy at the end of the bar wasn't new in town. Rusty had seen him around many times over the last couple of years—at the Publix or down at the local gas station. He was probably in his mid-forties and drove a black Mercedes, one of the big four-door models that cost as much as a house. From the way he usually dressed it'd been obvious the guy had some jingle in his pocket. The arm candy Rusty had seen him with a few times in the last couple of months looked like high maintenance, too.

A lot of people brought a ton of money down the long stretch of two-lane highway from Miami. Most came on vacation, intent on spending it all. But the guy now sitting at his bar wasn't one of those. He'd arrived with money and stayed. What he did for a living, Rusty didn't know for sure. But the fact that he'd made it for more than a month told Rusty he was good at whatever it was he did.

The guy'd struck him as too sophisticated to be a drug dealer, and Rusty'd seen a lot of those over the years. He'd first pegged this guy as being in real estate. There were plenty of those all up and down the Florida Keys. Or maybe he was a banker or stock trader.

But not a drug dealer.

He didn't look overly sophisticated now. His shirt was open at the collar, wrinkled, and had sweat stains under the arms. His pants

were rumpled, as if he'd slept in his clothes. And expensive leather shoes on his feet were scuffed and dirty.

"What can I get ya?" Rusty asked, absently wiping a beer mug.

"A new life'd be great," the man said, sounding dejected. "Or a second chance, maybe." He glanced around, as if suddenly realizing he was in a bar. "A beer, I guess," he said with a sigh.

Rusty turned, tilted the mug under a tap, then pulled the handle, letting the golden liquid half fill the heavy mug before straightening it to add a little head on the brew. He placed a coaster on the polished mahogany bar top, then set the mug on top of it.

"I've seen you around," Rusty said, then glanced out into the empty parking lot. It was past time for the lunch crowd and well before happy hour. "How'd ya get here? I don't see your Mercedes."

The man took a long swig from the mug and thunked it onto the coaster. "I walked," he replied simply.

The Rusty Anchor Bar and Grill sat nearly half a mile from the highway on the ocean side of Key Vaca. Rusty didn't get many walk-in customers, since there wasn't much of anything near the entrance to his property to indicate there was a restaurant and bar at the end of the shell driveway. No hotels or restaurants within easy walking distance either.

He might've come around the canal from a path through the woods which led to Sombrero Beach Road—a few locals came that way. But most of the Rusty Anchor's clientele arrived by car. There were also quite a few who came up his canal by boat. Some of the local fishing guides kept their boats at his marina. But they were mostly out on the water for the afternoon. Or else working a day job.

"Lives and chances are in short supply," Rusty said. "But beer I got plenty of. Want me to run you a tab?"

The guy dug into his pocket and pulled out a few bills and some

change, then laid the money on the bar. "I'll drink until this is gone."

"Might be a coupla fish tacos left over from lunch," Rusty offered. "Probly cold, but if they don't get ate, they'll just get tossed in the dumpster. On the house."

The man looked up, his eyes red and puffy. "I'm no charity case."

"Didn't say you were," Rusty said. "Just hate to see good food go to waste. Want something to eat?"

"Sure," the man mumbled.

"Coming up," Rusty said, slinging his bar towel over his left shoulder.

He hurried out the back and found his cook mopping the floor in the little covered outdoor kitchen.

"Rufus," he said, moving across the deck toward the old Jamaican man. "Got any fish tacos ready?"

"Not ready," Rufus replied. "But I and I can have some whipped up quick like. How many?"

"Five," Rusty said. "Some guy's in the bar, crying in his beer. Looks like he hasn't had a meal in days."

"I get right on it, mon."

Rusty returned to the bar, finding the stranger hunched over his beer.

"Rufus is gonna put 'em in the microwave for a second," he lied.

There wasn't a microwave oven on the whole property. The house and bar had been built almost two hundred years earlier, long before electricity, and built out of sturdy, Dade County pine. There was no electricity when the house and bar were built—electrical wiring was added to both when the island finally got power, but the most recent upgrade in wiring had been before the advent of microwave cooking and couldn't handle the load if he had one.

Rusty's family had always clung tightly to the old ways, each generation falling farther behind mainstream refinements and niceties.

Rusty went behind the bar and continued to pretend to polish mugs, while studying the man, and remembering what he could from past encounters.

James "Rusty" Thurman was good at reading people. He'd been a bar owner for over twenty-five years and had worked the bar under his dad for more than twenty years before that. Ever since he'd been big enough to look over the bar, he'd worked behind it. And he'd studied people. Most bartenders did.

He'd been called Rusty most of his life—it was only natural with the dark red mop he'd once had. Nobody he knew ever called him by his first name. He'd been born on Key Vaca sixty-two years earlier, in the very house he still lived in, and he came from a long line of Conchs. His father had been born in the same house, as had his father before him, and his father before that. Rusty's grandsons were seventh-generation Conchs.

The Rusty Anchor Bar and Grill had undergone many changes since Rusty's third great-grandfather had given up the sea and put down roots on the island. That was in 1838, when Captain Augustus Thurman had been a strapping young man of twenty-four, with a young wife and son.

Augustus had built the original house Rusty lived in not long before the Indian Key Massacre, just a few miles up island. Most of the inhabitants who'd lived on Key Vaca and Pigeon Key had fled in fear of the Seminole uprising. Augustus didn't leave, one of only three Key Vaca families who'd remained.

Initially, the bar had been built as a small general store, with the Thurman house behind it. The store had served the needs of the

small community, which mostly served the needs of the railroad. Augustus had made a lot of contacts in shipping ports up and down the Atlantic coast, from Canada down to his birthplace—Gloucester, Massachusetts—south all the way to Cuba. The general store became a hardware store, then a railroad depot before the turn of the last century.

When the railroad finally made it all the way to Key West in 1912, most of Key Vaca's inhabitants left again, the island being little more than a whistle-stop and encampment for the rowdy railroad workers. At the time, Rusty's grandfather, William Thurman, had been a young boy. By the time the boy became a man, he'd also become a bootlegger during America's Prohibition.

Rusty's father had been born during the cleanup following the Labor Day Hurricane of 1935. After the recovery, sport fishing became very popular, and the railroad turned into a road. The Thurman property also evolved, becoming a bar and bait shop. Rusty had finally done away with the smelly bait shop, tearing it off the back side of the bar, adding a deck and small outdoor kitchen, to turn the property into a restaurant and bar. Dredging the canal and adding the marina had completed the transformation.

But to many people, the Rusty Anchor was just a bar, first and foremost. A place where locals gathered to discuss the news of the day, weather forecasts and where the bite was on. It was a special place, not in architecture or amenities, though it had its share. What made the Anchor special was the people, the solidarity built through years of working and fighting the elements shoulder to shoulder. Not too dissimilar from the camaraderie Rusty had once had when he'd served in the Marine Corps.

Rusty had never advertised much in the past. He hadn't needed to. He and his father before him had developed a dedicated clientele

of locals, fishing guides, liveaboard sailors and cruisers, and every now and then a tourist who made a wrong turn and kept going. Over the years, quite a few had made that wrong turn and ended up staying.

Just as many folks considered the Anchor a bar first and foremost, Rusty considered himself a barkeeper above all else, and he knew what it took to make a life in these islands in the Stream.

Key Vaca had changed a lot in over 180 years. The town of Marathon had sprung up during the railroad days, as the crews had worked day and night to build the long bridge across seven miles of open water to the west. The whole island became a cement factory for a time, building the concrete piers the Old Seven Mile Bridge still stood on today, abandoned to time and the elements. The city of Marathon itself was fairly young, having only incorporated in 1999. The city limits included all or parts of thirteen different islands from Grassy Key to Knight's Key.

Through the 70s and 80s, Marathon had become known as a drinking town with a fishing problem. Now, as Rusty watched the man at the bar drink his beer slowly, but in large swallows, he wondered what events had brought him to such a state. A car breakdown? There would have been a lot easier places to get help. Hell, these days everyone had a cell phone and credit card. In Rusty's whole life, he only remembered one person *walking* in from the road after a breakdown, and that had been a friend of his father who knew his dad had the tools to fix his truck.

He glanced over at the man again. A long night out with old college buddies? He discounted that, as well. The man's spirit seemed broken.

Rusty had seen his share of broken men. Women too. Most recently after Hurricane Irma. A lot of businesses were hanging by a

shoestring before the storm, and they just never came back after it tore through the Middle Keys. He remembered the hollow faces of those who returned to find their life's work completely gone. He'd helped. The whole island had. But in the end, many people simply vanished over the weeks and months after Irma.

Rufus came in and approached the bar carrying a tray. "Only seven left, mon." He placed the tray full of tacos on the bar between Rusty and the man. "I and I had me fill," he said, winking at Rusty. "So, t'row away what yuh don' eat."

The old Jamaican had been privy to Rusty's generous nature for a long time. The bar owner often fed homeless people or out-of-work fishermen, and regularly put them to work doing odd jobs left partially finished by a previous recipient of Rusty's kind nature.

Rufus lived in the small shack on the back of the property where Rusty's grandfather had once made illegal rum, and he'd helped Rusty help others on many occasions. Though the two men were of different races, cultures, and nationalities, they came from similar upbringing, where people helped others when they needed it. And this guy sure looked like he needed it.

"Thanks, Rufus," Rusty said, picking up a taco and looking around discreetly. He leaned over the bar toward the stranger and whispered, "If ya see a tall redhead, give me a heads-up. Woman's always trying to get me into skinny jeans."

He took a bite and let his eyes roll back. When he swallowed, he nodded toward the tray. "You won't believe what that old Jamaican can do with a piece of fish and some island herbs."

The man looked at the food, then reached over and picked one up, taking a big bite and leaning over the tray.

Rusty laughed as a hunk of blackened mahi abandoned ship, plopping onto the edge of the platter.

"Ya know," he said thoughtfully, reaching under the bar, "it might be a good idea to have a spare tortilla or two when eatin' tacos. Then the first two can make the third."

He pulled two paper plates from a stack, then placed one next to the man's beer, while holding his own under the taco in his left fist.

When Rusty swallowed the last bite, he grinned. "Good, ain't they?"

The man reached for another.

"Knock yourself out, *mi amigo*," he told the man. "My wife's due back any second."

He moved down the bar a few feet, picked up another spotless beer mug and began wiping it. He often did this to occupy his hands, while seeming to be busy to anyone else. Nobody liked a nosy bartender.

"Name's Rusty," he said without looking up from a troublesome but nonexistent spot he was rubbing vigorously. "Rusty Thurman. I'm the owner, bartender, waiter, and chief mug polisher. Basically, I do anything and everything that needs doin' anywhere on the property."

The man took a napkin from the side of the platter and wiped his mouth. "Robert Grant. Thanks."

"No worries," Rusty said. "We usually have some left after the lunch crowd. I seen ya around town. Been here long?"

"Two years," Robert replied, then stared down at the food in his hand. He put it down on the paper plate and looked out the window toward the water, his expression vacant.

Rusty knew the man needed help. He'd seen his share of people come down from the mainland. The allure of living and working in paradise drew thousands every year. Most of them ended up

penniless and hitch-hiking back up Useless One, as many in the Keys called US-1, the famed Overseas Highway.

Some came with lots of money but no skills suitable for island life. Others brought the skill but no money, and since it was an island, everything but the land was trucked down, and there was only so much land.

In short, it was very expensive to live in paradise.

This guy had money when he'd arrived in Marathon. And since then, whenever Rusty'd seen him, he'd looked the part. So, he figured the guy had been able to maintain the status quo, at least. That said a lot. He didn't look like much now, in his rumpled clothes, but he'd been in the Keys for two years, which meant he'd had something of value to offer the community—some skill that made him employable or valuable. Or else he'd had a lot more money than most when he'd arrived. For the last couple of months, Rusty'd seen him a dozen times or more with a blonde, ten years younger than him, at least.

"Don't you usually drive one of those big ol' Mercedes sedans?" Rusty asked. "I bet ya gotta run the AC full blast in that thing."

Robert's head slowly slumped, and his already deflated shoulders sagged even further. "Not anymore," he mumbled. "It's all gone. I have nothing left. What a damned fool I've been."

CHAPTER SEVEN

I called the Rusty Anchor on my personal cell phone once we dropped anchor in Hawk Channel. Rusty still had a landline at the Anchor and usually left his cell on the charger in his office while he was tending bar, which was basically any time the place was open. Everyone who knew him knew to call the landline. I hadn't seen my old friend in almost a year, not since before I'd taken command of *Ambrosia.*

"Rusty Anchor Grill," a man's voice answered. "I mean Bar and Grill."

Rusty must have hired a new bartender.

"Is Rusty available?" I asked.

"Just a second," the man said.

There was a heavy thud as he set the receiver down. Rusty's landline phone wasn't one of those you plugged into an electrical socket to charge a cordless handset. It was an old-style, corded rotary phone. His reasoning was simple—in a storm, if power was lost, a corded phone still worked since it got its power directly through the phone line. The trouble was, the kind of storms that could knock out power in the Keys usually knocked out telephone lines, too.

In the background, I could hear voices, but couldn't make out what anyone was saying. It seemed like about a dozen people talking

at once, a typical Wednesday night at the Anchor—the weekly blue-collar celebration known as Hump Day.

"Hello," Rusty said.

"It's me. Did you hire a new bartender?"

"Jesse! Damn, it's good to hear your voice. When ya getting' in?"

"Feet up. Anchor down," I replied. "We cleared through Customs in Key West and the crew's putting the launches in the water now. All set to feed about twenty hungry people?"

"Thought that boat had a bigger crew."

"It does," I replied. "Several stayed ashore down in Key West and will meet us later or are flying home from there."

"Dink came in about an hour ago," Rusty said. "I was his first stop and bought twenty-five pounds of mahi from him."

"Twenty-five pounds of whole fish?" I asked.

"No, bro," Rusty replied. "Twenty-five pounds of fillets, all bulls. Plus, I still got a bunch of last season's stone crab claws on ice."

The season for stone crab had ended just a couple of months earlier, but Rusty almost always had some left, well into July.

"We'll be there in less than thirty minutes," I told him, then ended the call.

"Will he be able to feed everyone?" Savannah asked, herding Alberto and Finn toward the hatch.

"And then some, by the sound of it. Go ahead on down. I want to stop in the bridge one more time."

They went out the side hatch and I continued forward in the interior passageway, opened the hatch at the end, and stepped onto the bridge. Matt and Val were busy on a pair of Metis tablets, running diagnostics.

"Everything okay?" I asked.

"Oye, Cap'n," Matt replied. "So far, at least. We're gonna run

through a full inspection with Mr. Silva, then we'll come ashore on the next launch."

"See that you both do," I said to Val. "Two of the security guys will be up shortly. They'll be relieved at zero two hundred by two more. They're the only assigned watch."

"We will," Val said. "We just woke up a couple of hours ago, so we're in no hurry."

"I'll see you there," I told them both, then hurried down to the cockpit.

As I descended the steps to the work platform, Jocko was helping Savannah get Finn aboard. He seemed very anxious, as if he knew where we were and what lay ahead.

The ride to the new dock Rusty had built alongside the new boat ramp was very short and we were soon tied up.

"There've been a few changes," Savannah observed, as we were walking across the back lawn toward the bar.

My little seaplane, *Island Hopper*, wasn't on her tie-down pad. She was a 1953 deHavilland Beaver, and a great little plane for taking charters out to remote spots. She could take off or land on water no more than a couple of football fields long.

I'd bought a hangar way down at the end at Marathon Airport, just big enough for *Island Hopper* and her big sister, *Ocean Hopper*, a twin-engine Grumman Mallard flying boat that I'd gotten in trade from a salvage operator in Key West by the name of Buck Reilly.

"Change is inevitable," I said. "But it seems to happen slower here than anyplace else I know."

As we approached the steps to the deck, the back door flung open, and Rusty stepped out. "Somebody call the Shore Patrol! There's a rowdy jarhead running loose!"

He'd lost even more weight. While not down to what he'd been

in the Corps, I doubted he weighed any more than I did. And I had ten inches on the man.

He stepped lively as he descended the three steps from the deck and gathered both me and Savannah in a big bear hug. "Hot damn! It's good to see you two. Happy birthday, Savannah!"

"Thank you," she said, as he released us.

"Where's Alberto?"

I looked around and spotted him practically being dragged by Finn, who was running back and forth along the rocks at the water's edge. He seemed to be working his way down a receiving line, saying hello to old friends.

"Just let him go!" I called to Alberto.

He reeled the dog in and unclipped the leash. Finn shook his head vigorously, then tore off across the yard to the boat storage pad, where a number of weekend anglers kept smaller boats on trailers.

Alberto came running toward us as the crew gathered.

"Welcome, everyone!" Rusty shouted. "*Mi casa es tu casa.* Your skipper's got the meal tab, and your drinks are on me. I'm Rusty Thurman, owner of the Rusty Anchor Bar and Grill."

The door opened again, and Rusty's wife Sidney came down the steps to stand beside her husband.

"And this here's my wife, Sid," Rusty said, slipping an arm around the tall redhead's waist.

Rusty stood five-six and Sidney was at least four or five inches taller in her bare feet, and her feet were rarely bare. She wore two- or three-inch heels nearly everywhere. Rusty had fallen in lust with her when we were in the Corps together and she'd appeared in Playboy Magazine as a young college girl. When he saw her driving a beer delivery truck decades later, he'd wasted no time charming,

then marrying her.

"Welcome to the Anchor, everyone," Sid said, stepping forward and giving me and Savannah hugs. "We have plenty of room. Make yourselves at home."

Rusty did a fist bump with Alberto, then led the way inside. "Sit anywhere ya want," Rusty told everyone. "Robert, Naomi, and Sid will come around to get your orders."

Jimmy Saunders, my old first mate, and now captain of my charter fleet, rose from a bar stool and came toward us, smiling broadly.

"*Hola, Capitan*," he said, shaking my hand vigorously. "Man, it's good to see you guys again. Happy birthday, pretty lady."

He hugged Savannah and motioned us toward the bar. I put Alberto up on a stool and sat down next to him with Jimmy beside me. Savannah and Sid drifted over to a table where two other women were seated.

I looked around and saw a few familiar faces and a few I'd never met before. One was a man moving from table to table, carrying water glasses and taking orders.

"His name's Robert," Jimmy offered. "Not Bob, or Rob, or Bobby."

"I think I've seen him around," I said.

"Been here a coupla years, man. Was pretty rich up until recently."

"Keys disease?" I asked, referring to the number one cause for people losing their way in the Keys—alcohol.

"Dunno," Jimmy replied. "Rusty said he just wandered in earlier today."

I looked over at my old friend behind the bar. "And of course, you put him to work. Do you even know his last name?"

"The man was down to his last four dollars and some loose change," Rusty replied with a shrug. "And his last name's Grant. He's an investment banker who got swindled somehow—ain't got the whole story yet. Rufus offered to put him up down at the shack."

"There's barely enough room for one," I said.

Rusty had cleaned and remodeled the former rum-making shack on the back of the property. It had two small rooms and a porch—nothing more. Irma tore the roof off and high water ruined the interior, so Rufus moved in with Rusty for a couple of weeks until they could restore it.

"Just temporary," Rusty said. "Till he's back on his feet. Now, what can I get ya?"

"Beer me," I said. "I'm officially off duty for a week."

"What about you, little man?" Rusty asked Alberto.

"Beer him, too," I said with a wink.

"Coming right up," Rusty said, as Alberto looked up at me in surprise.

Rusty placed two stubby brown bottles in front of us. Mine was a Red Stripe lager and Alberto's an A&W root beer.

The back door opened, and Axel let Finn in, then held the door for Crystal Santiago. The young couple came toward us, and Finn went around the room greeting people he knew and making friends with those he didn't. Finally, he made his way to a corner, where I noticed Rusty had placed a water bowl and blanket. He lapped up a short drink, turned around twice on the blanket, then plopped down.

"Will you be coming up to the island tonight?" Jimmy asked.

"Not tonight," I replied. We'll stay aboard, then head up that way in the morning."

"Your Grady's here," Jimmy told me. "When you emailed you

were coming home, Naomi and I brought it down."

"Thanks," I said. "Hope I can remember the way."

"Nice place," Axel said, stopping beside me, then leaning over to where Savannah sat. "Happy birthday, Miss Savannah."

She thanked them both with a hug and then I introduced him and Crystal to Jimmy and Rusty. They shook hands, then moved off to sit with Ross and Kassandra.

"I remember meeting your first mate, man," Jimmy said. "The English guy. What was his name? Mac or Matt or something? Where's he at?"

"Matt," I replied. "And don't let him hear you call him an Englishman. He's Cornish."

"Cornwall's still in England, last time I checked."

"Not according to Matt," I said with a grin, then broke into my most piratical accent. "Once you've crossed the River Tamar, you're not in England anymore."

"Is he coming?" Jimmy asked.

"He and Val, our yeoman and second mate, stayed aboard to run some diagnostics."

Rusty nodded over toward where Axel and Crystal had joined the others. "That young fella Axel who stopped to say hi. What's he do?"

"Axel is one of the helmsmen, and the guy he's sitting with is Ross, one of *Ambrosia's* navigators. The two women are sisters—Crystal and Kassandra Santiago. Crystal works in the laundry and Kassandra in the galley with her dad, one of our chefs."

"You have two people for every station on the boat?" Jimmy asked.

"Most, yeah," I replied. "We sometimes operate twenty-four hours a day for weeks on end. Val has a nearshore captain's license and Matt's is an unlimited sea captain's, like mine. One of the three of us is on the bridge at all times."

"You've come a long way," Rusty said. "Ever miss the old days?"

I looked around at the very familiar surroundings, the knotty pine walls and beams, the louvered storm shutters on the many windows, the ornate mahogany bar top, complete with a bullet hole still in the front edge from looters who'd tried to rob us after Hurricane Wilma back in 2005.

I fingered the hole and looked up at him, grinning. "Don't miss all of it, brother."

CHAPTER EIGHT

The party continued well into the night. I started yawning before 2300. I worked out daily, but these days it was more often on a treadmill in *Ambrosia's* small gym than swimming in open water, which is what I preferred. But *Ambrosia* didn't often stop long enough for that. Even though I was feeling as strong as I ever had, I'd noticed that I needed more sleep in the last couple of years.

So, we said our goodnights early, rounded up the kid and the pup, then went out to the docks where Jimmy had my little seventeen-foot Grady-White tied up.

The 140-horse Suzuki fired up with a mere touch to the starter.

"I'll get the lines," Savannah said, helping Alberto down into the boat.

Finn leapt over the forward rail, landing lightly on the forward casting deck and sniffing around. He looked back at me and barked, as if telling me, "Hey, I found our boat!"

He seemed more like himself than he usually did. At twelve, he had some white hairs around his muzzle and eyebrows—hard to see, due to his color, but they were there, just like in my beard and hair. They say dog years are seven to one, making him eighty-four years old. He looked happier now than I'd seen him in quite a while.

Savannah cast off the stern line, then the bow, and used a small boat hook to push us away from the dock. I waited as the front of the boat came around, then clunked the outboard into forward, turning toward the middle of the canal.

"Has Jimmy been keeping it up?" Savannah asked, as we passed *Salty Dog* at the end of the canal and moved into the channel.

I bumped the throttle up slightly. "Said he starts everything once a week and does a turnaround once a month."

"How far?" Savannah asked.

I shrugged "Knowing Jimmy, at least out past the reef, where he can hoist the sails."

It only took a few minutes to get to *Ambrosia*. She sat on the calm water inside the reef line, seeming to float on a cloud, thanks to the many recessed lights mounted in the hull below the waterline.

I was quiet during the ride, thinking about the new guy Rusty'd hired. I'd had a chance to talk to him for a few minutes and without seeming to pry, I'd learned some things. Not that it was difficult. The man seemed like an empty boat, going through life with nobody at the helm. He wasn't talkative, but he told me a few things.

Savannah pushed off the leaning post and looked over the tinted windscreen. "Looks like we have company."

I stood beside her and saw a boat about the size of the Grady tied off to *Ambrosia's* work platform. "It appears so," I said.

"Something's troubling you, Jesse," Savannah said, once we got the boat tied off alongside the strange boat. It was also a center console, a Mako about sixteen feet.

She hadn't asked a question. We'd been together for a while now, and the woman knew me better than anyone.

Finn led Alberto up the steps to the cockpit, and we followed them.

"That guy, Robert," I said.

"Sidney and I were talking to two other ladies about him," she said, as we started up the steps. "The man had everything and lost it all."

"Yeah," I said. "Including the trophy wife."

"I hate that phrase," she said.

"What else would you call her? From what he and Rusty have said, she sounds like a B-rate actress, too old or just never good enough to get a chance to audition for anything more than commercials. She's ten years younger than him and still beautiful enough to turn his head. She wanted the things he and his money could provide. From what I gathered, she'd bled him for what she could before he got swindled, then just up and left when he didn't have anything else to give her."

"Is that the way you see me?" she asked, stopping one step above me at the top and turning to face me. "Your 'trophy' wife?"

I grinned up at her and slipped my arms around her waist. "Last time I checked, your net worth was more than mine."

"That's because I invest in things that go *up* in value," she retorted. "How many boats do you have again?"

"Well, the *island* has definitely increased in value," I countered. "Pam, over at the bank, called me three times in the past twelve months with offers to buy. The last one was middle-seven figures."

She bent her head and kissed me. "Tell her we'll start considering offers when they reach eight figures."

"You're tall," I said, pressing my head to her shoulder. "I think I like it. Maybe Sid can take you shoe shopping. You'd look hot, perched on four-inch heels."

She stepped back and punched my shoulder. "Put a pole up, out on the terrace?" I just stood there grinning up at her until she laughed. "Are you *ever* going to grow up?"

I stepped up beside her and with my arm around her waist, guided her toward the outside stairs up to the bridge deck and our quarters. "You keep me young, babe."

The fact was, I was starting to feel some of the aches and pains age brings. They came on subtly at first. The sound of my knee popping as I stood, something nobody else ever seemed to hear. I couldn't swim underwater as far or as fast as I once could, the real measure of overall strength and endurance.

At first, I'd chalked it up to not being able to do my usual three-mile swims every other day. But there was more going on. I was slowing down.

We got to the bridge deck and entered the hatch to the interior passageway. "Go ahead on," I told her, turning left. "Matt and Val never came ashore. I want to check and see if everything's okay and who the mystery guest is."

"Don't be long," she said, giving me a tight hug. "You need your rest."

Okay, so maybe she'd noticed it too and maybe she'd heard my knees, but her Southern charm and politeness wouldn't allow her to mention it.

Or *maybe*...she didn't mean *rest* at all.

I went forward, opened the hatch to the bridge, and stepped in.

Matt and Val weren't alone.

Jack Armstrong rose from the helm seat, extending his hand. "Ah, Jesse. We were just talking about you."

"I didn't know you were coming," I said, surprised, but happy to see him.

"I just flew over to discuss a matter with Matt and Val here."

"Oh?"

"Nothing that concerns you," Jack said. "You're on vacation and

when you return to work, it'll be as captain of the *Phoenix*."

"Will ye be needin' anythin' else, Mr. Armstrong?" Matt asked.

"No, Matt," he replied. "And thanks for dinner."

Matt turned to me. "Mr. Meachum should be up dreckly, Cap'n. Let him know there's nuthin' to report, yeah?"

"Will do," I replied, then turned toward Jack as Matt and Val went down the steps to the crew quarters. "Last you told me, *Phoenix* wouldn't be ready until fall."

"She's out of dry dock, Jesse," he said, sitting back down at the helm. "Work is slightly ahead of schedule, but it will be fall before she's fully operational. There are still a thousand and one things to do; crew and equipment to bring in, that sort of thing. But she'll be ready for sea trials in less than a month. Work will continue into fall, even as we conduct the trials. But I want you there the first time she moves under her own power."

Phoenix was Jack's latest endeavor—a nuclear-powered, 328-foot research vessel. While a nuclear-powered vessel in the private market was still some years away, there were already a number of commercial vessels with nuclear power plants. *Phoenix* was kind of a hybrid—not fully commercial, nor a private yacht. The power came from a small, fully self-contained molten salt reactor that produced fifty megawatts of energy, enough to keep the lights on for all of Key West.

I'd been there when *Phoenix's* keel was laid and Alberto and I had put a coin under the mounting frame for the reactor, which was about the size of a standard cargo container. The tradition was a throwback to a time when a ship's owner and captain would put coins under the mast when it was first stepped onto the keel. Jack had placed an identical coin under the other side of the frame. Another reactor had been installed at the shipyard and provided

electricity for most of North Bimini.

"I'm still not following you," I said. "What will I be doing for the other three weeks?"

"Matt's taking *Ambrosia* over to Bimini in three days," he replied. "She'll be in dry dock for a week for some needed refitment, then he's taking her to Ecuador. I was wondering if we could use your airplane to move some equipment and people in?"

"The Mallard?"

"It *can* carry over a ton of cargo or people, right?"

"Ten passengers," I replied. "Or the equivalent weight in cargo."

"And it has good range?"

Jack would already know the answer to that question. He wouldn't be asking me to use my plane if he didn't know for certain that it would do the job.

"Not long by today's standards," I replied. "I had it professionally restored to one-hundred-percent original, including the old Pratt and Whitney radial engines. But fully loaded, *Ocean Hopper* can fly twelve hundred miles."

"Perfect," Jack said. "As we near the end of the build, dozens of specialists will have to be flown in, along with their tools and other equipment. Didn't you tell me once that when you were a kid, you'd dreamed of being a pilot for Chalk's?"

He was recalling a conversation we'd once had, comparing our boyhoods, and I'd told him about my first ride in a flying boat. When I was ten, I'd flown with my grandfather in one of Chalk's Airline's Grumman G73 Mallards. We'd taken off from Miami and spent the weekend on North Bimini, staying at The Compleat Angler.

Chalk's Airline was *Ocean Hopper's* most recent owner before Buck Reilly. I'd done a little salvage work for the Key West treasure

hunter, moving fake cannons from one place to another. It might have been a sketchy deal—I'm still not completely sure—but Buck had signed over a barely airworthy Mallard as payment. I'd then spent more than a quarter million dollars to restore it to original condition.

I often wondered if *Ocean Hopper* was the same plane on which Pap and I had flown way back then.

"Sounds like fun," I said. "And *Ocean Hopper's* engines aren't broken in yet—this will give me a chance to do it right. Where and when do you want me?"

"North Bimini, at the end of next week," Jack replied. "Bring Savannah and Alberto if you'd like. She will probably be a great asset in the design of your stateroom and the common areas. Bring whatever you'll need for two weeks, and you can spend the weekend settling in before you start shuttling technicians in and out the following week. Your wife and son can stay aboard while you're flying back and forth, and you'll likely spend every night aboard, as well."

"Looks like you've thought of everything," I said.

"Not likely," Jack countered. "During these last months, we have to stay very fluid to remain on schedule, which is why I want you flying, rather than utilizing the airlines. If you're halfway from New York to Bimini, you might be diverted to Atlanta or Miami to pick up something that suddenly becomes a priority."

"Makes perfect sense."

Jack grinned. "I thought you'd agree."

"Are you staying aboard *Ambrosia* tonight?"

"No, I have a plane standing by in Marathon," he replied, rising to his feet. "I was only waiting for you to return."

"There is one other thing," I said. "With *Ocean Hopper* not yet

broken in, I want to bring someone along, a mechanic."

"Do you have someone in mind?"

"His name's Ray Floyd," I replied. "He was in charge of the plane's restoration and knows her better than anyone. He's a partner in Last Resort Charter and Salvage out of Key West."

"See if you can get him," Jack said, moving toward the hatch. "I'll see you in nine days."

He opened the hatch and went aft, leaving it open. A second later, Walt Meachum stepped through.

"Evening, Captain," he said, glancing back. "Wasn't that Mr. Armstrong?"

"Yeah," I replied, hearing an outboard start up. "Nothing to worry about. You're on duty now?"

"Midnight to oh-four-hundred," he replied. "I was supposed to relieve Matt. Did he give you anything to pass on to me?"

"He said he had nothing to report," I replied. "And it's doubtful you will at the end of your shift, either. I'll see you tomorrow."

I went through the interior hatch and walked the long passageway to our quarters. The lights were low, and I could see Savannah out on the terrace.

"Everything all right?" she asked, looking off toward a half moon, low in the western sky. "Who was that on the other boat?"

"It was Jack," I replied, stepping up beside her and leaning on the rail.

She turned her head quickly in surprise. "Jack Armstrong? What's wrong?"

She knew it was rare for Jack to make a personal visit and she was worried he'd asked me to do something dangerous.

I smiled, staring down at her beautiful features, softened and made more radiant by the moonlight. "Nothing at all," I whispered.

"He just wants me to do some flying week after next, before *Phoenix* is ready for her first sea trial."

"What kind of flying?"

"Moving equipment, parts, specialists and their tools in and out on a tight schedule, it sounds like. It'll be a great chance to break in *Ocean Hopper's* engines the way they're supposed to be."

I'd told Savannah once about the trip I'd taken in a flying boat all those years ago and how landing on the water off West End that first time still stuck in my memory. She also knew of my boyhood dream of being a Chalk's pilot.

"You mean..." she began.

I smiled. "We're taking an old Chalk's flying boat to North Bimini."

CHAPTER NINE

We woke late the following morning and I tried calling Ray Floyd. It rang three times and went to voicemail. I left a message, asking him to call me at his earliest convenience about a proposition I had for him.

I got dressed in comfortable clothes—khaki cargo shorts and a turquoise T-shirt with the Smokin' Tuna logo on the pocket. The Tuna was an open-air restaurant and bar down in Key West that featured live music just about every night. It sat back down an alley off Duval Street and was overlooked by most cruise ship tourists.

When we informed Alberto that we'd be flying *Ocean Hopper* over to Bimini, he wanted to leave right away.

"We've got a lot to do before then," Savannah told him. "We have to pack everything up. This will be Matt's quarters in a few days."

The enormity of what lay ahead suddenly hit me. We had three days to pack everything and move off *Ambrosia*.

The thought brought a sense of melancholy. *Ambrosia* had been our home for over a year now, the only home Alberto had known with us. We'd only returned to my island in the Content Keys a couple of times since he'd come to live with us.

"She's right," I said. "We need to move everything up to the

island and it'll probably take two or three trips in the Grady. Then we'll have to pack for two weeks to fly over to the Bahamas."

"I have a better idea," Savannah said. "Why not fly *Ocean Hopper* here, load everything, then fly up to the island. That way we can already have everything aboard when we fly to Bimini to move onto *Phoenix?*"

"Because...that's not what Jack said to do," I replied, though her idea did make a lot more sense.

"Oh, you and your string of command."

"*Chain* of command," I corrected her.

"Whatever," she said, waving a backhand dismissively, her signal that anything I'd said no longer mattered. "Just leave Jack and the details to me, okay?"

We spent the morning packing what we'd need for two weeks into two large suitcases. We wouldn't need a lot—there were laundry facilities on North Bimini, as well as aboard *Phoenix*, though the onboard laundry might not be operational yet. If our quarters weren't ready or Jack had some other reason for us to make the move in stages, we'd just leave what we didn't need for the first two weeks on the island or maybe store it all in a corner of one of the hangars, then just live out of the suitcases while we were on the island.

But Savannah managed to convince Jack that her idea was less time- consuming than moving everything twice. Once we were all packed, I would bring *Ocean Hopper* down in Hawk Channel and tie off to *Ambrosia's* work platform, where we could load all our belongings directly. Then we could fly up to the island and just leave everything on the plane until it was time to head to Bimini.

My phone vibrated in my pocket as we were packing the last suitcase. When I took it out, I saw that it was Ray and stabbed the

MAN OVERBOARD

Accept button.

"Ray Floyd," I said, glancing over at Savannah. "How've you been?"

"Surprised to hear from you," Ray said. "What's it been? Six months since we delivered your plane? No problem, I hope."

"Not a one," I said. "I wanted to talk to you about a job I have for you if you're interested. It might be a couple of weeks."

Ray hesitated, then said, "Starting when? And where?"

"In eight days, I'll start flying the Mallard daily in and out of North Bimini. It'd be a great opportunity to break those engines in the correct way."

"How many hours flying time?" he asked, an edge of excitement in his voice.

"Lots. We'll be flying daily, five hundred to a thousand miles a day, it sounds like."

"That's the way to do it," he said. "Put a lot of easy hours on those Wasps and they'll last a lifetime."

"Not exactly easy hours," I said. "We might be fully loaded on some hops."

"Fully loaded, empty, doesn't matter," he said. "The wings do the heavy lifting. A good break-in needs long, steady engine hours."

"Then you'll do it?" I asked, looking over at Savannah and Alberto, who were paused halfway closing the suitcase.

"Buck and I are... ah... between projects. Exactly what dates are you thinking?"

"We're flying from my island on Friday, the fifteenth. I can bring you back a week later, but maybe plan on two weeks, just in case."

"I normally charge five grand a week, plus expenses," he said.

"I'll send you ten to book you for two weeks," I said. "Your old payment method still good?"

"Yeah. You want me up there the day before?"

I'd figured on flying down to Key West to pick him up, but if he could drive up the day before, it'd save us half a day, and I told him so.

"Not a problem," he said. "I can be in Marathon by mid-afternoon the day before departure."

"Then I'll pick you up Thursday afternoon at the Rusty Anchor. Don't forget your passport."

"See you then," he replied and ended the call.

I shoved my phone in my pocket and grinned at Savannah. "We have our flight engineer."

"Good," she said, returning a smile. "That will ease my mind while you're out playing Chalk's pilot."

I looked around the living room. We didn't have a whole lot, both Savannah and I being minimalists, but it was all boxed up and would be a lot more than could be carried in the Grady in two trips.

"We're about finished here," I said. "Y'all wanna go with me to get the plane?"

"You two go ahead," she replied. "And take Finn. I'll finish things up here and get Jocko and Al to help get it all down to the cockpit."

Finn perked up at the mention of his name.

I ruffled Alberto's hair. "Feel like flying, little man?"

"Yeah!" he exclaimed.

"Let's go, Finn," I said, as we headed toward the hatch.

The word "go" had always been Finn's favorite. He liked to go for boat rides, go fishing, go swimming, go flying, go eat, and go to bed.

"How long will it take?" Alberto asked, as we descended the cockpit steps to the swim platform and the massive, hydraulic work deck mounted behind it.

"To get to the airport?" I asked. "Maybe half an hour. We gotta go to the Anchor, where my truck is."

"I meant to fly back here."

I pointed slightly to the right of the Rusty Anchor, which was about a mile away. "The airport's just over there. We'll barely get off the ground."

He frowned as I pulled the Grady closer.

"Maybe we can shoot out over the reef for a little bit, but we don't want Mom doing all the work, do we?"

"I guess not," he said, climbing over the boat's gunwale.

Finn put his paws up on the side and looked back at me with what I could only describe as a look of embarrassment. In the last year or so, even more so since Woden had died, Finn seemed to lack the energy to do a lot of the things he once relished. He still wanted to, but, like getting in and out of the boat, he needed help with some things.

I squatted and got my arms under his belly, then lifted him enough so he could get over into the boat, where he moved up to the forward casting deck and stood, wagging his thick tail.

After climbing in, I started the outboard and untied the line. I let the boat drift with the wind and current until we were clear, then dropped the 140-horsepower Suzuki into gear.

In no time at all, we were skimming across the water toward Rusty's little marina. The sea state was calm, almost no chop. That would make for a much easier open-water landing.

Ocean Hopper was bigger than *Island Hopper* but putting either of them down when there was more than a twelve-inch chop wasn't easy. The Coast Guard used to fly the much larger Grumman HU-16 Albatross for search and rescue. It was capable of landing in much rougher conditions.

When we reached Rusty's barge at the end of the canal, Alberto helped me tie off while Finn went exploring. We left the barge and started across the backyard toward the deck. As we did, the back door opened, and Rusty came out.

"That's about an ugly shirt, bro," he said, bounding down the steps. "Whatcha call that color?"

I looked down at my shirt and shrugged. "Turquoise, I guess."

Rusty didn't like it because it was from a competitor's bar, even though the Smokin' Tuna was fifty miles down island.

"On you," he said, with a chuckle, "I'd call it aqua-*marine.*"

Alberto laughed at Rusty's dumb-dad joke of the day.

"Thought you'd be moving up to the island this morning," Rusty said.

"Change of plans," I replied. "We're taking *Ocean Hopper* out to the boat so we can just load everything at once, then fly up to the island until we leave for Bimini next week."

"That makes a lot more sense," he said. "Lemme guess; Savannah's idea, right?"

"How'd you know?" Alberto asked.

"Cause your dad's a grunt," Rusty replied. "And your mom's the thinker."

Alberto grinned, then made a noise like a foraging chimp. "Ooo-ooo. The world needs grunts."

Rusty laughed. "That it does, Mr. Alberto." He jerked a thumb toward me. "So, you goin' *flyin'* with this grunt?"

"We're gonna fly out over the reef," Alberto replied.

"You got time to come with us?" I asked my old friend.

"No can do, bro. Got a delivery coming in an hour and I'm the only one here."

"Where's your new guy, Robert?"

"Him and Rufus went shopping," Rusty replied. "And Sid and Naomi are up island."

"Is he still moping around like an abandoned pup?"

"Sure wish he'd snap outta the funk he's in," Rusty replied, shaking his head. "I'm bettin' he's a decent guy when his head's on straight."

We said our goodbyes, then climbed into my ancient International Travelall, dubbed *The Beast*. It was only old in outward appearance—the way I liked it—but the interior was more or less new. At least newer than the outside, which was mostly light blue with ruddy brown surface rust and streaks down the sides. It looked like a typical "Keys car," which made it undesirable to thieves. Though the truck itself would be fifty years old in the fall, everything inside or under the body, including the upholstery, suspension, engine, and drive train were only fifteen years old.

The powerful diesel engine started with a touch of the ignition key and settled into a low rumble. The drive over to the airport wouldn't even be enough to get the engine up to normal operating temperature, so I let it idle for a bit before pulling out from under the tree that shaded it. The odometer showed slightly over six thousand miles since the rebuild fifteen years ago.

I don't drive much.

Rusty's tropical jungle enveloped us as soon as we left the parking lot, idling slowly up the winding drive cut through the mangroves a century before. Rusty, with help from Jimmy, Rufus, and a succession of out of work locals, had replaced the plants that had been killed or washed away during Hurricane Irma almost five years ago. Some parts of the island chain still bore the scars of the Cat 4 storm, especially down island toward Cudjoe Key, where it made landfall.

There was no traffic when I reached the end of the drive and turned right onto US-1. Dead leaves were blown out of the edges of the hood and from the wiper blades as we accelerated north.

The airport entrance was less than two miles up the highway, then another half mile around to my hangar near the end of the runway. I parked next to the building I'd bought late last year, and we got out.

We'd decided that once we got the plane loaded and moved up to the island, Jimmy and I would return to the Anchor, bring *The Beast* back to her shade tree, and take the Grady back up.

Living on an island that was only accessible by boat—or helicopter, though one hadn't landed there in a while—had its perks, but there were also a few obstacles, not the least of which was logistics. In many places, the local grocer was a short walk, or maybe a brief drive. Living on the island, a grocery run involved a twenty-minute boat ride, tying off, and then a short drive to the Publix.

"We gotta get those big doors open," I said to Alberto as we entered the smaller side door.

Finn trotted in ahead of us and sniffed at everything he encountered.

"I'll help you," Alberto replied.

The red fuselages and wings of my two planes shone brightly in the dim glow from a single filtered skylight. I switched on four breakers in the panel by the inside of the door and two dozen fluorescent lights came on at random intervals all around the skylight in the high roof.

I unlocked the hangar door from the inside, grabbed the handle, and looked down at Alberto. "Start pushing when I get it open a little."

The tracks were blown clear of debris every morning by the

fixed base operator's grounds maintenance crew, and the wheels on the multiple door panels were well greased, so it started sliding with little effort. But I made out like it was harder and the kid pushed with all his might.

"Keep your elbows bent," I advised. "When this panel picks up the next one, you can absorb the impact with your arms to keep it going and get the second one moving, too."

The doors clanged together and the second one started rolling open just as easily as the first. We repeated the process on the other side and with the four door panels extending out beyond the side walls of the hangar, we had an opening that measured one hundred feet across. Not enough to park the planes side by side, since they had a combined wingspan nearly fifteen feet greater, but *Island Hopper* wasn't nearly as tall as her big sister. So, half of her starboard wing was a couple of feet below *Ocean Hopper's* port wing but well short of the prop on that side.

Savannah was right; I did have a lot of toys—seven boats and two airplanes—and they were all old. At eighteen, my primary charter boat, *Gaspar's Revenge*, almost twenty years old and on her third set of engines, was the newest of my boats, not counting *Knot L-8*, the small wooden boat my former caretaker and I had built together. They were all well maintained, and each had a different role. The same with the two airplanes.

Island Hopper was just that, a short-range bush plane that could land on the water. With her, I could whisk clients to parts of the backcountry that skiffs would take hours to reach, even up into the Everglades.

• *Ocean Hopper*, with her large fuel tanks and twin engines, had almost three times the range, was faster, could carry a lot more, and could also land on the water.

Alberto and Finn followed me to the back of the hangar, where I unplugged the charger from the tow dolly.

"We'll need this to move her outside before we start the engines," I told him. "Let me wheel it over and get it hooked up, then you can pull the plane outside."

It only took a couple of minutes to connect the tow bar to the front landing gear.

"See this paddle on the right?" I asked, giving the reverse control lever a tap to pull the slack out of the two tow-bar connections. Alberto nodded. "This one's for pulling," I continued, "and the one on the other handle is for pushing. All you gotta do is grab the handle and pull, then just guide it straight out and a little to the left, okay?" He nodded his understanding and I added, "Wait till I pull the chocks out."

I went around to the pilot's side of the plane first, pulled the wheel chocks out, then ducked under the belly and pulled the starboard chocks.

"All clear," I called out. "Pull her out and a little to the left."

He started pulling and the electric motor on the tow dolly did all the work, but he still leaned into it as if he were pulling the big Grumman flying boat all on his own.

They were called flying boats rather than seaplanes or floatplanes for a reason. Airplanes like *Island Hopper*, a de Havilland Beaver, were primarily built for ground use, but could land or take off from water on long floats mounted in place of the landing gear, and the floats had retractable wheels for ground takeoff and landing. But a flying boat was just that—an enclosed boat hull with wings. It also had retractable landing gear for when it came up out of the water or landed on a runway, but flying boats were designed first and foremost for waterborne operation.

I'd gotten my multi-engine pilot's certification years earlier and had been on the lookout for a Beechcraft King Air when Buck Reilly made me an offer I couldn't refuse—the 1951 Mallard in exchange for some salvage work. There were only fifty-nine of the planes built and *Ocean Hopper* was number fifty-eight.

I'd hired Ray Floyd to do a complete, ground-up, one-hundred-percent original restoration, which had taken over a year. From the Grumman factory, the G73 Mallards had Pratt & Whitney Wasp radial engines—big nine-cylinder, air-cooled monsters producing six hundred horsepower each. Chalk's had replaced some of them with more efficient turboprop engines, but I'd asked Ray if he could find a couple of original radials to rebuild. He did better than that and managed to locate a pair of like-new remanufactured Wasp radials with zero hours. He even found a buyer for the turboprops.

Sure, the turbos were more reliable, more efficient, and more powerful, but there was just something about the low hum of those big radials that took a person back. At least me, anyway.

Ocean Hopper had only flown five times since Ray'd delivered her six months ago. And four of those flights had been in the first week with Ray checking me out.

Although Jimmy wasn't a licensed pilot, he came out to the airport once a week and started all three engines on the two planes, following the same laminated preflight sheets Ray had given me for the Wasps and the Wasp Junior in *Island Hopper*.

"That's good enough," I called to Alberto, once the plane was clear of the hangar doors. "Let's lock up and get this bird in the air."

CHAPTER TEN

Fifteen minutes after returning the dolly to the hangar and locking the doors, we were taking off into a clear blue Florida sky.

"Wheels up," I said, moving the landing gear lever.

"Three blue lights," Alberto said over the headset, as he watched the dash. "The wheels are up and locked."

"How'd you know that?" I asked, looking down and checking them myself.

He grinned. "I watched you and Mr. Floyd. Green for land and blue for water."

"We'll have you flying in no time."

"Really?"

"When you get a little bigger," I said, raising my hand and pulling back slightly on the overhead-mounted throttles.

Alberto sat up as high as he could in the seat but could barely see over the dash as I leveled off at two thousand feet, heading due east and angling out over the reef line. I banked right to give him a better view out the starboard window.

"Look at all the boats," he said, gazing down.

"It's summertime," I replied. "All the semi-locals come down for the diving and fishing."

Semi-locals was a term Rusty used for Florida's mainlanders who drove down to the Keys on vacation all year long, especially in the summer. Some stayed for a week or two at a time and some just for the weekend.

"Keep an eye out for Jimmy," I said, continuing my turn. "He might have a charter today."

"There's *Ambrosia*!" he shouted.

The super-yacht-turned-research-vessel dwarfed every other boat within sight, lying sedately in the turquoise waters of Hawk Channel.

"We'll head down island a ways," I told him. "Then we can turn back and land into the wind close to her. How's Finn doing in back?"

Alberto turned in his seat and looked back into the passenger area. *Ocean Hopper* was configured for ten passengers, and we'd strapped Finn into the nearest seat.

"He's part way out of his seatbelt," Alberto said, concern evident in his voice. "He's got his paws up on the side to look out the window."

"He's fine," I said. "When we start our approach, you can go back there and straighten him out."

The engines droned as I flew a course parallel to the highway. I stayed low and slow, where we had the best view of the island chain as we followed the Seven Mile Bridge, then on past Big Pine Key.

"How far are we going?" Alberto asked.

"We should probably turn around and go help Mom, huh?"

"Yeah," he replied. "It feels weird having fun when I know she's working."

I looked over at my miniature co-pilot and smiled. Alberto had come from tough beginnings, having lost his father at an early age, and then having to watch his mother get strung out on drugs. She'd

been murdered over a year ago, and Alberto set adrift in a small boat, left to perish at sea. He'd barely survived as the boat drifted all the way down to the Keys from Fort Myers.

On that particular day, Savannah and I had been participating in the annual Seven Mile Bridge Run and had seen a bunch of runners stopped and looking at the little boat. The moment we realized someone was aboard, my wife and I had jumped from the bridge and swum to it. We managed to get him to Pigeon Key, fighting against a strong current, where an ambulance took him to the hospital.

For several days, Alberto couldn't remember who he was or how he'd gotten there, but soon recovered, and then we'd discovered that he was an orphan. It took some string-pulling by Jack Armstrong, but we'd adopted Alberto in record time. Already very bright, he was now maturing faster than his years.

"That's a good feeling to have," I told him, "Any time you see someone struggling to do something, you should lend a hand."

"One human family, right?"

"Yeah," I replied with a chuckle, then turned my attention back to the controls. Banking right, we flew across the highway above Summerland Key. Then I made a lazy left turn, crossing the road again just south of Sugarloaf to avoid the parachute drop zone.

"Go ahead and unstrap," I said to Alberto once I'd leveled off. "Tell Finn to lie down in his seat so you can tighten up his harness."

Alberto took his headset off, unbuckled his belts, and climbed into the back of the plane as I announced my intent on the Unicom frequency for any other planes in the area.

A moment later, Alberto got back into his seat, buckled up, and put his headset back on.

"It's really loud without these," he said. "I got Finn all squared

away."

"Thanks," I said. "With his sensitive ears, maybe flying around in these noisy planes isn't such a hot idea."

Alberto looked thoughtful for a moment, then lifted his head high to see over the dash.

Reducing power, I added flaps and pointed the nose of the plane toward a spot about a mile off the far end of the Seven Mile Bridge. There, just beyond Knight's Key, I could make out East Sister Rock and *Ambrosia*, anchored near it.

I turned on the marine VHF radio Ray had installed to allow me to talk to boaters, and hailed *Ambrosia* on Channel 68, her standby channel.

"Already got a boat in the water, Cap'n," Matt replied when I told him we'd be landing within a few minutes. "Saw you pass by a few minutes ago. And the crew's movin' your crates down as we speak."

"Let whoever's on the boat know that we'll land about a quarter mile behind you, and I'll cut the engines a hundred yards away."

"Roger that, Cap'n."

I turned to look at Alberto. "Once we get slowed down, I'm going to need you up front to catch the line. Think you can do that?"

He ducked his head and looked under the dash, where a small door could be opened to access the large forward cargo hold.

"Yeah, I can get through there easy," he replied.

We came in low, half a mile out from the bridge, angling away from it. Flying boats used to be a fairly common sight in South Florida and the Keys—one that, as a kid, had always stirred an adventurous spirit in me. Dreams of flying to destinations in the Bahamas and Cuba, where few airports existed at the time. Places where pilots with nerves of steel, who could land and take off from

the water in their flying boats, were in high demand.

"There she is!" Alberto said, jolting my mind back to the present. "I see *Ambrosia!*"

The air speed indicator showed we were flying at eighty knots, and I glanced over at the bridge, I could only imagine the curious looks we were getting from people traveling across the bridge at only a slightly slower speed.

I double-checked that the landing gear lights were blue for a water landing and reduced power a little more as we came down close to the water. The air speed dropped to eighty knots, well above stall speed.

We were just a quarter mile south of East Sister Rock and lined up slightly to *Ambrosia's* starboard side when the stepped hull contacted the water.

"We were a plane," I said. "And just like that—we're a boat."

"Cool!" Alberto shouted as the plane slowed and started to settle into the water.

I reached up and pushed the twin throttles forward again, adding power to keep us slightly up on plane and give the rudder some purchase to steer until we got close to *Ambrosia*. Once *Ocean Hopper* stopped planing and settled deeper, the engines were the primary means of directional control.

Two hundred yards out, I reduced power and allowed the bird to settle fully into the water. With the wind barely five knots and a forward speed of only six, the plane's rudder didn't provide much steerage. So, I added power to the starboard engine, and it beat heavily against the air, slowly turning *Ocean Hopper* toward *Ambrosia's* stern. A Sea-Doo was making lazy circles just off the boat's port side, waiting for me to cut the power. Headed straight for the work deck, I brought both engines down to idle.

"Okay, head on up there and open the nose hatch," I told Alberto. "Antonio's on a Sea-Doo and will throw you a line. All you gotta do is hook it to the bow cleat."

"Roger that," he said, unbuckling his harness excitedly.

Alberto had picked up some expressions from my old friend, Tank. Probably a few of mine also. I nearly lost it the first time Tank had asked the boy how he was doing, and his reply had been, "Right as rain, Master Guns." He'd heard me calling Tank by his rank a few times and 'right as rain' was always the man's response when he was asked. I figured it was a Montana expression.

I switched the engines off and as we drifted slowly toward the yacht, I ran through the post-flight shutdown, checking each item on the laminated card.

The nose hatch opened on the other side of the windshield and Alberto's head popped up. He turned around and very carefully lowered the hatch back onto the plane's nose as Antonio came racing toward us on the Sea-Doo.

The PWC came alongside and there was no mistaking Antonio's voice when he called out, "Hiya, Alberto. How you doin'?"

Alberto waved, then looked up at *Ambrosia's* cockpit. Savannah stood there, along with most of our belongings. "Hi, Mom!" he shouted.

After she waved back, he looked down at Antonio and then stretched his arms out wide, just like I'd shown him.

Catching dock lines was sometimes more luck than skill. They were usually thrown from or to a moving boat and a coil of rope wasn't the easiest thing to catch. If the thrower on the boat was new to boating or looked clumsy, offering them a bigger target often calmed them and they could just toss the line over your head with your arms out.

Alberto caught the line and quickly secured the loop at the end around the nose cleat. I grabbed my handheld VHF radio and went aft to the rear hatch.

"Tie that off to the starboard cleat on the work deck, Antonio," I said into the radio. "Leave at least forty feet of slack, then come around to the aft hatch on the port side."

I opened the hatch and got a fifty-foot dock line from the aft storage compartment. Once I put the loop through a cleat just inside the hatch, I waited for Antonio, and when he came around the tail, I handed him the coiled line.

"Hell of a landing, Captain," Antonio said, letting out a few of the coils. "Tie this one to port, right?"

"You got it," I said. "Then we can turn her broadside to the platform and pull her in closer and keep the wing clear of the hull."

He idled off toward *Ambrosia*, paying out the line as he went.

I leaned out of the hatch and yelled forward, "That's it, Alberto. Come on back here and let Finn out of his harness."

Jocko and Al were on the work deck, ready to assist. Antonio went wide on the port side, using the Sea-Doo to pull the tail around, then untied the end of the line and handed it to Jocko.

"Pull us in tail-first," I called out to the big Bahamian. "So the wings will clear the starboard side of the boat."

Jocko leaned back and started pulling hand over hand, pivoting the plane around. With a wingspan of almost sixty-seven feet, the forty feet of slack in the bow line plus the length of the work deck insured the wingtip wouldn't come anywhere close to *Ambrosia's* hull.

Once we were at more of a tail-first angle, Jocko nodded over at Al, who started pulling in the nose. Soon, *Ocean Hopper* was secure against the fenders of the work deck and her port wing extended

beyond the side of the ship.

Alberto and Finn jumped across to the work deck and the dog shook his head vigorously. Alberto knelt and took Finn's big head in his hands, pulling him close and whispering in his ear.

"That was like something out of a classic movie," Savannah said, coming down the steps. "Very nostalgic."

She hadn't accompanied me and Ray on the initial flights, when Ray had shown me the finer points of the seventy-one-year-old flying boat. Nobody had. I'd wanted to focus only on what Ray was demonstrating.

"Yeah, I suppose it is," I agreed, surveying the big red and white Grumman.

The juxtaposition of the antique aircraft and the modern yacht wasn't lost on me. *Ambrosia* had the latest in high-tech instruments and equipment, but *Ocean Hopper* didn't have so much as an autopilot; the gauges were all analog dials and sweeps.

I did have Ray come up with a pair of mounts for digital notepads on each yoke, both loaded with the latest GPS software for both aviation and nautical charts. They were also capable of sending and receiving messages and data via a communications satellite.

"You're not goin' to just up and fly away, are ya?" Matt said, coming down the cockpit steps.

I looked around at the several crew members assembled on the work deck. When we flew up to the island there'd really be no reason to return, and that didn't sit well with me.

"No," Savannah replied. "I asked Marcos to arrange a final dinner aboard for this evening."

He and Val both smiled. "That will be nice," Val said. "Grady and Mr. Santiago have been ashore all morning, trading tips with your friend at the Rusty Anchor. The Jamaican gentleman?"

"Rufus," I replied, following Savannah's lead. "No telling what those three will come up with."

"For now," Savannah began," we need to get all this stuff into the plane. Everything was weighed before it was brought down: there's a little over fifteen hundred pounds. Where should we put it all?"

Fifteen hundred pounds? Where and how did we accumulate so much stuff? That old George Carlin skit started running through my mind.

"We'll only need five seats when we fly to Bimini," I said. "So, anything heavy, we can put in the middle and aft seats, secured by the seat belts. The light stuff can go half-and-half in the front and rear luggage compartments.

Matt looked at the boxes and suitcases stacked on the deck. "She'll be able to fly with all this stuff *and* five passengers?"

"No problem," I replied. "With full fuel tanks, she can carry up to three thousand pounds."

"Those motors are huge," Antonio commented, looking up at the port engine.

I laughed. "Yeah, they're big, all right. Each one of those nine cylinders is more displacement than that Sea-Doo's whole engine."

"No way!"

"Yep, 1344 cubic inches of American muscle."

"Each?" Antonio asked incredulously.

"Each," I replied, spotting Heitor Silva, the ship's chief engineer, coming down the steps.

"That's a beaut," Heitor said, his accent somewhere between Portugal and Boston.

"Thanks," I said. "It took a lot of time and energy, but she's almost like brand-new."

Heitor walked the length of the work platform, touching the plane's fuselage here and there. "I remember you telling me you were having an antique Grumman restored." He ducked his head through the hatch, then turned to face me. "Whoever you had do the work did a magnificent job, Captain."

It took a lot to impress the ship's engineer—he was in charge of keeping *Ambrosia's* powerplants in top shape.

"The nose art is a real throwback," Al commented.

On both sides of *Ocean Hopper's* nose was a painting of a woman lying back on a partially fallen palm with a green flash sunset in the background and *Ocean Hopper* stenciled below it. It was almost identical to the paintings on either side of *Island Hopper's* cowling.

Al looked over at Savannah, then back at the nose art. The design was a relic of days when WWII flyers painted pictures of scantily clad women on the noses of their bombers, but in this case, the painting of the woman had been from a photograph I'd taken.

Al looked back over at Savannah and exclaimed. "That's you!"

"Yes, yes, it's me in the picture," Savannah said, somewhat embarrassed. "Can we get this stuff loaded now, gentlemen?"

CHAPTER ELEVEN

Once the plane was loaded, I started the starboard engine, the one farthest away from the boat. It stumbled, belched, and misfired—as radial engines do—then came up to a rough idle, firing on all cylinders. Once it was idling smoothly, I nodded to Alberto, who was once more standing in the forward hatch.

He pulled on the line to get some slack, then let it loose from the nose cleat and dropped it in the water.

"Make sure to dog the hatch tight," I yelled through the little crawlway. "Then come on back here and sit with Finn."

The wind and current slowly pushed the nose away from *Ambrosia's* work deck as Alberto scrambled through the little opening below the right side of the console. I yelled back to the rear of the plane, telling Savannah to pull in the stern line. Through the side window, I saw Jocko untie the line and it quickly tailed across the water like a ribbonfish.

I began the startup procedure on the port engine while I watched the light for the hatch. The engine fired, coughed a little, then settled into an even idle.

The open-door warning light turned off, letting me know that Savannah had secured the rear hatch. A moment later, she appeared beside me and settled down in the copilot's seat, strapping in and

donning her headset.

I turned and looked back. Alberto was in the first aisle seat with his seatbelt and headset on. He had Finn's big head on his lap with a towel wrapped around it, covering his ears. Alberto held the towel with both hands on the sides of Finn's head.

I couldn't help but laugh. "Everybody ready?"

"All set," Alberto replied over the comm.

"I'm anxious to get home," Savannah added.

Once I announced my intent on the Unicom frequency to any aircraft in our vicinity and moved the flap controls to full, I checked out both sides to make sure they'd dropped into the right position. Then I reached up and pushed the right throttle to half power.

The bird started turning to windward, moving out and around *Ambrosia*. I did the same to the left throttle and held it there for a moment, listening to the engines.

The sound of a radial engine was unmistakable. With nine cylinders set at forty-degree angles around a center hub, it created a sort of deep, droning sound.

With the engines running perfectly, I moved the throttles to takeoff power. The triple-bladed props bit into the air, creating a sound all their own, pummeling the air into submission at over two thousand revolutions per minute.

Ocean Hopper gathered speed, quickly climbing up onto the step and skimming across the water. When we reached sixty knots, I eased back on the yoke, bringing the nose up just a little to reduce water friction as the wings began to produce the lift needed to pull us into the sky. When we broke free of water tension, we accelerated even faster, slowly climbing into the clear blue sky.

"She was a boat," I heard Alberto whisper over the comm. I looked back and noticed he had his face close to Finn's covered right

ear. "And just like that, she's an airplane."

I looked forward again with a grin, remembering the dog I'd had as a kid and how I'd have conversations with him, as if he could talk back.

At just one hundred feet, I retracted the flaps and eased the throttles to maintain 125 knots airspeed, then banked slowly out to sea.

"You going to Cuba?" Savannah asked over my headset.

"Just thought you'd like to get the full effect," I replied.

When I came out of the turn and leveled off on a compass heading of 305 degrees, we were flying straight back toward *Ambrosia* and the high arch of the Seven Mile Bridge beyond her. Much of the crew, all people we'd grown to know as family and had relied on in many tight spots, were on deck, all waving. I waggled the wings as we approached, flying low and slow, just off her stern.

"She's such a beautiful boat," Savannah said, waving down at the crew as *Ambrosia* flashed beneath us.

"So is *Phoenix*," I said.

But I knew what she meant. *Ambrosia* had been built as a luxury yacht, then pressed into service to do quasi-research, always moving around to study the seafloor in different locations—almost always near where trouble was brewing on land. She'd been our home for some time now and I knew we were all going to miss her terribly.

I climbed slightly to five hundred feet as we approached the bridge, giving us a bird's-eye view of it and the highway—the lifeline to civilization in these parts. Past it, Big Pine Key stretched out and mutated into the backcountry on the edge of the horizon.

Beyond the last of the roads and houses on northern Big Pine, the predominant feature was the water. Varying shades of blue and green morphed from one to the other, punctuated by white and

gold sandbars, all seeming to flow north and south, like paint spilled on an inclined canvas.

"It's beautiful," Savannah said quietly. "All this time, and I've never seen this area before."

Savannah had accompanied me several times, kayak fishing in the shallows west of my little island. We usually fished the outside, around Upper Content Key and down the natural channel just to the west of it.

But we'd never ventured way back, since we were always able to catch what we needed within a mile or two.

Crossing No Name Key and the northern tip of Big Pine, I banked slightly left, flying deep into the heart of the backcountry— way back, as it's often called by locals. Down below us, if you didn't know your way around, it would be easy to get lost. What might look like a promising channel would wash you up onto a sand flat. It was almost like stumbling through a maze.

Way back was where only experienced guides dared explore, and then, only in a kayak, because the water was sometimes only inches deep. There were places down there where it looked like you were in the ocean and half a mile from any dry land, but you could get out of your kayak and walk without getting your knees wet.

Even experienced guides carried a handheld GPS. Channels and sandbars shifted constantly, so it was a good thing to have. Sitting low in a kayak, the surroundings looked the same.

I'd flown this same trip quite a few times in *Island Hopper*, so I knew the landmarks for my turn, and where to line up to be sure I landed in at least waist-deep water, rather than ankle-deep flats.

Ocean Hopper was bigger and heavier than *Island Hopper*, so I flew her deeper over the primordial landscape. I wanted a longer approach and she needed deeper water than *Island Hopper's* floats

did. Not really to land—at forty knots, she could skim across water less than a foot deep—but once power was decreased and she settled into the water at less than fifteen knots or so, she drew a little over two feet. So, I was planning to overshoot my usual landing mark. The water just north of my island got deeper a little father to the east.

"It looks like this area hasn't changed in a thousand years," Savannah said.

"Not drastically," I said as we passed Big Torch Key just under the port wing. "But even a passing squall makes subtle changes in the maze of channels and flats down there. Hurricanes have rearranged it a lot over the centuries, washing out islands and building new ones. But the beauty has probably stayed much the same."

"This is the area Julie wrote her song about, isn't it?"

"Yes, it is," I replied. "There's the backcountry where you and I've kayaked before, but out here locals call it way back. About a hundred square miles of water, dotted with islands and laced with cuts and channels that create a maze that's easy to get lost in."

With Cudjoe Key due south of us, I started my turn, keeping the right wingtip pointed down at the natural curve of Cudjoe Channel. When we came out of the turn, I leveled off and reduced power as we crossed Sawyer Key.

"There's our island," Savannah said, pointing slightly right of dead ahead. "I can see the roof of our house!"

I glanced over at her and smiled. It'd taken her a while to change from saying *your* island and *your* house to *ours*.

Reducing power, I added half flaps. *Ocean Hopper* slowed even more, until the air speed indicator said eighty knots. I came down low over Content Passage, lining the nose up with the shallows

between two small islands to the west and northwest of our island.

From Harbor Channel, a tongue of deeper water came into the flats north of where I'd built our house. From there, Harbor Channel turned northeast, adding even more deep water to land and take off from.

I knew the water in the tongue was four to six feet, depending on the tide. At my dock, it was three feet at low tide.

"Are you sure it's deep enough?" Savannah asked, as we came in low over the water.

"Mom," Alberto said from behind. "Dad always knows what he's doing."

She turned and smiled back at him, then turned forward and craned her neck to see over the dash. "It still looks very shallow. I can see the bottom."

I looked over at her and smiled. "We'll find out how deep it is in a few seconds."

CHAPTER TWELVE

Passing the two small islands, I reduced power a little more and dipped the nose. Just a couple feet above the water, I flared slightly and reduced power a little more. *Ocean Hopper* settled and the rush of water against her hull slowed us even more. Adding a little more throttle, I kept the flying boat up on the step at about thirty knots as I turned and lined up with the floating north dock.

Jimmy and Naomi were running out to greet us.

As I reduced power, *Ocean Hopper* settled deeper into the water, headed toward the left side of the T-head. I wanted to try a maneuver Ray had shown me, using reverse pitch on the propellors to make the plane move backward. The Mallard didn't come with reverse pitch propellers, but Ray had scrounged a pair of hub assemblies from an Albatross, the Mallard's big sister, and *Ocean Hopper* was, as far as he knew, the only Mallard that could back up.

Still a hundred feet from the dock, I moved the starboard propellor to full reverse pitch and gave the one on the port side about half a bite forward.

"Go aft and throw a line to Jimmy," I said to Savannah.

She nodded and quickly got unbuckled as the plane continued turning.

The flying boat did just as Ray had demonstrated, turning

sharply to the right. When we were turned almost completely around, I moved the port engine's prop to full reverse pitch also.

Ocean Hopper began to move backward very slowly. I opened the sliding window and looked back. The tail of the plane was a lot higher than the dock, and the horizontal stabilizer would be about chest-high, easy for Jimmy to fend off.

Still twenty feet from the dock, I reduced power to an idle, feathered the props, then shut down the engines.

"Gotcha!" I heard Jimmy yell.

I knew the tide was incoming, and the wind was out of the east, as always. The two forces would push the nose toward the dock once the tail was tied off.

I glanced back at Alberto, who was unwrapping Finn's head. "Do you think that helped?"

"It didn't hurt," he replied, unbuckling his seatbelt and the dog's harness.

I went through the rest of the shutdown checklist and joined Savannah and Alberto at the back of the plane. Jimmy had a line looped around a cleat on the left side of the T-head, easing out slack as the plane crabbed sideways toward the dock.

"Welcome back," Naomi said, as we gently bumped the fenders.

"It's good to be back," Savannah replied, stepping over and giving her a hug. "It seems like ages."

Finn began barking, suddenly recognizing his surroundings.

"Go ahead," I told him. and he was off like a shot, running and barking toward the foot of the dock.

I opened the rear cargo hatch and got another dock line out.

"Want me to go back up through the front?" Alberto offered.

"I think I can lasso the cleat from the dock," I replied.

I doubled the line, creating a long loop that I held in my right

hand, so it crossed my palm in opposite directions, widening the loop slightly. Leaving several feet of line dangling, I held another loop in my left hand.

I'd done a lot of solo sailing and boating, and more often than not, there wasn't anyone on the dock to catch my lines. Lassoing a dock cleat was easy once you got the hang of it, and this time, I was throwing at a stationary cleat just a few feet beyond my reach.

Still, I missed it on my first try, but managed to yank the line back before it fell in the water. A wet line is heavier and more difficult to throw. I got the loop over the cleat on the second try and handed one end to Alberto.

"Make this fast to the middle cleat," I told him.

He quickly tied the line off with a perfect cleat hitch and I pulled it tight around the bow cleat on the plane's nose.

"Now watch this," I told him. "If this was a fixed dock, we'd have to leave some slack for the tide and the line might come off the bow cleat."

I flipped the line so that it rolled behind and then over the bow cleat, then pulled it tight, making a double loop around the nose cleat. Then I tied the bitter end to the last deck cleat.

"Now she's all secure," Alberto said, crossing his arms.

"Whoa!" Jimmy exclaimed, looking in the plane. "You got a lot of stuff in there, man."

"There's more in the forward and aft compartments," I said. "Most of it will just stay aboard until we get to Bimini. There are three bags in the aft compartment for our stay here."

"Now I know why Jack built the new ship," he said grinning. "You need a bigger place to put all your stuff."

Finn barked several times. I looked over and saw him standing by the foot of the pier, his big tail wagging. I would swear it looked

like he was smiling. He ran out onto the pier a few steps and barked some more, then turned and ran between the two bunkhouses, where he stopped and spun around in the sand, barking one more time before tearing off again at a dead run.

"I think he wants you to come and play," I told Alberto. "I don't think you were here long enough last time for him to show you all the cool places and things he knows about."

Alberto started to run toward shore but stopped short and looked back. "What's for lunch?"

Savannah and I both laughed. The kid was always thinking about what was next on the menu.

"Crawfish étouffée," Naomi replied.

His face scrunched up in a puzzled look. "Huh?"

"It's a recipe my grandmother taught me," she replied, and then her voice slipped into pure Louisiana Cajun. "De fav'rite dish of my Cajun peoples, non? Been simmerin' all morn, since Jimmy said you'd be coming."

"You didn't have to go to all that trouble," Savannah said.

"Don't be silly," she replied. "It's no trouble at all."

I ducked into the plane and opened the rear hatch, then handed our three bags out to Jimmy, who placed them on the dock. With that accomplished, I went forward to the cockpit and got my go-bag stored under the pilot's seat.

I shouldered the biggest bag, my old Marine Corps-issued seabag, and started toward shore.

"How's everything been on the island?" I asked, as we followed behind the women.

"One of the aquaculture pumps failed last week," he replied. "So, I replaced both of them and ordered two more."

"Thanks," I offered. "Anything else?"

"It's almost time to replace the batteries," he replied.

It was a chore we'd done many times since adding an electrical system on the island. We were completely off the grid, living so far from the nearest road, and had installed our own means of power.

The big, deep-cycle marine batteries provided power to the whole island through the use of a large inverter, and they were kept charged by solar panels and a backup generator.

During the day, the electricity we used on the island came from a solar array that tracked the sun across the sky like a huge sunflower, while also recharging the batteries, then it would fold itself up at night, turn back to the east and wait for the sun to rise again. But the batteries had a life expectancy of only four years, and we'd replaced them every three. Changing them out was backbreaking work.

"Well, let's get them ordered," I said. "We can install them before we leave next week."

"There's a better way," he said. "It's pricey, man, but Tesla makes a single battery system called a Powerwall. It's about 350 pounds but gives almost six kilowatts of continuous use all night."

"That's not enough for the whole island," I said. "Even just running the bare essentials."

"That's why it'd be pricey, man," he replied, as we reached shore and continued between the bunkhouses toward the clearing I'd carved out in the middle of the island. "We'd need two of them—one for our two houses and another one for the bunkhouses and garden."

"How pricey?"

"Ten grand each," he replied. "But that's professionally installed."

"Twenty thousand?" I asked, but my mind was already doing the math.

The deep-cycle batteries we used cost a lot less, but we'd replaced them many times already, including when Hurricane Irma had nearly wiped out our little slice of paradise. At $5,000 each replacement cycle, we'd already spent a good bit more than twenty grand over the years, just in normal operation.

"How long do these Powerwalls last?" I asked.

"They come with a ten-year warranty," he replied. "But the original ones they installed ten years ago at a test facility are still working. I read that the actual life expectancy of the newer system is double the warranty."

"We'd spend that much on batteries in ten years, easy."

"And we won't have to move the old ones out and install the new ones," he added. "They send people out to do that."

"To a remote little island?" I scoffed, starting up the back steps to our house.

"Remote locations are what they specialize in, dude."

He had a point there. "Once we get settled in, you can show me," I said.

The idea of not going through the ordeal of moving all those batteries was definitely appealing. And with two of the systems he described, we'd have a little more electricity than we currently had.

I stepped into our house and saw Savannah already moving around, opening windows and vents, and checking the refrigerator and pantry.

Our house didn't need air conditioning. Vents in the floor allowed cool air to rise up from under the house, exiting through the ridge vent in the exposed roof. The water under the house rarely got warmer than eighty-five degrees in summer or cooler than seventy-five in the winter, keeping the house comfortable all year long. Well, at least not scorching hot.

"Just set everything there by the bedroom door," I told Jimmy.

"We'll get out of your hair," Naomi said to my wife. "Once you're settled in, come on out to the tables and we'll catch up."

"Give us ten minutes," Savannah said. "We didn't bring much."

When they left, I followed Savannah into the bedroom, dropping the seabag on the floor by the bed. She opened the windows on the east and south sides, creating a nice breeze through the room.

I grabbed her around the waist and pulled her close. "You should have told her half an hour," I said mischievously.

She kissed me and pulled me close. "It's so good to be home," she whispered in my ear. Then she pushed me away. "But half an hour wouldn't be enough time for what you have in mind."

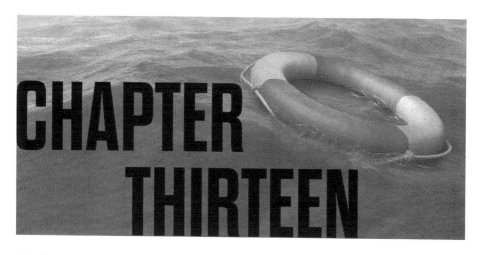

CHAPTER THIRTEEN

Naomi's lunch, cooked over a driftwood fire in the stone fireplace next to the tables, was delicious. Afterward, Jimmy brought his laptop out and connected to the Internet by using his phone as a hot spot.

While he pulled up the website he wanted to show me, I looked around the clearing. I hadn't realized just how much I'd missed this place. It was a lot different than it was the first time I'd visited and shown it to Rusty.

After Hurricane Irma, there hadn't been a whole lot left. The fireplace had survived since it was anchored on a thick concrete pad below ground level. It was six feet tall, made of stone, and had a built-in grill at counter height. One of the tables had crashed through the wall of the eastern bunkhouse and lodged there. The other table had disappeared, and I figured it'd been swept away and destroyed in the violent wind and waves that'd lashed the island. But two weeks later, I found it washed up on the north side of a nearby island.

Of the four structures, only my house had survived, but even it had had its roof ripped off. We'd rebuilt, with help from Jack Armstrong and a small army of hired professionals. We'd built the other three houses on stilts like mine, and everything was

constructed to Cat-5 standards, including the tables, which were now anchored five feet deep in solid bedrock.

"Here it is," Jimmy said, turning the laptop so I could see.

"That's it?" I asked, seeing a picture of a smallish box mounted to the side of a house.

"Yeah," he replied. "It's the shape of the future, man. Those big, heavy batteries we've been using are meant for boats or trucks. People adapted them to use for backup shore power, but they're still just marine batteries, ya know. This bank is the larger one Tesla sells. It provides five-point-eight kilowatts of continuous power and ten kilowatts of peak power for up to ten seconds. That's for, you know, when an air conditioner or pump first kicks on."

I looked at the spec sheet he was showing me. The unit measured 45.3 inches tall and 29.6 wide, with a depth of only 5.75 inches. Both could easily fit inside the battery shack, with lots more room between them than we had between the two banks of marine batteries. The aquaculture system, as well as all four houses, were each on a separate circuit, so rerouting them would be easy.

"That small and it can store that much?"

He nodded enthusiastically. "Yeah, man. The sunflower provides all we need during the day, while charging the Powerwall. Then the Powerwall provides any electricity we'd need at night."

Our solar array, or "sunflower," as Jimmy liked to call it, was composed of twelve pie-shaped solar panels that opened up like a flower. It was located on the smaller island just a few feet away from the main one, and it tracked the sun across the sky all day, folding in its "petals" and returning to face the direction the sun would rise the next morning.

"With the sunflower and two of these," he continued, "we can run everything, twenty-four hours a day. Even the air conditioner in

your house."

"My house doesn't have an air conditioner," I reminded him.

"You'll find one in your closet," he said with a grin. "I was going to install it before you got back, but the work on the pump took priority."

"I don't need—"

"But maybe Savannah and Alberto would like it."

He did have a point. And the truth was, I'd grown accustomed to the conditioned air aboard *Ambrosia*.

"Order them," I said. "We'll just stay on the batteries until they can come out and install them. With the time we save not swapping out the batteries, we can install the air conditioner. What is it? One of those noisy window units?"

"It can be installed in a window," he replied. "But I think it'd be better if it was installed in the wall."

"Why?"

"Trust me, man," he said, with a knowing smile. "Those things are a lot quieter when they're built in."

Time management had always been one of the biggest problems living on the island. Even something as simple as going to the grocery store took planning. There was no such thing as popping out to a convenience store when we ran out of sugar. The shortest trip was to Old Wooden Bridge Marina on the north end of Big Pine and that was a twenty-minute boat ride. If it rained, you got wet. If it was hot, you sweated. And if it was cold, you shivered.

"Changing out those batteries would be an all-day job," I said, more thinking out loud. "We could probably frame out a spot in the living room in a day."

Jimmy practically buzzed with excitement. "I'll get right on it, man."

"I need to give Rusty a call," I said, rising from the table. "We're planning a big dinner aboard *Ambrosia* tonight. You and Naomi, as well as all the regulars at the Anchor, are invited."

Out of habit, I headed back up to the deck surrounding three sides of my house. It had once been the only place I could get a cell signal, and then, only if I held my tongue in my cheek just right. Since they'd put a new tower up on the north end of Big Pine Key, we could get two bars just about anywhere on the island.

Alberto and Finn met me at the bottom of the steps. Finn danced around us excitedly, his tongue hanging out.

"You seem happy to be home," I said, scratching his neck when he sat on my foot. "What have you two been up to?"

"Picking mangos," Alberto replied. "We found six that were good and ripe."

"Did you give them to Mom?"

"Yeah. Well, five of 'em anyway. She said we could eat them by the fire tonight. Are we gonna have one?"

The old fire ring was one other thing that had survived the hurricane. It was made of thick steel and weighed nearly two hundred pounds. Over time, sand had piled up around it, so it was sunk a few inches in the ground when the storm hit. At first, I'd thought it too had been washed away and was surprised to find it had only been filled and covered with sand—the whole island was under ten feet of water at the peak of the storm. I could tell by the water marks on my stilt house.

"A fire's almost a necessity here," I replied. "When the sun goes down, the bugs come out in force."

"And the fire keeps them away?"

"Smoke from some kinds of wood will," I replied as we went up the steps. "But biting gnats and mosquitoes are drawn by heat, so

any kind of fire will draw them in and burn them up."

"What kind of wood? Do we have any?"

"I know cedar, sage, and lemongrass work, but I don't think there's any on the island."

"Can we go get some?"

"I'll add it to the list," I said. "I'm sure Mom wants to make a run to the store."

He and Finn went inside, and I stepped over to the south-facing part of the deck. When I'd built the house, it was barely visible through the trees growing around it. Now, after Irma had practically swept the island of vegetation, the house itself was the southernmost thing on the island and remained in full sun all day. We'd replanted some trees—mangos and oranges mostly, and the mangroves were coming back. All that sun on the house was another good reason to put in an air conditioner.

I took my phone out and pulled up my old friend's landline number at the bar. Robert answered on the second ring. "Rusty Anchor."

"Hey, Robert. It's Jesse. Is Rusty around?"

"He's out back with Rufus and the two cooks from your boat. Want me to get him?"

I said yeah, and he clunked the old rotary phone's receiver down on the bar. I could hear the back door open and close and a few faint voices from inside the bar, probably at a table. The door opened and closed again, then Rusty came on.

"What's up, bro?"

"A duck's ass when he eats."

"Har-har," Rusty said. "Get that one from Alberto?"

I chuckled. "Hey, we're having a dinner party aboard *Ambrosia* tonight and everyone from the Anchor is invited."

"Kinda short notice, ain't it?"

"Well, yeah, but—"

"Just yankin' your chain, bud. Savvy called two days ago."

"Oh, it's like that now, huh?" I said with mock indignation.

"Hey, you got a lot on your plate and she's a planner. Let her do whatever she can to take some of your load. That's all I'm sayin'."

"So, you'll come?"

"We're closin' down at four and bringin' the pontoon boat and a designated driver."

"Pontoon boat?"

"Yeah. Remember that tiki bar taxi that blew away during Irma? Big sister Bertha arrived today."

"I'm almost afraid to ask," I muttered.

"Thirty-six-foot custom-built pontoon boat with twin Suzuki one-forties."

"Will you be able to bring everyone at once?" I asked, looking forward to hearing whatever whacky deal Rusty'd made to get it. "I can have one or both of the tenders sent over."

"Just gonna be about nine or ten of us," he replied. "She'll seat twenty easy. Or stand thirty."

"So, you know what time, then?" I asked.

"Sure do," he replied, then chuckled. "Do you?"

"I'll see you at eighteen hundred," I replied.

"Eighteen-thirty," he corrected

"I want you there early, jackass!"

He laughed and hung up with a clunk of the receiver.

CHAPTER FOURTEEN

With the sun still high above the horizon to the west-northwest, we boarded the little Grady-White I'd bought years ago up in Beaufort, South Carolina. While Jimmy got the lines, I started the engine and checked the gauges and controls. As always, Jimmy had everything in good running condition.

Savannah and Naomi stashed their purses and phones on the small dash, then moved up to sit on the little seat just in front of the center console. Alberto and Finn went past them and up onto the forward casting deck.

"You won't be able to ride there, once we get up on plane," Savannah reminded him.

"Aw, but this is the best place to ride."

"Too much weight," I said. "If you and Finn move aft it's a transfer of more than three hundred pounds."

Alberto looked at me, puzzled, then looked at Finn. "How much does he *weigh?*"

"About a hundred pounds," I replied. "But since you're moving aft of the center of gravity..."

I saw the light go on behind his eyes. "The weight's doubled! His one hundred and my sixty times two."

"You got it," I said with a laugh. "It'll take one-sixty off the bow

and add one-sixty to the stern."

"You're very smart," Naomi said as Alberto moved aft. "How'd you get so smart?"

"I don't know," he replied with a shrug.

"It might be because you've had some smart teachers," Savannah said.

"But you and Miss Mayra have been my..." He paused, then a sly smile came to his face. "I see what you did there."

Alberto had turned ten just a couple of weeks earlier, but when he first came to live with us, we knew he was gifted and since then, he'd been absorbing anything Savannah and Mayra could teach him, including adult humor and sarcasm.

I idled slowly through my channel toward the deeper natural channel less than a hundred yards from my house. When I'd first bought the island, I was keeping *Gaspar's Revenge* at Dockside and dug the first channel by hand while building the house. I'd made the channel just deep and wide enough to get my little flats skiff through, but it still meant moving a lot of sand and limestone by hand. Later, I'd used Rusty's big salvage barge and backhoe to make it wider and deeper in order to allow the *Revenge* to be brought out and docked under the house.

"High tide was less than an hour ago," Jimmy said, checking the small chart plotter's depth reading. "There's still plenty of water over the flats south of Mac's place."

I turned into Harbor Channel and slowly brought the speed up, listening to the engine.

"How's he been?" I asked. "Any trouble since the incident on Boot Key?"

Nearly a year ago, Jimmy had told me about a run-in my nearest neighbor, Mac Travis, had had with a bunch of squatters and

vagrants on Boot Key, on the southwest side of Marathon. There'd been several people murdered.

"Been quiet as a church on Saturday over there, man," he replied knowingly. The way sound traveled over water, little happened out here that he didn't know about. "Unless I see his boat," Jimmy continued. "I wouldn't even know they were there."

Mac and his girlfriend, Mel Woodson, lived on an island over a mile from mine at the upper end of Harbor Channel. Her father had purchased it years earlier and Wood, as everyone called him, had built a little stilt house there. Mel had inherited it when he was killed up on the mainland and later, the house was torched by some nefarious characters and Mac had rebuilt it.

"Let me guess," I said, pushing the throttle forward until the Grady reached planing speed and raising my voice to be heard. "Trufante hasn't been around much."

"He and Pam have been laying low, man. I think what happened out there spooked him. He's not a bad dude, he's just a bad magnet."

Reaching twenty knots, I pulled back on the throttle a little and steered toward the unmarked cut through the shallows. I looked over and didn't see a boat tied up at Mac's place, but that didn't mean much. He had a small boat he could winch all the way up into the tree line behind a gate.

I weaved through the cut, watching the water surface, then turned south in deeper water, heading toward the Seven Mile Bridge. Jimmy checked the depth and chart plotter regularly. Though we both knew the water very well, the bottom was constantly changing, and our knowledge had to change with it. I was trusting him to warn me if anything was new, but with a slight chop on the water, seeing the shallows was a piece of cake.

After passing under the bridge, I began a wide turn around

Knight's Key and East Sister Rock, then *Ambrosia* came into view. The women began talking excitedly, though I couldn't make out what they were saying.

"That sure is some boat," Jimmy said.

"Wait'll you see *Phoenix*," I said. "She's half again as big."

"I remember the pictures you sent me last time you went to Bimini," Jimmy said. "Pretty weird-looking boat."

It was, I had to admit. Jimmy rarely saw anything as being odd or off-kilter though—that was normal in the Keys.

Was *Phoenix* so unusual looking it would even be regarded as odd by those who saw odd on a daily basis? If so, it meant it was really out there, which I also had to admit was true. I'd seen my share of weird, but for some reason, I seemed to be drawn to *Phoenix*.

The overall concept was sort of like old-Spanish-galleon-meets-Cousteau-meets-the-twenty-first century. She was high at both ends and low in the middle, reminiscent of the galleons and naos that plied the Atlantic from Europe to the New World four hundred years ago.

Alberto squirmed his way in between us. "We're flying to Bimini in Dad's airplane next week. After that, we'll live on *Phoenix*."

"Oh yeah?" Jimmy asked, looking down at him. "What are you gonna be doing there, little dude?"

"I'll be in school most of the time," he replied. "Me and Roberto and two more kids."

"Two more, huh?" Jimmy said, looking up at me.

"Deuce will be head of onboard security," I said. "He, Julie, and the boys will be living aboard."

"How many people in all?"

I slowed as we neared *Ambrosia*. "She'll have a round-the-clock crew of forty," I replied. "With liveaboard accommodations for up to

twenty scientists."

"Didn't you tell me once that *Ambrosia's* crew was about that?"

"You're wondering why a ship that's fifty percent bigger has the same number of crew?"

"Yeah, man. Seems to me you'd need more."

"Fewer, actually. A lot of things are automated, and everything aboard is state of the art. From what Jack says, she can literally be crewed by just three people."

I could see *Ambrosia's* underwater lights were on, as well as those on the work platform and the cockpit above it. With the sun behind us, they weren't really needed, but it did create a warm, welcoming glow.

Fenders were situated all around the platform, so we didn't have to deploy any from the Grady.

Peter Jarvis, the ship's bosun, stood in the middle of the work deck, flanked by Al and Jocko. Peter was in full uniform, with his bosun's whistle dangling around his neck on a braided cord.

Bringing the Grady in at an angle to the work deck, I reversed the engine and spun the wheel toward *Ambrosia*. The boat stopped, and as the stern began creeping toward the platform, I shifted to neutral and stepped over to hand Jocko the stern line. Jimmy was forward and, once he'd passed the bow line to Al, the two men pulled the little boat alongside.

Peter blew the signal for *Attention*, then spoke into a microphone clipped to his collar. "Captain McDermitt and party, arriving." His whistle and announcement echoed from speakers inside the yacht.

. Savannah and Naomi grabbed their stuff from the console and stepped over to the work deck, while Jimmy and Alberto helped Finn get down.

"Need me to carry anything, Cap'n?" Jocko asked, with a big, toothy smile.

"Nothing to carry," I said, as Matt and Val came down the steps from the cockpit.

"*Gorthugher da*, Cap'n," the Cornishman said, crossing the deck and extending his hand.

"And a good evening to you," I replied, shaking hands with him. "Have you had a chance to get out on the reef since we got here?"

"Val and I took a bit of a plunge this afternoon, yeah? No big walls or anything, but plenty of life down there."

"What about moving into your new quarters?"

"Hung up a few things," he replied. "I'll get to the rest dreckly, I s'pose."

Dreckly was a Cornishman's way of saying he'd get to something sooner or later, but it wasn't a high priority.

A horn blared and we both turned to see the longest pontoon boat I think I'd ever laid eyes on. It was turning toward *Ambrosia's* stern, and I recognized Rusty standing at the front.

"That's Rusty," I said, looking at my watch. "He's early. And it appears he has a new toy."

"The only difference between men and boys..." Savannah said to Val.

"Is the price of their toys," *Ambrosia's* new first mate concluded.

"Pull the Grady around to the port cleat," I said to Al, "then let her out on a good rode."

As the massive pontoon boat approached the stern, my Grady drifted back, swinging on its painter in the current, leaving plenty of room for Rusty to pull up bow-first beside it.

Jimmy moved toward the middle of the platform, ready to catch a line from Rusty, who had moved over to the starboard rail on the

bow.

He tossed a line underhanded to Jimmy, then moved to the port side and did the same, throwing a line to Jocko.

As the two men pulled the long pontoon boat closer, Rusty activated some controls by the center gate and a ramp slowly extended out from between the pontoons. It stopped about three feet beyond the edge of the work deck, an easy step down.

"Just tie her off snug to the fenders," Rusty said, stepping out onto the gangplank and raising two handles at the end.

Robert killed the engines, then came forward to hand Rusty a pair of lines with carabiners attached to the ends. Rusty clipped them to the tops of the two uprights and Robert tied the bitter ends off to the forward rail, creating an easy handhold for the passengers.

"That's pretty cool," Jimmy said. "But what if the deck was higher or you pulled up on a beach?"

Rusty stepped down and put a hand on one of the uprights. "The gangway comes out ten feet," he said. "Puttin' the engines more'n fifteen yards from the beach. Then the plank can be raised or lowered, and these end poles ratcheted down into the sand or used to hold the boat against a pair of fenders."

Sidney, Rufus, Marcos, and Grady, along with a few regulars from the Anchor, began to file off, joining Savannah and Naomi, all talking together.

Matt stepped over to Rusty and nodded toward the massive pontoon boat. "What do ya call a vessel such as this, mate?"

"I don't reckon y'all have anything like this in England," Rusty said with a grin. "Around these parts, it's called a party barge."

"A party barge?" Matt asked, a whimsical expression lighting up his face. "You mean like a...floating do?"

"If a 'do' means a bunch of friends gettin' together for a good

time," Rusty replied with a nod, "then, yeah."

Matt looked back at the stern. "And it needs two-hundred-eighty horsepower to move the do?"

Rusty nodded again, a broad smile on his face. "If ya wanna move yer do at forty knots, it do."

Matt laughed as one of the local fishing guides, a man called Dink, stepped off last. "Heck of a boat, Jesse."

"Sure is," I said, moving over to the gangway and looking down the middle of the boat.

"I meant this big ole yacht," Dink said with a chuckle.

"Oh, yeah, thanks," I said. I never knew quite how to respond to compliments on *Ambrosia.* "Feel free to look around."

"Thanks," he replied, then followed some of the others up to the cockpit.

I looked at my old friend. "Permission to board."

"C'mon," Rusty said, leading the way.

Matt followed behind me as I crossed over and stepped down onto the foredeck.

"This is Miss Bertha," Rusty said proudly, as he swept his arms wide. "She's thirty-six feet long and ten feet wide—three hundred and sixty square feet. The arch has four big woofers facing aft and four more forward, with another eight speakers all around the deck. There's a pair of eight-foot sun pads aft and half of one of 'em can be raised up four feet, with a privacy curtain surrounding a small Porta-Potty."

"Almost as big as my first house," I said, looking around at the expansive seating area.

"Bigger'n mine," Matt added.

"There's a gas grill under this seat, big enough for twenty lobster tails at once," Rusty said. "In five minutes, it can be rigged

outboard the forward rail and warming up."

The set-up was very functional and for a pontoon boat, pretty damned luxurious. "Everything looks brand-new," I said.

Rusty chuckled. "It is. The engines only have four hours on them, and most of that was idling at the dock before we came out here."

"Brand-new?" I asked dubiously.

Rusty had made a living for many years by scrounging boatyards, buying hulls, engines, and assorted parts and hardware, then putting them together with other parts and selling running boats. But this didn't look like any boat project he'd done himself. Not that he couldn't, but it was obvious the boat had been built by a team of skilled craftsmen.

"Factory new," he said. "Always wanted one of these and this is the biggest and best they come. Go big or go home, bro."

Robert was seated at the helm, his legs stretched out alongside it, arms folded across his chest, as he stared across the boat and out over the water toward the lights of Key Colony Beach and Coco Plum. He looked adrift. It was a Marine Corps term. Marines don't get lost; we just go adrift sometimes. Robert looked like he was reminiscing over some great loss.

"You're not joining the party?" I asked him.

He turned his gaze upward, as if seeing us for the first time. "Hmm?"

"The dinner party," I said. "You'll be joining us, right?"

He glanced over at Rusty, then back at me. "I thought I was just driving the boat."

CHAPTER FIFTEEN

Whenever you can put like-minded people together, people who are skilled in what they do, then remove ego from the equation, you foster a medium for sharing and an intertwining of abilities where the whole is much greater than the sum of the parts.

That was dinner aboard *Ambrosia*.

Rusty told me that Marcos and Grady had spent most of the day ashore, just hanging out with Rufus at his little outdoor kitchen behind the Anchor.

Rufus's kitchen and walk-in freezer took up most of one side of the outdoor deck area. In the opposite corner was a small stage overlooking the marina and backyard. The deck wrapped around the other side of the building, with a great view of the marina and sunsets filtered through mangroves beyond the canal.

I'd always thought it was that deck, the yard, and the marina with the full panoramic view of the ocean beyond that fostered a sort of communal thinking.

Rufus, Marcos, and Grady were excellent chefs, each in a different way. Their age range was generational. Rufus was old enough to be father and grandfather to the other two men, though nobody knew for sure just what his true age was. He was Jamaican and had been the head chef in one of his country's finest

restaurants. He'd retired years ago and worked for Rusty part-time, in exchange for his little shack by the beach.

Marcos was Venezuelan and, along with his entire family, had run a high-end resort in Maracaibo, working mostly in the kitchen while his wife Mayra ran the day-to-day operation, and their three daughters did most of the manual labor.

Grady was the youngest of the three. He'd been the sous-chef at one of Atlanta's best barbecue restaurants when he'd been hired by Jack Armstrong. He was smart, quick-witted, and got along with everyone he met.

Rusty told me that while the three cooks had talked, occasional orders were placed and they just all chipped in, working together, quickly picking up on one another's techniques, recipes, methods, and ideas. He said it was like watching three masters of the guitar, talking, picking, and strumming, none following any known melody, but all improvising and playing off each other.

So, by the time the three men came out to *Ambrosia*, they'd already planned the menu, but had raided Rusty's freezer and made two trips over to the Publix in Rusty's pickup. The odd thing was, Grady was the only one of the three who had ever driven a car.

As the evening progressed, I got several opportunities to sit and talk with Robert, trying to feel him out without seeming too pushy. I sensed that something huge had recently happened and it was almost like he was experiencing shock.

In previous talks, and from what Savannah and I had learned from Rusty and the others, I knew that Robert Grant had been, to all outward appearances, a wealthy and successful businessman.

Until it all suddenly went away.

Nobody wanted to pry, and he'd volunteered only a few details about what had happened, fragmented and out of sequence. From

what others said, he'd been living the good life, settling into the Keys lifestyle, while apparently working from home and doing quite well. What had brought him to the Rusty Anchor with nothing more than beer money in his pocket was a mystery.

So, naturally, rumors started going around. It was a small town and people liked to talk. One rumor had him recently married to a Russian spy who'd drained all his assets. Another said he'd put everything he owned on the line for some stock option that tanked. Other notions offered had run the gamut from his having had Mafia connections up north and been cut off, to his being a drug smuggler, or smug druggler, as the locals would say.

The coconut telegraph was arcing and burning with speculation.

It was close to 2200 when Savannah and I went up to the flybridge to enjoy the night air one last time. We found Robert sitting there, staring off toward the northeast, toward the houses, apartments, and high-rise condos that lit up the sky over Key Colony and Coco Plum.

It was the third time I'd seen him just staring in that direction. Rufus's little shack, where Robert had been staying the last few nights, had the same view.

I'd spoken to Rufus about him, and he'd told me that Robert was only there at night and most of the time simply sat in a recliner and stared out the window toward the water.

"I'm sorry," Robert said, as we came onto the fly bridge. "I'll go back down below."

"No, no," Savannah said, quickly moving and putting a hand on his shoulder. "We're interrupting *you*. Please sit back down."

He did and looked back and forth between the two of us. "But it's your boat."

117

"We don't own her," I said. "I was the captain, but this is my last night aboard. Matt, the young Cornishman you met earlier, will be taking over when *Ambrosia* leaves here to head back to Bimini for her annual inspection and refit."

"May we join you?" Savannah asked, smiling at him as if Robert was an old friend.

"Um, sure."

We sat down and his eyes drifted toward Key Colony again.

"Did you used to live over there?" Savannah asked. "I've seen you looking that way a few times, like you'd lost a puppy over there."

He blinked, then looked at her. "A puppy?"

"Or a mother," she said softly, "or a wife."

His eyes drifted back to the horizon. "Yes, I used to live there. Do you see that tallest building?"

"Bonefish Tower?" I asked, looking toward the fourteen-story condo. "It's lucky to still be there after Irma."

"Four previous hurricanes would argue that point, Mr. McDer... um... Captain?"

"Just Jesse and Savvy are fine," I said.

Savannah never introduced herself by the shortened version of her name and that was the first time I had. But those closest to her sometimes used it and I wanted Robert to feel more comfortable. His nerves seemed on edge.

"So, you did live over there?" Savannah coaxed.

"I owned the penthouse," he replied. "Until I met her."

An hour later, as we were getting ready to leave *Ambrosia* for the last time, Jimmy said he and Naomi were going to stay at her place

and asked if Alberto might want to spend the night.

My eyebrow moved a fraction of an inch as I turned my eyes on Jimmy.

"*No dentro de cien vara, mi capitán.*

Jimmy believed that in some previous incarnation, he'd been a sixteenth-century foot soldier in the Spanish army—a *conquistador*—and he often slipped into "Spanglish" or full-blown Castilian Spanish.

But in his *current* life, the only one in which I employed him, he partook of the ganja. My rule was simple. I didn't want it around me. Not on my boats. Not in my car. And only when he and Naomi were alone on my island. I didn't know if she smoked it or not and didn't want to know. It was none of my business what a person did in their private life, unless they were someone I cared for, and they were hurting themselves or others. Jimmy was the consummate professional when he was on the job.

What he was telling me was that he would extend and widen my boundary to include Alberto. He'd told me once that a *vara* was one of the first units of measure in Spain and was about thirty-two inches, a few inches shy of a yard. So, *cien vara* was a little short of a hundred yards. In other words, he was promising there was no weed in Naomi's apartment.

"Naomi knows a special place where the water glows at night," Alberto said. "Can I stay?"

"Finn will probably miss you," I said, knowing that the dog—in his eighties in dog years—could probably use a break from the energetic boy.

"We have all week," Alberto said. "And besides, maybe he needs to just lay in the sun for a while."

Savannah giggled at her reference to the times I often liked to

just be alone and soak up the sun.

"Okay," I replied and turned back to Jimmy. "You'll bring him out in the morning?"

"Late morning," Naomi said. "We're going to splash around for a few hours."

So, with just Savannah and Finn aboard, we headed west, keeping East Sister Rock well off our starboard side. I brought the throttle up to just under planing speed, the bow high, and the engine still quiet enough to talk over.

"So, what did you make of all that?" Savannah asked.

"I think they just thought we might like some time alone."

She looked over at me with the moon shining down from the port side and slightly ahead of us. Savannah and Luna had a good thing going. The light played across her face in a most seductive way.

"I wasn't talking about them," she said, bursting my fantasy bubble.

"Robert Grant?"

"Yes, and the people who swindled him out of everything."

I looked over at her and by just the moonlight, I could read the fire in her eyes and the firm set of her jawline. Savannah had a very defined sense of right and wrong and was a strong-willed Southern woman who wouldn't turn her back to wrongdoers.

"He's an islander, like us," she said. "It doesn't matter where he came here *from*, or what he does or used to do. He chose to make these islands his home. And from those I've talked to, he contributed to the community in a good way."

"You want to try to get his money back or something?" I asked, already knowing the answer.

She looked over at me and I guess she saw the same thing in my expression. I didn't like thieves, con-artists, and swindlers. And from

what he'd told us, eyes vacant, as if recounting a dull news story, he'd fallen victim to all three. And on top of that, he'd been tricked into falling in love with a woman who at first wanted to rob him and then when his business deal went south, wanted to help him create a new identity. But it turned out that robbing Robert Grant was the goal all along. Only the version of the scam changed.

Savannah's features softened. "Nothing we can do tonight," she said, eyes sparkling with mischief. "And we *do* have the whole island to ourselves."

I grinned and pushed the throttle forward, bringing the little center console up on plane and heading north into the backcountry.

CHAPTER SIXTEEN

The man who would soon be Bart Mason sat at a table on a second-story balcony overlooking Duval Street. The noise from below was a cacophony of voices, shouts, laughter, cars, mopeds, and live music from at least half a dozen venues just on the one block.

He was invisible—a shadow looking down from above, like some great horned owl in the darkness. In the minds of the people in the street below, he didn't exist. Nobody ever looked up, especially when they were enjoying themselves and having a good time with friends.

Even if he were on the street with them, he'd be an average-looking guy. His hair was now cut very short in a modern-day version of a crew cut. It was several shades darker than it had been and looked darker still due to the shadowy brown stubble on his cheeks.

When he'd arrived in town, everything had worked just as he'd been told it would. He'd had no trouble at the airport in Miami and no issue with his credit card when he'd checked in. He'd done everything as instructed, and spent a lot of money, glad-handing the local waitstaff and bartenders, store clerks, and street vendors. He'd made Thom Smythe known and recognized all over town.

Spencer had him buy two round-trip tickets—one using his fake name, bound for Paris, and another under his new name, making the short hop from Miami to Key West. Spencer had even hired

someone who looked enough like him to fly to Paris in his place, using his real credentials.

"Oh, there you are."

Smythe turned as the blond Czechian woman who would soon be pretending to be his wife stepped out onto the small terrace. Her hair was styled exquisitely, pinned up, with a curl dangling down on one side of her face. She wore a tight-fitting red dress with long sleeves but bare shoulders. He guessed the sleeves were connected to the dress under her arms. She slowly tipped a champagne flute to full, red lips.

"Just trying out my invisibility cloak," he said, then looked up the street as a car honked.

"You have nothing to worry about," Katya said, her Rs just a little thick with lightly accented English. "We have done this many times. Do you like the name I chose for you?"

"Bart," he said flatly. "Cowabunga, dude."

She took a couple more steps toward him, heels clicking on the boards. A slight giggle escaped her lips as she covered her mouth. "It is a manly name. Not for a little skate-boarding cretin. They should have called him Tommy."

"I have to admit," he said, "the ID and everything worked just like Mr. Spencer said it would."

For the short flight from Miami to Key West, he'd used his new ID and credit card. Bart Mason arrived without fanfare, stepped off the plane and fell right back into his old persona as Thom Smythe.

"Are you ready for *Act One*?" Katya asked. "I like this one better than the 'mail-order bride' plan."

He looked at her dubiously. "Is all this really necessary?"

"It is a game," she said. "Like smoke and mirrors. We will get people to notice and remember you, Mr. Thom Smythe, the luckiest

124

man in Key West. Pretending is a fantasy, is it not?"

"I still think it's ridiculous," he muttered as he stood.

She set her flute down on the table and approached him, straightening his shirt, and smoothing imaginary wrinkles from his chest and shoulders. She traced her hand lightly across the stubble on the side of his head and face.

"I like this cut," she said. "It is like Jiří Procházka."

"Who's that?"

"He is a famous Czech MMA fighter," she said, pouting a little. "You do not know him?"

"I don't have much time for watching sports," he replied. "And I still think all this isn't necessary. But, as you say, you've done it before."

"We can make it fun, can we not?"

To say Katya Popova was a beautiful woman would be a massive understatement. Smythe stared into her eyes, as bright and blue as a glacier. The woman was sensual beyond belief without even trying, seductive with nothing more than a passing glance, and she exuded a pervasive, wanton attitude with a simple smile. She was probably two inches shorter than his five-nine, but her heels put her at eye level at least, maybe slightly taller. Her body was lean, yet wide in the hips, where the dress flared from her tiny waist, hugging her thighs tightly.

He looked into Katya's eyes and could see a hunger lurking in those ice-blue orbs.

"When you come to the bar, do not be surprised if there are one or two men ahead of you," she said seductively, running her fingertips down his arm. "But I am what you would call a sure thing. So, you will not have to try so hard."

Tonight, would be their "first meeting," which would take place in a public area. He'd made friends with the bartender on the first floor and was already known as a big spender. Katya would go to the bar first and he'd wait half an hour before also going down. Then he was to strike up a flirtatious conversation and before the night ended, everyone would see him score the hottest woman on Duval Street. The two would celebrate their newfound love for the next several days, making it clear that their futures and destinies were entwined.

According to Spencer, the best way to not stick out like a sore thumb was to be a sore thumb in a sea of sore thumbs. At least half the people on the little island at the very tip of Florida were looking for someone of the opposite sex, and for a good many, the same sex.

Katya Popova and Thom Smythe would be the hottest couple in the Keys since Bogey and Bacall. Their meeting, quick affair, and subsequent marriage would be the talk of the town. Everyone would know who they were.

"A sure thing, huh?" Smythe asked.

She smiled seductively. "Mike and I have an understanding," she began, then lightly raked her teeth over her lower lip as she looked at him with eyes as deep as arctic ice. "Even with his little blue pill he knows he cannot satisfy me."

"I can't shake it out of my head that this is all some elaborate ruse," he said, "put on by those who want me dead. Any minute, I'm expecting your husband's gonna bust through the door and shoot me."

She stepped even closer, their faces only inches apart. He could feel the heat radiating from her body.

"If Mike wanted to kill you," she whispered, "you would be dead. You have hired us to help you and that is what we are doing."

"He's doing it by allowing his wife to share my bed?"

126

MAN OVERBOARD

She took both his hands and placed them on her hips, then slipped her arms around his neck, cradling his head. "You speak as if I have no say in this matter," she said softly, her breath moist on his lips.

When he kissed her, she responded with intense passion, crushing her body against him as her tongue played across his teeth, searching for his. Her lithe frame squirmed against him like a slow-moving constrictor.

He kissed her more deeply, letting his hands roam down her back and across her voluptuous hips.

She broke the kiss and pulled his head down onto her neck, arching her back, and pushing her pelvis against his growing manhood.

Finally, she pushed away from him, her breathing a little ragged. "I think we can most definitely have fun with this, Bart."

"Eat my shorts, man."

She giggled again, then kissed him lightly on the cheek, whispering in his ear, "This too may happen."

Katya broke free of his embrace, turned, and walked seductively back toward the door. She stopped and turned sideways, leaning against the door frame and arching her back. Then she smiled sensually and raised her left leg high, bent at the knee, baring her thigh and just a little bit of her butt cheek.

"Do not keep me waiting," she breathed huskily, and then she was gone.

Smythe heard the room's door click as she exited, then went back over to the table where she'd left the champagne flute still half full.

He picked it up and raised the glass to the heavens. "To new beginnings," he said before drinking the bubbly.

He sat back down at the table and checked his watch. The sounds from the street reached his ears, but he could still hear Katya's words hanging in the air.

For the next thirty minutes, he thought about what he might have done differently to have avoided the situation he was in. Finally, he stood, deciding he'd played his cards right and fate had just dealt a better hand to someone else.

He had no family, but he'd miss the group of friends and associates he had in his previous life. Over time, he'd be forgotten. But Bart Mason would live on.

Leaving the room, he took the elevator to the ground floor and entered the first of La Concha's three bars. It was still early, the sun had only been down for an hour, but there were a good many people there, mostly sitting at the bar.

But no Katya.

The next bar was smaller, a bit more intimate. That was where he found her, sitting, legs crossed, on a bar stool with her back against the dark wooden bar. Two men, both dressed as tourists, were laughing with her.

The bartender, a woman slightly older than Smythe, smiled at him, recognizing him from the previous night.

Smythe put on his game face, smiled back at her, and strolled confidently toward the bar. "Hello, Coral," he said, eliciting an even brighter smile from the woman.

Coral LaRoc hadn't needed to tell him where she was from; the first words out of her mouth had told him that when he'd first sat down at her bar. The previous night, she'd told him she'd been in Key West for twenty years and still couldn't shake her Boston accent.

Smythe remembered things people told him. He'd always had uncanny recall, which likely contributed to his success in some small

way. People liked it when you remembered them.

She'd also told him that she'd only come to Key West to visit an aunt and ended up staying. The aunt had been a fortune teller who'd lived on the island since the 1970s, when she was a young woman.

"The Macallan, Mr. Smythe?" Coral asked as he slid onto a stool two down from Katya.

Coral also had a good memory for details, he thought, figuring it was a good trait for a bartender.

"Yes, please," he replied. "And didn't we agree it was just Thom?"

She smiled as she produced a highball glass, deposited a single cube of ice in it, then poured the golden Scotch whisky over it until the cube floated.

She placed the drink in front of him and smiled again. "Anything else, Thom?" she asked with a bright smile.

She was a pretty woman, waifish, with blond hair past her shoulders and brown eyes. He remembered that she'd said she was also a dancer and aerobics instructor for a while, but she'd given up the teaching after her first child.

Smythe looked around the bar, then smiled at Coral. "Yes, there is," he replied, lifting his voice slightly. "I'm celebrating. Another round for everyone!"

CHAPTER SEVENTEEN

I woke early the following morning, still somewhat exhausted from the events of the previous night but feeling very good overall. Better than I'd felt in quite a while. We were back home, if only for a week. I'd forgotten how much I'd truly missed my little corner of paradise in the backcountry.

Quietly getting out of bed so as not to wake Savannah, I pulled on a clean pair of skivvies and padded barefoot into the living room, the aroma from the automatic coffeemaker filling my nostrils.

Finn lay on his rug in the middle of the room and lifted his head as I quietly closed the bedroom door. He watched me as I crossed the room and poured a mug.

I jerked my head toward the door, clicked my tongue, and Finn rose and followed me outside. The air felt dryer than usual for this time of year. July was typically hot and humid, with both official measurements nearing three digits. While it was a warm morning, it wasn't nearly as muggy as it usually was.

It was barely light; the sun still below the horizon, but ready to spring forth at any moment. All around, everything was tinted in shades of morning gray. We went to the rear steps and then down to the ground.

There'd been a time when Finn would have torn across the deck and run down the steps in a blur of legs to get to his favorite tree. But we were both older now, so we walked down the steps at a slower, more relaxed pace.

At the bottom, I followed Finn to the corner of the house. He

stopped and looked to the left, then up at me. His eyes said it all.

"It's gone, buddy," I reminded him.

The massive gumbo limbo tree that had once stood at the corner of the house by the foot of the pier and shaded half the deck had been blown over during Hurricane Irma. It had probably fallen against the house, causing the roof to go flying off before tearing off some of the siding and the deck's railing as it fell to the ground.

Finn trotted straight across to the young mangroves now beginning to grow back between my house and Jimmy's. He hiked his leg on a random root, then sniffed the ground around a few others before returning and starting back up the steps.

"What?" I whispered. "You're not gonna roust the pelicans from their roost?"

Finn didn't like the big, ungainly birds. When he was younger, his first duty, after relieving himself, had been to chase off the pelicans who often roosted in the mangroves on the windward side of the island.

Finn stopped halfway up the steps, turned his head to face me, and barked once.

Over by the firepit, several pelicans took flight, vacating the higher branches of the only mangroves that had survived the storm five years ago. They were probably old timers who remembered him from before.

"What's he barking at?" Savannah asked, coming into view beside Finn.

She was wearing one of my work shirts and only the bottom few buttons were fastened. Below it, she had on a pair of cutoff jeans that looked a lot like the ones she'd worn the first time we met.

"Pelicans," I replied, heading up the steps after Finn. "He doesn't seem very enthused about it, though."

She squatted beside him and ruffled the loose skin on either side of his head. "He doesn't need to be enthusiastic," she cooed at him. "One bark and they all fly away. Right, boy?"

His tongue lashed out and slurped her wrist.

MAN OVERBOARD

Savannah stood and looked toward the rising sun. "It looks like it's going to be a nice day. Where do you want to start?"

"What do you mean?" I asked hesitantly.

The previous night, we'd run all around the island, as bare as newborns, chasing one another, rolling in the sand, swimming in the lagoon, and making love on the pier. I wasn't sure I could handle much more.

"Robert Grant," she said, popping my mind back to reality. "We said we were going to help him. You have all the *high drag* friends. Who do we need?"

"High speed, low drag," I corrected her.

"Whatever," she said with a dismissive wave of a hand. "Who do we bring in? Tony? Andrew? What's the plan?"

"Not so fast," I replied, leaning on the rail, watching the dawn of a new day. "We don't even know what we don't know yet. Let's invite Grant up here to spend a day or two. Maybe we can come up with an idea that way."

"You don't have a plan?" she asked, joining me at the rail.

"That's not how these things work," I replied.

"Oh." She stared off toward the rising sun for a moment. "So, you didn't have a plan when you went up into the Honduran mountains? Or that time up in Fort Myers?"

"A plan never survives first contact with an opposing force."

"You mean to tell me you go into these things with no idea what you're doing?"

I turned and grinned. "Just a basic outline of who and what the objective is. The when, where, and how are fluid."

"I see," she said, sounding a bit surprised. "Is that the way you did things in the Marines?"

I laughed. "I was just a grunt then. Somebody else did all the planning."

"Okay. Then when do you want to go get him?"

"I'll call Rusty and see if he can cut Robert loose for the day. Maybe he can send him out when Jimmy and Naomi bring Alberto

back."

She reached into the pocket of her shorts and handed me my phone. "You need pockets in your boxers."

I took the phone and called Rusty's cell.

"Hey, bro," he answered. "I was just gonna call you."

"Why? Something wrong?"

"No," he replied. "I just looked out and saw *Ambrosia* gone. Just wanted to make sure you didn't stow away. Man, that's some boat."

I pushed the speaker button and said, "You're on speaker, Rusty. I'm up at the island with Savannah. Jimmy's headed this way in a while to bring Alberto home."

"They're loading the boat now," he said. "Looks like they bought out the store."

I glanced at Savannah, but she only shrugged.

"Holler at him to not leave yet," I said.

His voice sounded muffled as he told someone to go catch Jimmy.

"Is there something else you need him to bring up there?"

"Robert, if you can spare him," I replied. "We thought he might like to chill up here for a while."

"Uh-huh," he said, a knowing inflection in his tone. "What're you planning, bro? And do ya need any help?"

I grinned at my wife. "Savannah's the planner, remember?"

"We just want to see if we can help him," she said, leaning closer to the phone.

Rusty was quiet for a moment. "Yeah, I think that's a good thing," he finally said. "That sorry SOB seems like a man overboard who just don't care to swim."

"Good," I said, giving Savannah a wink. "So, we can expect to see them within an hour."

"Probably less than that," he said. "The man's like a pinball. He just bounces around doing whatever anyone tells him."

We said goodbye, I ended the call, and turned to Savannah. "We'll put him up in the eastern bunkhouse."

"You get dressed," she said, heading down the steps. "I'll make up the bed by the window."

Finn followed me inside, turning around twice on his rug before plopping down on it. I put on a pair of tattered cargo shorts and a faded Rusty Anchor T-shirt. Whether we had a guest coming or not, there was work to be done.

I was checking the fish tanks ten minutes later, when Savannah returned from the bunkhouse. "I'm going to go change before our guest arrives," she announced.

"I'll be here," I replied, noting that she'd completely unbuttoned my work shirt she was wearing.

I assumed it was hot in the bunkhouse.

She returned a few minutes later, wearing a blue, sleeveless blouse and loose-fitting khaki shorts. "Is everything working as it should?" she asked, coming up the steps to the shaded platform built around the fish tanks.

"We'll need to harvest crawfish soon," I replied. "There's getting to be a lot of them in the upper stage."

We had two large tanks, one for raising fish, rotating various freshwater species as demand changed, and the other for freshwater crawfish, hard to get in the Keys. Each of those tanks spilled into a lower, much longer tank with baskets suspended in the water containing a variety of plants growing in them, everything from asparagus to zucchini. At the far end, water spilled into a large reservoir tank set deep in the ground. From there, it was pumped back up to the fish tanks.

Digging a hole anywhere on the island, you'd hit seawater just a few feet below the surface. With the bottom of the reservoir five feet below ground, the water in the reservoir was kept cool in the summer.

Waste from the fish tanks provided nutrients for the plants, which in turn added oxygen to the water for the fish.

"We just had crawfish for lunch," Savannah said. "How can there be too many?"

I looked up at the fast-growing clusters of pygmy date palms that Jimmy had planted during the rebuilding process almost five years earlier.

"Guess Jimmy was right," I said. "He told me they'd grow faster if there was shade over the tanks for much of the day."

Finn lifted his head, his floppy ears cocked forward as he looked toward the south.

"What is it, boy?" I asked.

He glanced up at me, made a slight whining sound, and licked his chops before trotting down the steps and heading toward the south pier.

"I think company is arriving," Savannah said, following behind the big yellow dog.

I trotted after her and took her hand as we walked out onto the south pier. "What are we getting ourselves into?" I asked.

"He needs help, Jesse. And you just happen to be the man who can fix his problems."

"From what he said, I don't know that they can be fixed. He signed everything over of his own free will."

We stopped at the end of the dock, and she turned toward me. "Do you really think a man has *free will* where a beautiful woman is concerned?"

"You think men are that easily coerced?"

"Some men," she said, as Jimmy's skiff came into view beyond Water Key. "By some women. She tricked him into falling for her with the intent of stealing from him. As soon as she found out he was in financial trouble, she revealed who she really was and that she and her husband could help him. At that point, he should have booted her to the curb, but he didn't because he still loved her."

CHAPTER EIGHTEEN

I'd expected Jimmy to be in Rusty's boat, since he usually left his little flats skiff at the school where he and several other local guides volunteered, teaching troubled kids the fine art of fly fishing and the more difficult art of life.

Alberto rode in the front of the boat, sitting on the pedestal seat on the casting deck, and holding onto the sides of it with both hands. Behind him, Jimmy, Naomi, and Robert sat on the aft deck, Jimmy at the wheel in the middle.

When Finn saw Alberto waving, he started barking and dancing around the end of the dock.

"Even though Finn loves Alberto, I think he still misses his playmate," Savannah said.

I knew what she meant without her having to say the words. Woden, a big, burly Rottweiler she and Flo had owned for many years, had gotten sick and died less than a year ago.

The two dogs had been constant companions to each other for several years. They'd been an odd mix, the goofy Lab always wanting to play, and the usually stoic Rott always on the alert for danger. Over time, Finn learned tactics from Woden and Woden learned to play like Finn.

Combined, the pair had been a force to be reckoned with,

whenever danger came too close. They'd had a combined weight the same as my own—220 pounds—and the mere sight of the two of them running and snarling toward a possible adversary usually ended up with someone having to change their skivvies.

It had been painfully obvious in the weeks following Woden's passing that Finn was despondent without his canine friend. He cheered up a little, but never really seemed to get over the loss— never fully returned to being the goofy, playful dog he'd been before.

At twelve years old, we were likely facing the prospect of losing Finn in the not-too-distant future as well. I'd had him since he was a pup, just nine months old, and was dreading the day I would have to say goodbye.

But today wasn't that day.

I smiled, watching him excitedly greeting the party on the approaching vessel. Jimmy idled up to the dock and I could see dozens of boxes and canvas shopping bags on the deck in the middle of the boat.

"What all did you get?" I asked, as Jimmy stopped the boat.

Alberto handed me the bow line, which I looped around a cleat. He jumped over and knelt down with Finn, both seeming equally excited to see each other again. Then he got up and ran toward shore, Finn bounding after him.

I nodded at Jimmy, and he put the boat in gear and turned the wheel toward the dock. "Just essentials, man," he replied as the boat started to move. "I usually stock up on dry goods the first of the month, but what with Independence Day and all, I got behind."

The line I held looped around the cleat became taut and I put one foot on the bow to keep the skiff off the dock. With the wheel turned, the boat started to pivot.

MAN OVERBOARD

Once past the halfway point in the spin, Jimmy took the engine out of gear and shut it off, before raising it out of the water. The little craft continued to drift around until it was facing the other way. Jimmy tossed the stern line to Savannah, who quickly pulled the boat in, and we tied it off.

"Welcome to our home, Robert," Savannah said, smiling at him.

He looked up at the little house on stilts. "All of you live in that one little house?"

I laughed. "No, we have four of these little houses on our island and you'll have one all to yourself."

He looked up at me, puzzled. "Why did you tell Rusty to send me out here?"

"You need help, Robert," Savannah said, extending a hand to assist him onto the dock. "And we think we might be able to get back what you lost."

He stepped up beside me, a surprised look in his eyes. "Why?"

"I don't like bullies," I said flatly. "Or thieves or con artists."

"But why help me? I don't even know you people."

"You're an islander, man," Jimmy said, placing two boxes on the dock. "We stick together."

He looked around at all of us. "What can you do?"

Savannah smiled and took his arm, leading him toward the foot of the pier. "Jesse has... certain skills," she told him. "He and his friends are very good at what they do."

He looked back at me as Jimmy started handing me canvas shopping bags. "What does he do?"

"He fixes things," she replied.

I slung two bags on each arm and picked up one of the boxes. Naomi grabbed two bags, and Jimmy did the same, picking up another box.

I followed Savannah and Robert toward the steps at the end of the dock, then turned to Jimmy. "Where's all this go?"

In the past we'd made weekly grocery runs, stocking up two freezers and two refrigerators with what we'd need for a week, plus dry goods, like rice and canned foods, which we'd always stored in a closet in Jimmy's second bedroom. But we rarely bought this much canned and boxed foods.

"Just head out to the tables," Naomi said. "We can sort everything there, but most of it will go to the bunkhouse."

"The bunkhouse?" I asked, stepping off into the sand at the foot of the pier.

"I built a storage shed under it," Jimmy replied, coming up beside me. "Nothing fancy. Just a place to store non-perishable stuff. Doing the same under mine."

I glanced over and saw the partially framed walls of a small addition under the middle of Jimmy's house, and ahead, I could see the same built under the eastern bunkhouse.

I'd missed both last night, but we'd been a little preoccupied.

After dropping my load off on the table, I followed Savannah and Robert up the steps to the bunkhouse. He looked around at five other unmade beds, then went over to the north-facing window and looked out.

"You sure have a nice place, Mr. McDermitt."

"Now, I told you," Savannah scolded, shaking a finger at him but smiling, "It's Jesse and Savvy, savvy?"

He turned and grinned. It was the first expression I'd seen that was positive. Until then, he'd seemed an empty shell of a man. The words from a song I'd heard a local band play up island came to my head—he seemed like a *Hollow Man*.

Robert nodded. "Thanks for all you're trying to do, but I really

screwed the pooch this time."

"There are ways," I said. "Just because you got the dirty end of the stick this time doesn't mean you can't turn it around on them."

"What do you mean?"

Savannah turned and enthusiastically clapped her hands. "He's coming up with a plan!"

"Not a plan," I said. "But from what you told us last night, we know the who and what. On paper, what they did was legal. But two can play that game and I think I might have an idea about the how part. That just leaves when and where."

There was a banging sound below and I could hear Jimmy and Naomi talking but couldn't make out what they were saying.

"I should go help Jimmy," I said. "You get settled in and we can—"

"Nothing to settle," Robert said. "I didn't bring anything."

"Didn't Rusty tell you you'd be here a couple of days?" Savannah asked.

"He did. But I don't own anything. The clothes I'm wearing are someone else's."

Savannah and I exchanged glances. "We'll fix that later today or tomorrow," she told him, stepping back to appraise his size. "If you need anything before then, Jesse's pants and Jimmy's shirts will fit you okay."

Robert looked back and forth at us in disbelief. "I can't let you buy me clothes."

"Call it an investment," I said. "And when we get your life back in order, you can pay it forward."

His once-vacant brown eyes took on a spark, as if he was finally seeing some hope—a light at the end of the tunnel that wasn't an oncoming train.

"I've heard people talk about you," he said. "Mostly gossip at bars or coffee houses. I've been here two years and have heard people say you're everything from a federal agent to a hit man, a cop, a drug dealer, and everything in between."

Few people had their own private island, and the truth was, I'd bought the island for a song more than twenty years earlier, using money I'd inherited. But perception was often reality in many people's minds.

"They were close with some of that," I said. "But I'm not a smug druggler."

"Federal agent?"

"Twenty years in the Marine Corps and working with Homeland Security in some form or another for the last twenty."

"So, that yacht we had dinner on last night...?"

"Owned by a private corporation, conducting discreet DHS projects."

"What interest would DHS have in what happened to me?" he asked.

"Probably none," I replied. "I'm on vacation."

"Those two down there?" he asked. "Can we talk in front of them?"

"I'd trust Jimmy with my life," I replied.

"Same with Naomi," Savannah added.

"Then since I don't need to unpack anything, can I help you? I think better when I'm working."

"You're fortunate," I said with a grin. "There's lots of time to *think* here on our island."

CHAPTER NINETEEN

"I meant to ask," I said to Jimmy after we'd brought the rest of the stuff up from the boat. "Why'd you bring your boat instead of Rusty's? I thought you kept it at the school."

He grinned over at me. "We're hosting a genuine Cajun feast at Chyrel's house, man. Her and Naomi are cooking up a hundred pounds of crawfish."

"A hundred pounds?" Savannah asked.

"It's a fundraiser," Naomi replied.

"The school's self-sustained," I said. "If more money is needed, there's no need for a fundraiser."

The Alex DuBois McDermitt Fly Fishing Lodge, named for my late wife, had been housing and teaching kids for almost thirteen years. Alex had been a fly-fishing guide in Oregon and had opened a sort of Outward-Bound school there for troubled inner-city kids. They taught fly fishing, mountaineering, and outdoor survival skills, as well as a regular school curriculum. Her partner in the school, which was called Catching It, was a woman named Cindy Saturday, and a couple of years after Alex's death, she'd come to Marathon to fulfill my late wife's dream of opening another school in the Keys. Jimmy was one of the first guides the school hired.

"It was the kids' idea, dude," Jimmy said. "Don't know if you

know it or not, but one of the school's first success stories was a kid who was one step away from Raiford Prison. That was ten years ago. Today, Gary Burch is one of the school's biggest advocates and mentors as well as being a successful builder up in Palm Beach."

"So, what would the money from this fundraiser go toward, then?" Savannah asked.

"Some of the kids thought it'd be cool to learn to sail," Naomi said. "So, a friend and I took them out in her twenty-foot O'Day. We've been teaching small-boat sailing for over a year."

"So, they're raising money to buy a sailboat?" Savannah asked.

"Nothing extravagant," Naomi replied. "But a little bigger would allow us to take more kids."

"I used to sail," Robert said. "I worked my way through college as a sailing instructor. A boat in the twenty-six to thirty-foot range is a good size for teaching."

"You were a sailing instructor?" Naomi asked.

"A long time ago," he replied. "But my Coast Guard and ASA certifications are still good."

"Neither Ashley nor I are real instructors," she said. "Maybe you could help us out?"

He shrugged, not committing to anything.

"What about a big ketch?" I asked. "One you could take the whole school out on."

"*Salty Dog?*" Jimmy asked. "I don't know if they could raise enough for something like that, *hermano.*"

"Think they can raise enough to cover what I paid for it?"

Jimmy and Savannah both grinned, already knowing the story. *Salty Dog* was practically given to me by Charity Styles after her fiancé was killed and he'd left it to her. Never one to accept gifts, I got her to agree on a low price, and I was to handle the fees for the

paperwork.

"How much was that?" Naomi asked.

"Two hundred dollars."

"Somebody got taken," Robert said under his breath, shaking his head. "Was it a derelict?"

"It's the sixty-eight-foot Formosa at the end of Rusty's dock," I replied. "She's as clean and functional as the day she was splashed back in '81. A friend wanted to gift it to me, but I got her to accept a hundred bucks, plus the cost of transferring the title."

He glanced up, a deep appreciation in his eyes. "Heck of a gift. I've been wondering who owned it. Beautiful boat."

"Thanks. Now, about your problem. You said they had you do a transfer from your bank to a numbered account?"

Robert looked over at Jimmy and Naomi, who smiled at him.

"What's said on the island stays on the island," Naomi said.

He nodded, then took a deep breath and sighed. "Yeah, I was in a financial bind—extended beyond my ability, having covered an investment promised by a South American firm. I'd met Katya through a dating site and after several weeks, I thought we were both in love and on the same path, so I shared that business information. She seemed to be a godsend when she told me she knew someone who could create a new identity for me. I hate to admit it, but the only way out of the deal that I could see was to give up and lose a very substantial investment. So, I made moves to do just that, and the South Americans became angry, threatening to kill me if I didn't invest their money for them. At best, I'd come out with a loss, at worst, maybe dead."

"What did you do?" Savannah asked.

"Katya introduced me to this guy in Miami, Mike Spencer. He claimed to have a team of tech people who could solve my problem.

He said they could create a new identity for me and move what money I had left, without it being traced. Anyway, long story short, I agreed to pretend to be married to Katya, which, to my amazement, she'd gone along with. We would make it appear as if I was the victim of a scam where she'd drained all my assets and run off. It was all very public. She was on board a hundred percent. We were going to go to Australia together."

"So, the people in South America wouldn't come looking for you?" Jimmy asked. "Knowing you were broke?"

Robert nodded. "What they were supposed to do was liquidate all my assets and move everything, in one big transfer to a shell company's offshore account. Then it was supposed to be split up and moved all over the world by these tech people to other numbered accounts in half a dozen countries—hundreds and hundreds of small transfers being handled by their computers—before it all came back to me in a new account set up under the new identity. The South Americans would think I'd been sucked dry, and I'd lose the investment I'd already made, but I'd be able to keep what I still had."

"How much was that?" I asked.

He looked over at me. "Two point two million."

"That's a little bit?" Naomi asked.

"The lost investment was well north of eight figures."

Jimmy whistled. "Wow! That's a lot, man."

"But it didn't come back to you." Savannah said.

"No, it didn't. Everything went down exactly like they said it would. We did the fake marriage—did I mention that Katya was already married to the head of the outfit?"

"Seriously?" Jimmy said. "How long was she pretending to be your wife?"

"A month," he replied. "During that time, we appeared to be

happily married newlyweds, as the liquidations began. When everything was gone, she and I had a big, public row and she said she was going home to her family."

"How far did this sham marriage go?" Savannah asked.

Robert's face flushed and he looked around at the four of us. Then he lowered his gaze to the table. "When we met, she said she was single. I would never have seen her again if I'd known."

Jimmy looked shocked. "Wait...what? Did you *sleep* with her?"

"I honestly didn't know," he said. "Looking back, I'm not real proud of these past two months."

"You found her on a dating website?" I asked. "But she was already married? And you didn't find until later that she was not only married but her husband was the money launderer she'd helped you set up the deal with?"

"Yeah, well, like I said. Not one of my finer moments of clarity and perception."

"You were blinded by love," Savannah said.

"Men are so easily manipulated," Naomi added.

Savannah nodded her head, then looked at Robert. "Thinking with the wrong head."

People make mistakes, I get that. It's what a person learns from those mistakes that counts. He'd made a series of blunders but what got him in his current situation was a bad business deal with unscrupulous people. I knew enough about how business was done in some parts of South America to know getting out of a deal often meant a person's life. I wondered what I'd do if I was faced with similar circumstances.

"So, this big initial transfer you made?" I began, just thinking out loud. "How was it done?"

"Computers," he replied, cocking his head slightly. "All done

through secure servers involving dozens, if not hundreds, of accounts."

"Or so you were told," I said. "Maybe it was just the big transfer and it's still just sitting there." I turned to Jimmy. "When's this big crawfish boil?"

"Sunday," Naomi answered for him. "About two dozen supporters are coming, along with their plus ones."

"And you're taking the crawfish over to Chyrel's this afternoon?" I asked.

Jimmy grinned. He was a bit of an electronics and computer whiz, but nothing compared to Chyrel Koshinski.

Savannah smiled. "What are you thinking, Jesse?"

"I'm thinking if someone were to get this guy to open that virtual door again, a certain person might be standing beside it waiting to snatch everything that was inside."

"Think she can do it?" Jimmy asked.

"You know I don't know crap about computers." I shrugged. "Won't know until we ask her."

CHAPTER TWENTY

Once we got everything put away, Jimmy, Robert, and I worked on the storage space under Jimmy's house for a couple of hours. It was a simple structure, using treated lumber for the studs and resting right on the sand. Long metal straps held each stud firmly to the underside of the house, carrying as much of the weight as the ground it rested on.

Alberto helped, holding two by fours while I cut them to length with a handsaw. We could have used power tools but living off the grid was something we took seriously, and using a chop saw or table saw meant draining the batteries unnecessarily. Besides, it'd take longer to run an extension cord and set it up. A handsaw took less than two minutes per stud and there just weren't a lot of boards to be cut. A power saw would have saved us maybe five or six minutes. Cutting treated lumber with a handsaw wasn't easy, but I'd been lax in my exercise routine and needed the workout. As a boy, Pap had shown me how to use a handsaw equally well with both hands, so I alternated.

By lunch, we'd hung the door and finished the project, except for building shelves on the inside. We ate leftovers from the previous day, then began loading two coolers with water and crawfish. The crawfish were big, quite a bit larger than you'd get at a

restaurant in New Orleans.

"Robert and I will go with you to deliver the crawfish," I said to Jimmy, as we carried the coolers to the pier. "We can find out if it's possible then."

We'd discussed the feasibility of my plan as we'd worked, and Jimmy thought it was viable, if we had the right person doing it.

"Why not just call this person?" Robert asked.

Jimmy laughed. "She's the kinda person who prefers talking face-to-face, man. She used to work for the CIA but is quasi-retired now."

"And you think it's possible she can get my money back?"

I nodded. "If anyone can, it would be Chyrel. More than anything, it depends if the account they moved money into has anything in it. But I think it's worth a try."

As we loaded the coolers into Jimmy's skiff, I asked him why we were taking the crawfish over today, when the shindig was two days away.

"Kyndall's handling everything from Chyrel's kitchen," he replied.

Rufus's niece had come to Marathon several years ago and helped her uncle in the kitchen at the Rusty Anchor. At least, Rufus had introduced her as his niece. Some thought she might be his grandniece, myself included. Kyndall looked to be in her early to mid-thirties and Rufus was probably close to eighty.

"You plan to leave your boat there?" I asked.

"Yeah," Jimmy replied, sliding the second cooler in next to the first, in front of the small console. "Naomi's car's there. We can drive it back to the Anchor and I'll borrow one of Rusty's boats to get us back."

"Why don't you just call me when you leave Chyrel's and I'll

meet you there in the Grady?" Savannah suggested.

While she was a dynamite skipper on the blue, I wasn't really sure about her going out alone in the shallows of the backcountry yet. But it was bound to happen sooner or later. I wouldn't offer any advice unless she asked for it.

"Or that," I said with a shrug. "Keys are in the box, babe."

"What are we doing while you're gone?" Alberto asked as I untied the lines.

"You've missed a couple of days of schoolwork," Savannah said. "If you're to have the weekend off and go to this big cookout, you need to at least catch up a little."

We'd tried to impress upon the boy that a week had seven days and there was work to be done even on the days the traditional workforce took off—Saturday and Sunday. The only days that weren't workdays were the ones that didn't end with Y. Even workday did. But we often had more free time and occasionally took a whole day off. What day that was didn't matter. It was a day to relax and recharge the mental and physical batteries.

"But I'm way ahead already!" he groaned.

"How far ahead?" I asked him.

He hung his head. "Two months."

"And the plan is?"

"Get a year ahead before high school," he muttered.

I nodded as I stepped aboard. "Catch up a little today and when we get back, we'll go for a moonlight paddle."

He pointed west. "Out there?"

"From there you'll see more stars than you could imagine," I promised.

"Okay," he said, then turned and started running. "Come on, Finn! Let's race!"

The big, goofy Lab trotted after him, a trot being fast enough for his long legs to keep pace. There'd been a time when he would have bowled a person over who dared challenge him to a race. These days he seemed content to keep pace.

Jimmy guided the skiff through my channel, then brought it up on plane, turning left to head up Harbor Channel. Even in a shallow-draft, backcountry skiff, there were a lot of places to run aground, and trying to drive a straight, even though covered with water, would put us on the sandbar. So, we headed northeast toward Mac's place before turning southeast to run through some narrow natural cuts to reach East Bahia Honda Channel, a wide and comparatively deep natural channel that ran all the way down to the Seven Mile Bridge.

Once clear of the cut, Jimmy opened the boat's engine up a little on water that was rarely more than five feet deep, except when crossing the wide, natural channel that had once carried Spanish galleons in search of the Fountain of Youth.

We didn't go that way.

From the cut, Jimmy followed a rhumb line in his mind, straight toward the school on Grassy Key, knowing the route like the back of his hand. There was only one shoal between us and the school, and we both knew right where it was.

"How deep's the water way out here?" Robert yelled after we'd crossed East Bahia Honda Channel.

Jimmy pointed to a heron standing in the shoal waters of Elbow Bank just south of our course.

"What's it standing on?" Robert yelled again.

I looked over at the man, the wind whipping his hair back. "He's standing on the bottom," I said, loud enough to be heard over the wind, water, and engine. "Most of this part of the bay is five feet or

less."

His expression tensed for a few minutes as he looked at the two of us, but after a while, he seemed to relax and enjoy the ride.

As we approached the dock at Chyrel's house, I felt a pang of sadness. My old friend and mentor, Owen "Tank" Tankersley, had bought the house, knowing he was going to die there. He'd married Chyrel so his military pension and social security widow's benefits could continue.

His retirement was a pittance compared to what he'd accumulated over fifty-one years of service in the Marine Corps, always living and eating on Uncle Sam's dime. He'd amassed a small fortune and he figured it was more about the principle. He'd served so long, only to die a couple of years after retiring, that he felt he deserved more.

And the pale blue Medal of Honor ribbon he was buried with confirmed that. At least in my eyes.

I thought Tank was nuts when he'd first told me he wanted to ask Chyrel to marry him. I knew she'd never felt the need for a husband or family and was happy spending the rest of her life single. But initially, she'd seen it as a valid business proposition. By agreeing, she would inherit the house as well as his assets, which she would manage, adding his pension and social security checks to it every month and donating the interest his investments earned to a number of charities important to him.

Since he'd passed, she'd added substantial amounts to the trust funds he'd set up by making some very astute business decisions. She now sat on the board of directors for the school as well as several new charitable organizations, and she'd recently been appointed to the Greater Marathon Chamber of Commerce.

Jimmy idled up to the dock, where Chyrel was waiting with two

teenage girls.

"Jesse!" she shouted, as I stood and went forward to throw a line. "I didn't know you were coming! I was gonna come out and visit this afternoon."

"Come anyway," I said, handing one of the girls a line. "Savannah would love to see you."

I stepped onto the dock just as Jimmy reversed the engine and brought the stern close enough to the dock to hand the stern line to the other girl.

Chyrel hugged me tightly, her head against my chest. "It's so good to see you again," she whispered, then stepped back. "I want you to meet two of my girls. This is Andrea and Kris. That's with a K. Girls, this is Jesse McDermitt."

Both girls looked at me, surprise evident on their faces.

"The man who owns the school?" the taller blond girl asked.

"I don't own it," I said. "I only helped set it up."

"But it's named after your wife, right?" the other girl, a mousy brunette asked.

"My late wife," I replied. "The school was her dream, but she died a couple of years before it came about."

"Hey, girls!" Jimmy said, as he stepped up onto the far end of the dock. "How'd the morning session go?"

"Okay, I guess," the blonde said, her head down slightly and her straight hair covering much of her face.

I still wasn't sure which was which, but figured I'd find out soon enough.

"Come on, Andrea," Jimmy said, sounding more like a patient teacher than a California surfer dude. "Openness is key. One human family, traveling the road of life together, remember? Jesse here is as much a part of you guys learning to cope as any of us."

Andrea looked up and squared her shoulders. "We talked about the crimes we committed and what our feelings were leading up to them."

Jimmy smiled and put an arm around the girl, pulling her to his side as he smiled and looked over at me. "Andrea made some poor decisions in her earlier life, but I think she's on the road to a better one now."

The girl looked at Jimmy with genuine admiration. "Thanks, Mr. Jimmy."

He reached out and pulled the smaller girl toward him. "And this little fireball has turned out to be a Class-A lip ripper, man. She seems to be able to out-fish-think the fish."

"Is that right?" I asked, looking from one girl to the other. "Do y'all like it here?"

"I didn't at first," Kris replied. "I tried to run away, but Miss Chyrel caught me. She was waiting at the end of the driveway."

I laughed. "And now?"

"It's terrific!" Andrea said with enthusiasm. "We have fun, get to meet other kids like us, and the teachers here understand us. Kris and I just completed our exams last week to move up to twelfth grade."

Robert stepped up onto the dock and approached us.

"Chyrel, I'd like you to meet Robert," I said. "He's staying on-island with us for a while. Robert, meet Chyrel, Andrea, and Kris."

He nodded at the women, then said, "I'll need some help with the coolers."

"I'll get it," Jimmy said, turning back to the boat.

"Robert was once a sailing instructor," I said to Chyrel. "And we might have found a boat the school can get."

"Really?" Andrea said, the excitement in her eyes cranking up

ten-fold. "I love going out with Naomi and Ashley."

"What kind of boat did you find?" Chyrel asked.

"How's a sixty-eight-foot Formosa ketch sound?"

"Whoa!" Andrea shouted. "That's a ship."

"Sails just the same as an O'Day," I said. "And with practice and patience, she can be single-handed."

The young blonde's eyes went oval. "One person on a boat that big?"

"I sailed her solo all across the Caribbean," I replied.

"There's no way we can raise that much money," Kris said, as Jimmy and Robert hefted the big Yeti cooler onto the dock.

"We'll put whatever money you raise toward a maintenance fund," I said. "And I'll donate the boat to the school."

"*Salty Dog?*" Chyrel asked. "You'd do that?"

"It's just a boat, and with all I have going on, she's just slipping by the way. I think it'd make Charity happy to learn Victor's boat is being used and taken care of."

"Ooh, I could just kiss you!" Chyrel said, hugging me again.

"Think you girls can handle that smaller cooler?" I asked, as Robert set it up on the dock.

They went over and hefted each end, nodding at me.

"Y'all go ahead then," I said. "I need to talk to Miss Chyrel for a minute."

The girls bent and lifted the cooler, chattering excitedly, as Robert and Jimmy went ahead of them carrying the larger Yeti.

"That's a side of Jimmy I've never seen," I said, as Chyrel and I slowly trailed behind them.

"Understandably," she said. "From what I've been told, you've only visited the school twice in thirteen years, and one of those was the grand opening. The kids love Jimmy."

"It was Alex's dream," I said. "It's enough that I helped make it a reality."

"Sure," she said, stretching the word out. "Jesse, I know why you avoid it, so don't play coy with me. The death of a spouse is a lot different than a divorce or breakup. Not that I know anything about the latter."

"Yeah," I admitted. "But missing her makes me feel disloyal toward Savannah."

"I've been going to a support group for widows and widowers," she said, stopping to face me. "There's a couple of people in the group who are moving on...one's even remarried. Life goes on, old friend. An understanding spouse is key to that. Those who are able to find love in this life are lucky. Those who find it twice or even three or four times are immensely fortunate. Savannah would understand if you came around on occasion to talk to the kids."

"I don't really have a lot of time to be a teacher."

We turned and started walking again. "Who said anything about teaching? We have teachers. We get quite a few very successful people coming down to charter with our volunteer guides. They pay through the nose for the chance, and they spend a little one-on-one time with the kids."

"Okay," I decided. "I'll pay though the nose to go fishing with one of the guides and a couple of kids."

"Not a couple," she said. "That part's strictly one-on-one, usually while the guide is busy poling or something, and not paying attention.

"These kids are naturally curious—that's what got a lot of them into trouble in the first place. So, they ask questions. The school you created has had quite a few young people go through it and then go on to become successful adults. They come down a lot more than most and the kids seem to get more from them, knowing they were once literally right there in the same seat."

"The two girls seem to like Jimmy," I said, when we reached the end of the dock and started across the back lawn toward two large tents set up in the shade.

"He's one of the best," she said. "He's older than the kids by a few decades, but he seems to have a natural rapport, and they respond to his laid-back, 'ever't'ing is irie, mon' attitude."

"No problems with the weed?"

She glanced up at me, surprised. "I didn't know he smoked it. But so what? Everybody does. I even got Owen to try it and it really helped toward the end."

"Tank?" I asked incredulously. "Smoking pot?"

She laughed. "You really are a stick-in-the-mud, Jesse."

The idea of Tank Tankersley, recipient of the Medal of Honor, a salty old master gunnery sergeant and fifty-one-year combat vet smoking pot was crazy. But then again, I'd tried it and liked it, and he was my mentor for twenty years.

Chyrel stopped in the middle of the yard and faced me. "What did you want to ask me about, Jesse?"

"Robert has a problem," I began. "And I think you might be the one who can help fix it."

CHAPTER TWENTY-ONE

Just after dark, with a waxing moon on the rise, all six of us set out westward in a trio of big, two-person, sit-on-top kayaks. The SOTs were perfect for the backcountry, as they barely drew three or four inches, even with two people sitting in the recessed seats.

Robert proved to be a strong paddler, and Alberto rode with him as we paddled out. Savannah and I had another kayak and Jimmy and Naomi the third.

Just two miles west of our island, we were smack in the middle of Crane Key Bank, where a person could walk a mile in any direction and not get the bottoms of their shorts wet or step out of the water.

"This looks good," I announced in a low voice, knowing how easily sound carried over water. "Raft up and we'll anchor here."

The other two kayaks moved closer, and we used a single line to lash all three together and put out a small mushroom anchor. A mile from any land or mangroves, with a southerly breeze blowing at over five knots, I was unworried about bugs.

"What do we do now?" Alberto asked.

"Look up," I replied.

With a nearly full moon low in the sky off to our left, we had plenty of light to see by and it was low enough that it only blocked

out the stars to the east.

We'd made sure to leave on only a low-powered LED light out on the end of the south dock, and any lights from Mac and Mel's island three miles away were invisible. To the southeast, a faint glow showed where Marathon was, but the moon just above and a little north of it was brighter. So, we had a clear field of view for a good 270 degrees, from the southeast all the way around behind us and to the northeast.

The skies were clear, and the Milky Way stood out like a hazy band of light across the night sky.

"Whoa," Alberto breathed. "I've never seen so many stars."

"Didn't I tell you?" I whispered.

"It still amazes me," Savannah said. "I've spent a third of my life far from shore and it still just boggles the mind."

Robert leaned forward and tapped Alberto's shoulder. "See those two bright stars above and to either side of the moon?"

Alberto nodded.

"The one on the left is Altaire in the constellation Aquila, the great eagle that carried Zeus's thunderbolts in Greek mythology."

"Really?" Alberto said softly, as he gazed toward the moon. "What's the star on the right called?"

"It's not a star at all," Robert replied, his face turned up toward the heavens. "That's Saturn."

I appraised him in the darkness. I knew very little about the man—just that he had a good business head until the deal with the South American investors, and he'd been an upstanding member of the community, donating to local fundraisers and private personal charities—glass jugs on local convenience store counters.

He surprised me with his knowledge of the night sky. Most people who lived in towns rarely looked up at night. They knew the

moon and sun, and some might find the Big Dipper if they turned their porch light off. Fewer still knew that it could be used as a clock. The pointer stars indicated the direction of Polaris, the North Star. But if you imagined Polaris as the middle of a twenty-four-hour clock, the pointers also told the time, though it was backward, with 1800 on the right horizontal plane and 0600 on the left. But for those who ventured out on the water at night, away from other light sources, the stars were as prominent as leaves in a forest.

"I don't see any rings around it," Alberto commented.

I chuckled. "You'd need a telescope to see the rings."

"Make sure you go out and look at the moon on Wednesday," Robert said. "At midnight, it'll be the biggest supermoon of the year. Do you know what that is?"

Alberto looked over at Savannah and smiled, obviously recalling something from one of her lessons. "A supermoon is when the moon reaches its perigee and is closer than three hundred and sixty thousand miles from Earth."

I grinned as I stared up at Luna's nearly full face. The kid had a terrific knack for facts and figures.

Robert leaned over toward me, surprised. "Impressive."

"He picks up fast," I said, feeling sort of prideful, though Alberto's intelligence had little to do with me. "He's in fourth grade and our plan is for him to skip fifth by taking classes next summer and go right into middle school studies next fall."

"You're not worried about later, when he enters high school at fourteen?"

"He's home-schooled," Savannah said. "Or what we like to call 'boat-schooled,' because we spend most of the year on a boat. But when he reaches high-school level, he's going to go to a private charter school."

"Good idea," Robert agreed. "From what I've seen, he's a gifted young man."

"Just don't play chess with him for money," Jimmy said, looking off to the southwest. "Is that the ISS?"

We all turned and looked where he was pointing. After a second, I spotted a bright star that seemed to be moving. Most of them were moving, or at least appeared to be. Their apparent movement across the sky was the result of Earth's rotation. But this one was moving faster than the others.

"Must be a satellite of some kind," I said. "And the International Space Station is the largest thing up there. Robert?"

"Probably," he agreed. "I'm afraid I lost interest in space after college. I have no idea where it would be at any particular time."

We were quiet for a few minutes, each lost in our own thoughts as we looked up at the vastness of space. Alberto had his phone out and was engrossed in something.

Savannah turned slightly, looking back at me. "For that idea you had to work," she whispered, "you're going to need someone on the other side."

Alberto was looking at the moon through a pair of binoculars, seemingly oblivious to us talking.

I knew it'd been heavy on Savannah's mind since dinner, when we'd all discussed my idea. "Yeah, I know," I whispered back. "I was thinking Deuce."

"Too close," Jimmy said. "And he's kinda recognizable up island and in Miami. The dude you want to meet might have seen him before."

"Your friend seemed to be confident she could do it," Robert said. "I obviously can't be the one."

I looked over at Jimmy.

MAN OVERBOARD

He laughed, nervously glancing at Alberto, who was scrolling on his phone again. "No way, dude. I couldn't pull it off in a million years."

"Do you know if these people have ever...*helped* a couple? Like a married couple?" Savannah asked. "Something less elaborate than how they helped you?"

I thought about that a moment as Robert said he didn't have any idea. Talking about it openly, even obscurely, wasn't a good idea in front of sensitive ears, but Alberto was engrossed in an app on his phone, showing where the stars and planets were.

"You might be onto something," I said. "I'll call the bank in the morning and have Pam move half a mil into a new account. But we still have to...meet these people."

"That shouldn't be hard," Alberto said, looking through the binoculars again, this time toward the Seven Sisters. "Not with a name like Katya Popova."

I know we hadn't mentioned her or Spencer's names around him, he took off playing with Finn right after dinner, but with a virtual jungle of mangroves growing up around our island's perimeter, there were a million places for a boy to eavesdrop without meaning to. Our island was small—about the size of two football fields placed side by side.

When he'd heard the name, I didn't know, but he did have a point. It was doubtful that was her real name, but I'd have Deuce run both names for starters.

Robert steered the conversation back to the stars and Savannah passed around snacks and small aluminum cups she filled from a large water jug, as I thought about what we'd have to do. Out here, or on the boat, whichever boat that might be, Savannah was in her element. But going up to Miami to search for a con artist could be

163

dangerous.

I watched as she talked and laughed with the others. No, I'd first try to find a way for me to get inside their network. But I'd have to move very fast. We only had a week left.

After an hour of stargazing, with me, Robert, and Jimmy pointing out certain navigational stars and constellations, we decided it was getting late, and pulled the little anchor back aboard. We unlashed the kayaks and started paddling, the rising moon guiding our way.

"You're not going to let us try it as a couple, are you?" Savannah asked in a low voice.

"Not if I can help it," I said honestly. "It could be dang—"

"Did I ever tell you about the blue hole on Hoffman's Cay?" she interrupted.

She hadn't. But our daughter Flo had told me the whole grisly story.

"You don't have to," I said. "I know what happened to the men who attacked you, Flo, and Charity."

She flung her head around. "Who told... Charity, of course."

"No," I said. "Flo told me."

She was silent for a moment, staring straight ahead, her paddle resting across her thighs. When she turned her head again, I could see by the moonlight that her eyes were moist with tears. "I'd hoped she would have forgotten anything she'd seen that day."

Over ten years ago, Savannah and Charity had been forced to defend themselves when several men attacked them. Florence had been jumping off the cliff into the inland blue hole on Hoffman's and had seen it all, as she hid just below the edge. Woden killed one of the men by knocking him off the cliff onto the rocks below. And Charity knew only one method of stopping an attacker, especially if

it were multiple assailants.

All four of the men's bodies were probably still at the bottom of that hole.

"Our daughter thinks you're a badass," I said, grinning in the darkness.

She lifted her paddle and dug deep, slinging a bucketload of water on me. "I *am* a badass, Jesse McDermitt. Don't you ever forget that."

CHAPTER TWENTY-TWO

The man who would soon become Bart Mason stood by a table on the second-floor balcony at Rick's Bar on Duval Street. It was a five-minute walk back to La Concha and the fourth stop on his and Katya's nightly stroll.

At each watering hole they visited, the two of them had made themselves known as a happy, very wealthy couple, living life to the fullest.

But Thom Smythe would have never considered throwing around money the way he'd been doing since meeting Mike Spencer and Katya Popova, the husband-and-wife team who were going to make him disappear. Permanently.

Spencer and the woman had insisted that it had to be that way. "Look at it as an investment," Spencer had told him. Thom and Katya's short- lived romance, fake marriage, and subsequent breakup had to be so public that it would be the virtual talk of the town. If it made it into the papers, all the better.

Those looking for him would hear about it. And they'd hear the stories about how Katya Popova had catfished him and taken him for everything he owned. With nothing left to invest in the venture, they'd have no reason to continue looking. But Spencer had convinced him to go a step further. He'd said the people looking for

him, might not take his lack of funds as payment enough and could possibly try to kill him, so he'd agreed to the full-court press—faking his death.

He had no family and few close friends; his business associates would grieve over his death, but that had as much to do with his money as anything about him, personally.

He had two friends, a couple he'd met two years earlier right there in Key West. They had a home there, as well as up in the Florida Panhandle, a Manhattan apartment, a cliff-side home in Monterey, and also a few properties in the Caribbean and Europe. He'd miss Rudy Haverstock's sage business counsel, for which he'd asked nothing in return. But they'd move on, like everyone else. Like Thom, himself.

He'd be a free man and he'd have most of his wealth still intact. What he'd invested would be lost, of course, but he wasn't about to let them suck any more from him. Spencer's fee was high, but he'd have a whole new start in a different place, with enough wealth to start over.

Or maybe just head to the South Pacific and retire.

Katya returned with their drinks and placed his in front of him. "We should go, darling. The amateur contest next door is about to start."

"You're really going to go through with that?"

She smiled seductively. "It is a big part of the plan," she said. "The bar is full, and people will be taking pictures. You will escort me to the stage and introduce me as your fiancée. It will be a memorable occasion for everyone. And everyone will know your name."

"Yeah, but taking your clothes off in front of a bunch of strangers?" Smythe asked. "You're okay with that?"

"I look forward to it," she said, leaning against the rail with one hand on her hip. "And everyone will know where it is we will go when I step off the stage and you whiskey me away."

"Whisk," he corrected her. "Whiskey's a liquor."

She took a sip from her straw, looking at him with those pale blue eyes. Her makeup was flawless: smokey-gray eye shadow, a little color on her cheeks to accentuate her naturally high cheekbones, and glossy red lipstick that now tantalized him.

"I like 'whiskey me away,'" she said, smiling.

He picked up his drink, then turned to face her. There were more than a dozen people on the balcony and the lights and sounds from Duval Street filled their eyes and ears. Men with dates or spouses cast furtive glances at Katya, waiting for the chance when the women they were with were preoccupied.

"And I'm supposed to be the kind of man who's okay with his fiancée stripping? That's not who I am."

"Part of the smoke and mirrors," she replied. "Many people here know you now. Are you a scuba diver?"

"Yeah, why?"

"Tomorrow there is a big, underwater concert," she said. "They hold this every year, and it is covered by the media. I can make sure we get on television."

"How will you do that?" he asked, hearing more cash register sounds ringing in his head.

She smiled a little slyly. "Please hand me a napkin."

He produced one from the holder. She unfolded it, then tore about two thirds of it off and crumpled it, tossing it on the table. Then she carefully tore the remaining third into three small triangles, arranging two of them side by side pointing away from him. The third she placed much closer, pointing toward his crotch.

The layout of the three small triangles wasn't lost on him.

"When we dive tomorrow," she said, leaning toward him and speaking in a sultry, husky tone, "I will be wearing this much more than I will when I dance for you tonight."

She scooped up the tiny pieces of paper and sprinkled them over his head like confetti. Then she turned and sauntered through the door in a fashion that made many men, and a few women, stop and stare.

The couple made their way down the stairs and went next door to the Red Garter Saloon, where they showed their IDs just inside the door.

There were two small signs by the doorman's desk. One said *We Card Everyone No Exceptions*, and the other said the cover charge was $10. Katya whispered something in the bouncer's ear, and he waved them through with a smile.

"What'd you say to that guy?" Thom asked, as a hostess showed them to a table near one of the stages.

"I told him you are spending a lot of money tonight and I am dancing for you to celebrate our engagement."

Thom didn't visit strip clubs often. Almost never. He'd always been far too busy with work, sometimes late into the night and on weekends, leaving him no time for such frivolities.

The overpowering perfume odor assailed his nostrils as the two of them looked around. The dominant colors in the club were purple and red, both from the lights and the furnishings. The place was nearly packed, but Katya had reserved a table.

The hostess stopped at an empty table and said, "Your waitress will be right with you, Mr. Smythe."

The waitresses wore short shorts and tight-fitting tank tops with the Red Garter Saloon logo below ample breasts. Any one of them

could have been a dancer on the stage.

Thom and Katya were met at their table by an attractive server with long, straight blond hair. She took their drink orders and his Amex Black card, then started to turn.

Thom stopped her. "Open a tab on that card, please," he said, then handed the girl a hundred-dollar bill from a thick roll in his pocket.

Her smile ratcheted up, commensurate with the tip.

"Yes sir, Mr. Smythe!"

Then she hurried off as the couple sat down.

On the stage closest to their table, a redhead swung lazily around a pole as the song the DJ was spinning climaxed and began to fade, while on the other stage, a statuesque black woman hung inverted on the pole, her legs wrapped around it. Neither wore a stitch of clothes and as they finished, the crowd roared its approval.

"Put your hands together for Shaniqua and Mercedes," an amplified voice yelled. "It's amateur night at the Red Garter! And it looks like we have quite a few beautiful young ladies in the crowd."

The roar of applause, whistles, and catcalls rose as the lights on the far stage turned off, and the two dancers exited through a door in the back. Looking around, Thom could see that there were indeed quite a few women, which totally surprised him. The few times he'd visited strip clubs, he'd rarely seen any women who didn't work there.

Suddenly, the waitress was back with their drinks. She smiled at Katya and asked, "Are you going to dance tonight?"

Katya replied, loud enough for those at adjacent tables to hear, "We just got engaged! And yes, I want to dance for my fiancé. But only if he will come to the stage and introduce me."

"Do it, man!" one guy shouted from a crowded nearby table.

Several of his buddies joined in, looking hungrily at Katya.

"Okay, okay," Thom said, as if he were reluctant. But it was the way Katya had told him to be. Then he turned toward her. "But you gotta take it *all* off, baby."

The guys at the other table went crazy, whooping and yelling for her to do it.

She leaned over and kissed Thom so passionately it elicited more shouts, adding fuel to the fire in many of the men sitting near them. Katya broke away and confided excitedly to the waitress, "I have never done this before!"

The waitress asked her name and Katya gave it, having to spell her last name. She also gave her Thom's name, which the waitress also wrote down on her little notepad. She handed Katya the pen and turned the pad toward her.

"This is just a simple modeling agreement," she said. "Red Garter Saloon pays nothing for your performance, and you don't hold them liable for anything that happens to you while you're performing or after."

Katya signed it with a flourish, then the waitress hurried over to the DJ's booth and handed him the slip of paper.

Katya leaned toward him, sucking on the little drink straw with pursed lips. "You remember your lines?"

"Yeah," Thom replied, beginning to get aroused over the whole thing.

"Al-righty!" The DJ's voice was loud over the speakers. "We have our first contestant. Her name is Katya, and judging by her last name, I'm guessing she's Russian."

"I am Czechian!" Katya shouted, standing, then jumping up and down, and clapping her hands.

"And a very fine Czechian woman you are!" the DJ shouted.

MAN OVERBOARD

"Let's hear it for Katya!"

Katya seemed to revel in the attention, turning and waving to the crowd all around them, which erupted in lewd shouts and whistles again.

"Sorry, gentlemen, but Katya has requested that her brand-new fiancé introduce her!" the DJ announced. "So, come on over here to the booth, the very lucky Mr. Thom Smythe!"

Rising to stand beside her, Thom grabbed Katya's hand and they started toward the DJ's booth and the steps leading up to the stage. Katya had been right. Dozens of men had their phones up, taking pictures, maybe even video. Others cheered her on, whistling and yelling.

The DJ was Asian, a smallish man with shoulder-length hair, who was lost among a sea of electronic equipment.

He handed Thom a cordless microphone and leaned over the edge of the booth. "Don't drop that, man. Just walk her over to the stage and make a short intro, okay? Ya gotta hold it right up to your mouth. Got it?"

Thom took the mic and looked at the side. A button was slid toward the top and next to it was a green light. He nodded at the man, then turned toward the stage, put on a fake smile, and extended his arm.

Katya took it and the two walked to the stage and turned to face the audience. The lights over the crowd tilted down slightly, bathing them in a glare that made it difficult to see. The place was packed, and dozens of phones were pointed at them.

Thom turned toward Katya. She was smiling brightly at the audience like a red-carpet celebrity posing for the photographers. Her hair was up again, with waves of blond tresses cascading to her right shoulder. If it were even remotely possible, the lighting made

her look even more beautiful.

She was wearing a skin-tight, long-sleeved top that didn't reach the bottom of her ribcage. It revealed a trim, flat belly, with long straight lines of ab muscles. A matching black skirt tightly formed to the perfect contour of her waist, hips, and upper thighs, riding well below her navel and flowing down to just below her right knee. It was cut very high on the left, exposing most of her long, firm leg. Where the slit ended there were three elastic straps continuing the slit all the way up her hip to the tight spandex waist.

Thom stepped back, holding Katya's hand as he raised the mic to his lips and admired her beauty. "I don't know what to say," he began, although they'd rehearsed his saying just that. Then he turned toward the audience, raising Katya's hand high. "I'm Thom Smythe and I really am the luckiest man in the world." He looked across the room from side to side, playing it up as Katya moved her body as if she were a serpent hanging from his palm.

By then, the crowd was at a fever pitch. Thom had no idea how these amateur shows worked, but he figured they probably took a little longer to get rolling, as men tried to convince their women to do it. Everywhere he looked, Thom noticed lustful stares and men clapping and pounding tables as the noise grew louder.

After lifting Katya's hand higher, he gave her a little twirl. "Today, I asked this absolutely...*drop...dead...gorgeous* woman to marry me. And she said yes! So" —he paused and looked around— "for the next few minutes, I'm going to share Katya Popova with you! Bartenders! Drinks are on me while she dances!"

CHAPTER TWENTY-THREE

When I awoke, I was still tired. We hadn't gotten back to the house until almost midnight, and it was another hour before Savannah and I actually got to sleep.

"Growing old ain't for sissies," an old friend of mine by the name of Billy Rainwater used to say. Probably still does. He and I grew up together and we served in the Marine Corps, occasionally at the same duty station, during my first enlistment. He was Calusa, his father a full-blooded chieftain. His mother was also Calusa, but one of her grandparents had been Seminole. Billy, having more pure Calusa blood than any other of his people, had assumed leadership.

You're not married to a younger woman, I told Billy in my head.

I turned to gaze at Savannah's face as she lay motionless beside me. Her blond hair was splashed across the pillow as she clutched a sheet under her chin, The thin fabric disappeared over her left hip, the tangle of the sheet uncovering her legs, one of which was draped over mine.

I extricated myself from our bed carefully, so as not to disturb her, then stood and looked down at her while she slept peacefully. There was no doubt in my mind that I was the luckiest man in the whole world to have found such a beautiful woman to love me.

Quietly pulling a drawer open, I got out a clean pair of skivvies

and put them on. Pulling a pair of shorts over them, I slipped out of our bedroom into the living room.

Finn raised his head and looked at me. Then we went through the same familiar morning routine we'd done for ten years before moving aboard *Ambrosia*. He rose and trotted to the door, his tail wagging. It was easy to see he was happy to be home. He knew every square inch of the island, as well as others nearby.

I let him out, then checked Alberto's tiny room. He was sound asleep. From his window, gazing toward the island's interior, I didn't see Jimmy or Naomi moving around.

Grabbing my phone from the charger, I stepped out onto the deck and checked to see if Chyrel had come up with anything. Not seeing any message, I checked the time, then scrolled through my phone list to find Pam's number and called her. She was always in the office at 0800, even on Saturday. She answered on the third ring.

"Hey, Pam," I said, watching Finn sniff around one of the orange trees beside Jimmy's house. "It's Jesse. How've you been?"

We made small talk for a few minutes before I told her the reason for my call.

"Opening the account is no trouble at all," she said. "But new banking regulations mean you'll have to come to the bank and fill out a new signature card for it before I can transfer the funds."

"The card you have on file isn't enough?"

"Sorry, no," she replied. "Some of these new regulations are crazy, but we have to follow them."

"How late are you open today?" I asked, knowing that the branch opened at 0900 and closed at noon on Saturdays.

"We close at twelve," she replied. "But I'll be here until at least one o'clock. Maybe two."

"I'll be there as soon as I can get away," I said. "We're on the

island until next weekend."

"Well, good," she said. "Everyone needs some down time. Welcome home, Jesse."

We ended the call as Finn started back up the steps. I was about to put my phone in my pocket when it chirped and vibrated in my hand. It was a number here in the Keys but not one in my contact list, so I answered it with "McDermitt."

"Hi, Mr. McDermitt," a woman's voice said. "You probably don't remember me, but you helped my husband out of a bad situation about fifteen years ago. My name's Coral Trebor. Only then it was Coral LaRoc."

I did remember her. She'd had a boyfriend by the name of Michael Grabowski, a guy who'd ripped off a drug dealer in Pittsburgh. The dealer was once a famous football player and he'd tracked Grabowski to the Keys, showing up at the Rusty Anchor and throwing his weight around.

I also remembered the strange way in which Rufus had whooped his ass.

"Yes, I do remember you," I said, opening the door to let Finn back in the house.

"Remember who," Savannah mouthed, as she stepped out in one of my T-shirts and handed me a mug.

"Coral LaRoc is an easy name to remember," I said for Savannah's benefit. "And your boyfriend was Michael Grabowski."

"Yes, it was," she said, as I clicked the speaker button. "He changed it to Robert Trebor after that, but everyone calls him Bob."

"And your aunt is a palm reader or something," I said. "The lady with the shotgun."

"Aunt Dawn," she confirmed. "Dawn McKenna. She passed away about a year ago. Bob and I are married and have two kids now."

I looked at Savannah, trying to recall if I'd told her the story about the big shootout at Key West Bight that'd left five men dead. "I'm genuinely sorry to hear about your aunt, Coral. But happy to hear you have a family. What can I do for you?"

"There's something weird going on down here on the Rock."

"Well, it's Saturday," I said, grinning at Savannah. "Not that the day of the week has never defined the level of weirdness in Key West."

She laughed. "They don't call it Key Weird for nothing. But this is like *mystery* weird. You see, there's this guy in town; a guy I know I met here a couple of years ago. The reason I remember meeting him was that he was here on business, and, unlike his associates, he wasn't drinking, and was a very polite and professional man. Only now, he's acting like some sort of celeb or something. A Czechian woman has him spending money like it's going out of style. I heard through the coconut telegraph that they announced their engagement last night, just before he pushed her up on stage at the Red Garter's amateur night."

"A Czechian woman?" I asked, arching an eyebrow at Savannah, who sipped her coffee.

"That's the really weird thing," Coral said. "I know I've seen her before too. She's the same woman that was down here just a couple of months ago and started to pull the same thing with a guy who I heard was from up island—in your area. He must have come to his senses or something because they both just disappeared."

"You're a smart woman, Coral," I said. "What do you think is going on?"

"I think she's gonna rob this guy blind," she replied. "He's a nice man and I doubt the cops would do anything, so Bob suggested I call you."

"Is her name Katya Popova?" I asked. "And the guy from a coupla months ago, Robert Grant?"

"How'd you know?"

"They say that God takes care of drunks and fools and children," I said. "At one time or another, I've been all three. The guy she's with is *definitely* getting ripped off. That's what this woman does."

"I kind of figured that," Coral said. "She's got him buying her all kinds of stuff, melting his Amex Black card in a hurry."

"It's a whole lot deeper than her just getting him to buy her things," I said. "Look, I can be down there by ten hund—er, ten o'clock. I'd like to talk to you more about this."

"Sure," she said. "I'm working the pool bar today at La Concha. It opens at eleven, but I'll be there by ten. Just come there."

"I'll see you at ten," I said, and ended the call.

"How do you get so lucky?" Savannah asked.

I touched my mug to hers with one hand and drew her closer with the other. "I ask myself that every morning."

"Seriously," she said, kissing me on the lips, then moving toward the table at the corner of the deck. "Things like this fall into your lap a *lot*."

"Chance favors the prepared mind," I offered, using one of my favorite quotes—this one from Louis Pasteur.

"So, how does one prepare their mind for getting a tip from someone they haven't talked to in more than a decade?"

"Fifteen years," I replied. "I'd just gotten my first cell phone about then, and I remember giving her my number and telling her to call me if she needed anything."

"And she waited fifteen years?" Savannah asked, looking over her mug at me. "I wouldn't have shown so much restraint."

"She was just a kid," I said. "And she and Grabow—er, Bob, were

in love. When he changed his name, he chose one that was a palindrome, like hers."

"I remember you telling me that. Clever and cute."

"Ah, crap!" I said, realizing I'd left myself a very short time frame.

"What?"

"I'd just gotten off the phone with Pam when Coral called. I told her I'd meet her at noon to sign the paperwork for the new bank account."

"You could go there first," she suggested. "The bank opens at nine. If all you have to do is sign something, you might be a little late getting to Key West but not much."

"I have a lot of—"

"Just go do what you have to do," she interrupted. "Alberto and I can pitch in and help Jimmy get everything done you were going to do. And we've got Robert here, too."

I glanced toward the bunkhouse across the clearing.

"There's nothing to worry about," she assured me. "He's completely harmless."

I smiled at her. "You don't even know what I was planning to work on today."

"Neither do you," she replied. "There are always things that need doing here. So, we'll just find a few and do them."

CHAPTER TWENTY-FOUR

A little over an hour later, I was leaving the bank and headed south on Useless-1, crossing the Seven Mile Bridge. I had to slow down for the Key deer speed limit through Big Pine, but by the time I reached Key West, I was only fifteen minutes late.

The Beast stood out among Keys cars. It was nearly as long as two of them, way taller than all but commercial trucks, and to most, it looked like it'd been dredged from the channel and deposited with the spoils.

A car's vehicle identification number provided all sorts of information, including engine, transmission, differential ratio, even the interior and exterior color and date manufactured. Years ago, I'd checked *The Beast's* VIN to see exactly what the date was when she rolled off the assembly line. Her fiftieth anniversary was coming up on the first of November.

My old truck wasn't the only thing out of place as I drove slowly down Whitehead Street, looking for a spot. I too, stood out like a sore thumb among the tourists, predominantly young people, walking the sidewalks on both sides. They were mostly pale in complexion, which is unheard of under the bright Florida Keys sun in July.

It was Saturday, so I knew there was a cruise ship tied up at

Mallory Dock, probably two of them.

Ahead, a delivery truck was taking up two parking spaces across from The Green Parrot. I slowed, seeing the driver climb into the cab, and when he signaled and the front tires turned toward the street, I put my right signal on and flashed my headlights at him.

I rolled into the spot as he pulled out, waving a friendly hand, and he waved back. With my window already down, I stopped next to a young guy stacking boxes onto a hand truck.

"Expecting any more deliveries?" I asked.

"Huh, um no, man," he replied, looking through the window and raising his sunglasses. "No, you're good to park here. Our next delivery's at noon, so he might block you in."

"Thanks," I replied, setting the brake and shutting off the big diesel engine. "I'll either be headed back up island before then or come back and move it to a better spot for the day."

"What is this thing, man?" the kid asked as I stepped out.

"International Travelall," I replied, then turned and walked away.

I didn't have time for idle chat. Backtracking toward Fleming Street, I turned right, then crossed over and entered the large hotel that took up nearly a block of Duval Street.

Once inside, the air conditioning felt cold on my sweaty neck. I'd never been a big fan of air conditioning, although we were going to install a unit in my house at some point this week.

As I made my way through the lobby and out onto the big courtyard area, I immediately spotted Coral at the patio bar, stocking a cooler. The short blond dreads she'd once worn were gone; her hair now pulled back in a ponytail. She hadn't changed a whole lot, as I remembered, but she had added a few pounds, giving her a bit fuller figure. That was to be expected, having had two

children. The added dimensions looked good on her.

She looked up as I sat on a stool and started to say something. Then she must've recognized me—she smiled. "Mr. McDermitt," she said, her Bostonian accent rounding the R sounds into kind of a half-silent H. "I wasn't sure if you were still coming."

"It took a while to find a parking spot big enough for my truck," I said. "Sorry I'm late. No more dreads?"

"Drea..." —her hand went to her hair— "No, that was a young girl thing. I'm a mom to two adolescent boys these days. Can I get you something?"

"Water, if it's not too much trouble," I replied.

She pulled a bottled water from another cooler and placed it on a coaster. "It's good to see you again. You look well."

"Thanks," I said, twisting the cap off. "So, do you. Motherhood agrees with you."

Her eyes shifted to the ring on my finger. "You're married now?"

"Almost two years," I replied. "But I was a little slow on the uptake. Out daughter will be twenty-two later this month."

"Are you still working for the government?" she asked, changing the subject. "I heard from a friend that you were with Homeland Security or something."

"Not any longer," I replied. "I'm a partner in a security company up island."

It was a true enough statement, though I had very little to do with Deuce's private investigations and security work. I'd invested in his business early on and had more than earned back the venture capital.

"And the woman I told you about is someone you were already investigating?" she asked in disbelief. "That's some coincidence—my calling you."

"Robert Grant, the guy she ripped off a couple of months ago, is a friend of mine," I explained. "The woman, Katya Popova, if that's her real name, is supposedly married to a man in Miami named Mike Spencer. Together, they look for people who are in desperate need of a new identity and they provide it for a fee. If the client's wealthy, as in Robert's case, they convince them to fake a marriage and transfer all their holdings to them. The deal is, they're supposed to launder it and transfer it back to the new identity, and the fake wife is supposed to disappear, making it look like he got catfished. That way, the rich guy gets to keep his money and start over in a new place, for whatever reason."

"But they don't follow through," she said. "When will people ever learn? There aren't any shortcuts to success."

I smiled. "You're preaching to the choir, sister. So, is this guy Smythe staying here at the hotel?"

"Yeah," she said, continuing to stock the cooler. "Both of them are now. He checked in a few days ago and met her in the Wine-O a day or two later."

La Concha had three bars—the 430 Restaurant and Bar, Wine-O, and the pool bar. It was the first luxury hotel built in Key West, having first opened in 1926, fourteen years after the railroad reached the island. It was still the tallest building in town.

I didn't need to ask how she knew any details about Smythe and Popova. Key West was a small town and people in the service industries—waiters, waitresses, bartenders, and the like, probably numbered fewer than a thousand. People talked.

"Have you seen them today?" I asked, as a rail-thin man with long dreadlocks wheeled a dolly loaded with three cases of beer behind the bar.

"I haven't," she said, then turned toward the barback.

"Terrance, have you seen the glam couple today? The rich business guy and the blond Czechian woman?"

He nodded, with a quick glance at me. "I and I see dem early dis mornin', Miss Coral. De desk mon summoned a chariot to take dem to Key Largo to go divin'."

"That's right," Coral said. "I remember her mentioning going to a concert and they're having the annual underwater concert at Pennekamp today."

"Whut else do yuh need heah?" the Jamaican man asked.

She glanced down into the cooler, stepped over and opened another one, then glanced at the cases on the dolly. "That should do it until dinner. Come see me before you punch out and we'll get things set up for the party."

He nodded, pulled the dolly from under the beer cases, then wheeled it away.

"Do you know the man's name?" I asked her.

"Thom Smythe," she replied. "He spells his first name with an H and the last name's spelled with a Y and has an E at the end—S-M-Y-T-H-E, but he pronounces it like the regular old Smith. He's a businessman up in Palm Beach."

"Did he ever say what kind of business?"

"The stock market, I think. And he mentioned real estate."

"You seem to know a lot about him," I suggested.

"You know how it is," she said with a smile. "The bar is like an invisibility cloak and people say things."

"That they do," I agreed, knowing just what she meant. "What's Bob doing these days?"

"He works over at the airport," she replied. "He was a steel worker up north, you know. Now he works as a welder for a guy named Ray Floyd and he moonlights a little with a couple of

boatyards."

"He works for Ray?"

"You know him?" she asked.

"Bob didn't by any chance help Ray with a Grumman Mallard last year, did he?"

"That big twin-engine plane that lands on the water? He did a lot of custom work for Ray on that one."

"That's my plane, *Ocean Hopper*," I said. "Ray's joining me next week to fly some people and cargo into Bimini for several days, to help break the engines in."

"Well, that explains things," she said. "Bob came home the other day and said Ray'd be gone for a while but wouldn't say where he was going. I'll have to tell Bob that was your plane. He'll get a kick outta that."

That was the way things often happened in the Keys. Years ago, people talked about the six degrees to Kevin Bacon, and how anyone could be connected to even popular movie stars by as few as six relationships. In the Keys, it was more like three or four. With just over eighty thousand full-time residents in Monroe County, more than ninety-nine percent of them living on one of the many islands of the Keys, they tended to rely more on one another than they would on the mainland. In the Keys, people were closer.

"Anything else you can tell me about the woman?" I asked.

"She really likes attention," Coral replied. "Like I said, she was here a couple of days before they met at the Wine-O—I work weeknights there. I'm only working the pool bar today because one of my girls stepped on an urchin and her foot's swollen up real bad."

"One of *your* girls?"

"I manage all three bars," she said, smiling proudly. "Anyway, guys were literally crowding around her the first couple of nights she

was in town, following her from one bar to another. A real tease. Then she met Mr. Smythe."

"When was that?" I asked.

She thought about it for a moment. "Thursday night," she finally replied. "About ten o'clock, I think. She'd been in the bar for less than an hour and had already collected an entourage of men. Even after they met and started dating, if she was alone, it wasn't for long. She was flirting with every man she came across."

"She ever mention what she did for a living?"

"I could guess," Coral said, kind of under her breath with a shake of her head. Then she looked up, thinking. "But you know what? Now that you mention it, no, I don't remember her ever saying. Which is kinda weird, too, huh? I mean, everybody talks about what they do and where they're from when they're on vacation. I don't recall her ever mentioning it to anyone. But, then again, I don't intentionally listen in on people's conversations."

"Of course not," I said with a wink. "Off topic, but have you ever acted on anything you *accidentally* overheard?"

She glanced around, leaned across the bar, and smiled. "A few times," she whispered. "It's paid for our little house, our boys' future college, and a good start in life for both of them."

"Really?" I said, confirming a hunch I'd had for a long time.

I'd always known of the "invisibility cloak," as she'd called it. When people of means let their guard down in a bar or the back of a cab, they often ignored the fact that they were discussing sensitive information in front of a total stranger.

"This one time, about ten years ago," Coral continued. "Bob overheard two airline execs talking about a big deal they had coming up. We researched the company and prices were way low. So, we took a big leap of faith and invested all we had in the company.

After the deal went through, we sold for a huge profit and bought our forever home over by the cemetery on Olivia."

I grinned and lifted my water bottle in salute. "So, there are occasional shortcuts to success."

She smiled back. "I suppose so. But you gotta be ready when the golden ring appears."

Chance favors the prepared mind, I thought once more.

"That you do," I agreed. "I'm happy for you both. Do you think the 'glam couple' will be back this evening? Smythe and Popova?"

"I'm certain of it," she replied. "He reserved the pool bar for a private party. So, I get to pull a double."

"Whoa! That had to set him back."

"I'll say," she agreed. "I've been working here for over ten years, and it's only happened a couple of times that I know of. Usually, a big wedding reception or something. But we've never done one on a Saturday night. The pool bar makes a lot of money then."

I thanked her and we said goodbye. Then I left a ten on the bar and made my way back through the main lobby and out onto the street. I turned north, with no particular destination in mind, and considered what I'd found out as I dodged tourists on the busy Duval Street sidewalk.

There was no doubt in my mind that if he let it continue, this Thom Smythe guy would end up looking for work at the Rusty Anchor or some other place, just as Robert Grant had.

What would drive a person to want to abandon everything—their family, friends, home, all just to start over again somewhere new?

A few blocks later, I made the familiar turns through the shops that lined Mallory Square and found a shady spot to sit. A massive cruise ship blocked the view, but I knew from experience that it

would leave before sunset.

I pulled up Deuce's number and called him.

"I heard you were in town," he said without preamble. "When do you head to Bimini?"

"The ship's still a few weeks from sailing," I replied. "But you know that. We're flying over next weekend to get settled aboard. Then I'll be flying people and equipment in with *Ocean Hopper*."

"We'll be on one of those hops," he said. "But not for a couple of weeks. We ought to get together before then."

"Yeah, I'd like that, and I know Savannah would. Listen, I'm working on something solo down here in Key Weird."

He laughed. "I seem to remember you saying something very similar a long time ago. We don't have to go into Cuba, do we?"

CHAPTER TWENTY-FIVE

Sitting at a table at Sunset Pier, I enjoyed a blackened fish sandwich as the hordes of cruising tourists began to meander back to the ship like so many lemmings. The grouper was delicious and had probably been swimming earlier that morning.

Finally, my phone chirped an incoming email, which I opened and read. It was from Deuce—a preliminary report on Mike Spencer. I opened the attached file, dug my reading glasses out of my pocket, and read the report.

Apparently, Mike Spencer was a respected, upstanding citizen of Miami with a background in sales and marketing. He had no history of arrests, aside from the occasional traffic summons, and he was legally married to Katrina Popovich three years ago, a model who chose to keep her last name.

Interesting, I thought. Katya Popova and Katrina Popovich.

Nothing in the attached PDF file Deuce sent even hinted at anything illegal. Then there was the question of what did they hold over their victims? What was Robert not telling us? Could it just be the empty feeling of being a failure and so easily taken?

It was almost a certainty that Popova and Popovich were one and the same person, but I forwarded a picture of the couple to Savannah and asked her to show it to Robert. She replied in less than a minute—*He says that's definitely them. Did you find the guy Coral told you about?*

I started to type a reply, then "Young Jesse's" voice spoke inside my head. *It's a fancy telephone and your fongers are thick.*

So, I clicked the call button and put the phone to my ear.

"How's it going?" Savannah asked.

"I'm not sure," I said. "Katya Popova's real name is Katrina Popovich and she and Mike Spencer are, in fact, legally married. So far, they both look squeaky clean on paper. The guy she's currently with down here is named Thom Smythe, a businessman from Palm Beach. Still waiting for a report on him, but Deuce sent me a preliminary work up on Spencer and Popovich. Is Robert sure it was them?"

"Very sure," she replied. "He was angry at first, then his eyes glazed over and he's back to being empty inside. I'm really worried about him."

"She's using the same name with Smythe that she used with Robert," I said. "The two of them hired a limo service to take them to Pennekamp for the underwater concert. Tonight, they reserved the pool bar at La Concha for a big party. I can't get my head wrapped around why they'd do that."

"Do either of them have friends down there?"

"Not that I can tell," I replied. "Coral described him as being a very conservative professional when she'd seen him here a couple of years back. And both of them only just recently arrived in town."

"How can they throw a party if they don't know anyone?" she asked rhetorically. "Inviting friends from the mainland?"

"I don't think it's a party for friends," I said. "I think they're wanting people to know who they are."

"What for?"

MAN OVERBOARD

"I don't know. I think I'm going to stay for the night, see if I can learn anything at this party—maybe talk to Smythe."

"Be careful, Jesse. We don't know what these people are up to."

I ended the call as another email pinged my phone. Attached to Deuce's second message was a file on Thom Smythe. He was an investor out of Palm Beach and had holdings all up and down the Gold Coast. He was single, never married, no kids, no siblings, and both parents were deceased.

Nobody would miss him.

And Robert had also said that he had no family. Maybe these people looked for specific types of men—wealthy men with no familial ties who, once they disappeared, nobody would miss. They'd relocate and abandon them. The victims couldn't very well go to the police since they were at least complicit in identity fraud, if nothing else.

The waitress brought my check, and I left enough cash on the table to cover it with a nice tip. Then I made my way back to La Concha. It seemed as good a place to start as any. Finding lodging in Key West on the weekend could often be difficult.

I was lucky. La Concha had a last-minute cancellation and if I didn't mind a room with two beds and a sofa bed, I could have it for $780 for one night. I mentioned that Margaritaville, just down the street, had a room for under five hundred, though I didn't have any idea what their rates were. All I knew was that the desk clerk had a paying customer in front of him, it was nearly noon, and the hotel had an empty room.

He dropped the price to $495.

It was still an outlandish price to pay, but if I wanted to get close enough, I had to actually *be* close.

"Is your luggage outside in your car, Mr. Buchannan?" the man asked, handing my fake ID and credit card back, along with a little folder with a key card in it.

"Yeah, but it's a few blocks away," I replied. "Couldn't find closer parking."

"We have ample parking here, sir." He slid me another card. "Just give this to the valet when you bring your car in."

"What's the vertical clearance?" I asked.

"The what, sir?"

"My vehicle's tall," I replied. "A little over seven and a half feet."

"Oh, that's no problem. It's not a covered garage or anything like that. Just pull in off of Duval down at the end of the six-story hotel building. Just before the Sandal Factory."

I left and walked back to get *The Beast*, shaking my head. Whether the lot was covered or not didn't matter, the entrance had a roof over it, but if he didn't balk, I wouldn't either. Every scratch and ding on *The Beast* had a story to tell.

It wasn't quite noon yet, so when I arrived, there was no big delivery truck blocking me in. But a rental car had parked very close behind me, even though it had half a car length behind *it* to the next vehicle.

When I got in and started the engine, I noticed a piece of paper stuck under the windshield. I climbed out and retrieved it. Scrawled across the back of a receipt from Five Guys in Miami were the words *Too damn big for down here. Good luck getting out, asshole.*

I went back and looked at the red Camry parked on *The Beast's* bumper. Rental cars were easy to spot in the Keys. They were shiny, new, had little bar codes at the bottom corner of the windshield, and no smoking stickers on the side windows.

They were also fully insured.

After climbing back into *The Beast*, I put the truck in neutral, slid

the transfer case into four-wheel-drive low, then put the transmission in reverse. I backed up until I heard a satisfying crunch, then gunned the engine. With an empty weight of over two tons, a big diesel engine with tons of horsepower and torque, and giant all-terrain tires, *The Beast* easily pushed the lightweight rental car back five feet.

I put the transfer case back into two-wheel high, put the transmission in second gear, and pulled forward, hearing more crunching sounds as the big, four-way dropped hitch broke free from the rental car's grill.

Checking my mirror, I signaled and then drove sedately toward Fleming. Whoever the jerk was, he was going to be stuck in Key West a little longer than he anticipated and would spend part of his weekend trip sitting at a rental car agency arguing that he didn't plow into a sign.

I'm usually very accommodating toward others, as long as they're polite. But crowding *The Beast's* bumper like that was a bullying tactic and I don't have any trouble carrying the fight right back.

After making the right on Fleming, I waited on the narrow one-way street at the light, then turned left on Duval. A car was coming out of La Concha's parking lot driveway, so I waited for him to get out and pulled in. There was at least ten feet of clearance.

A kid dressed in the hotel's uniform came running from the parking lot behind the building, waving his hands to stop me.

"This is guest parking only," he said when he reached my open window. "We don't let just anyone park here."

Shutting off the engine, I climbed out and looked down at the kid. He was about twenty, half a foot shorter than my six-three, and at least sixty pounds under my two-twenty.

I handed him the card the desk clerk had given me. "Just let me grab my bag out of the back," I said, and walked around *The Beast* to open the right side of the double barn-style doors.

My emergency go-bag was there in the cargo compartment, packed with clothes and toiletries to last three days. There was also an assortment of fenders, dock lines, and boat parts, none of which I needed.

I grabbed the bag, closed the door, and returned to the valet, to whom I slipped a twenty along with the key and winked. "Keep an eye on her for me," I said. "All this happened last time I was down here."

I left him scratching his head in confusion and entered the hotel lobby, assaulted once more by the cold, dry air. Before going up to my room, I headed back out to the pool bar, the go-bag slung over my left shoulder.

"Back so soon?" Coral asked, serving Cokes to three teens.

"Got a room for the night," I said.

She smiled at the boys and accepted their money as easily as their stares. Coral was twice their age—but a very attractive woman—and boys will be boys.

"Who'd you have to beat up to get a room on short notice like that?" she asked.

"Got lucky," I replied. "They had a last-minute cancellation. At any rate, I want to be here when that party happens. Any idea how I can swing an invite?"

"As far as I know, it's open to everyone."

"Perfect. I'd also like to ask a favor."

"What's that?" she asked, smiling. "Just name it."

"Think you can introduce me to the happy couple?"

"Not a problem with him," she replied, wiping down the water

spots where the boys' drinks had been. "But I don't think she knows me from the furniture."

"That'll do," I replied. "But introduce me as Stretch Buchannan."

"Stretch Buchannan. Got it. Anything I can do to help. After what you did for me and Bob, we owe you a lot more, Mr. McDermitt."

"I'll consider the debt paid if you'd just call me Jesse. What time's this party start?"

"The pool bar's reserved from nine o'clock on," she replied. "So, everyone can hit Mallory Square for the Sunset Celebration before coming here."

"Thanks, Coral."

"I told Bob you were in town," she said. "He's anxious to see you when he gets off work."

"He's working on Saturday?"

"He's doing a custom dinghy davit for a boatyard over on Stock Island today."

I pulled my key card out, glanced at the little cardboard holder it was in, and gave her the room number. "Call me when he gets off. We can sit on this side of the invisibility cloak for a couple of drinks."

CHAPTER TWENTY-SIX

Once in my room, I switched on the TV and clicked the remote until a Miami news channel came on, then opened my go-bag on one of the beds and unpacked everything. As I was about to go into the head to take a shower, an English accented reporter on the screen caught my ear.

I sat on the edge of the bed and turned the volume up a little. The reporter stood on a dock, as if waiting for divers to exit a dive boat in the background. At the bottom of the screen, it said he was in Key Largo.

Suddenly, I recognized Popova as she stepped off the boat, wearing the skimpiest bikini I think I'd ever seen. Behind her, Thom Smythe struggled with two dive bags, but finally reached her side just as the reporter stepped up to Popova.

"Excuse me," the reporter said. "Were you diving the underwater concert? Can you tell our audience what it was like?"

The camera stayed zoomed out, so Popova was visible from the waist up, leaving little to the imagination.

"Yes, we did!" Popova replied enthusiastically, her body in motion for all to see. "It was wonderful and...exhilarating."

I had to give the cameraman props. I had no idea who he was, but the way she was bouncing up and down would have caused a few

men to clutch their chests and fall over.

"What's your name and where are you from?" the reporter asked, smiling at both the woman and the camera.

"I am Katya Popova," she replied. "And this is my fiancé, Thom Smythe."

The reporter shoved the mic in front of Smythe and asked how he enjoyed the show.

"Like she said," Smythe replied, as the camera slowly zoomed out just enough to show the bottom of Popova's bathing suit. "It was an exciting show."

"I'm sure it was," the reporter said, putting a finger to his ear. The camera zoomed closer, cropping the couple out. "This is Nick Harvey, on location at John Pennekamp Coral Reef State Park. Back to the studio."

I wondered what the producer had said into his and the cameraman's headsets. Normally, when interviewing someone, the cameraman went for a tight head shot. But with so much skin showing, maybe he couldn't resist.

The station cut back to talking heads at a desk and I rose from the bed, wondering why anyone would wear next to nothing when doing a dive that required you to do little more than rest on the bottom. She must have gotten very cold toward the end.

Then it hit me. The two of them were making sure that his name was known not just here in Key West, but all over. It just didn't make any sense if someone was looking for him and he was planning to disappear and assume a new name.

There was an element missing. Something they were doing with Smythe beyond what they'd done for Robert.

I called Savannah again.

"Let me talk to Robert," I said as soon as she answered.

"Hold on."

I heard a door open and close, then Savannah's voice in the background saying, "It's Jesse. He wants to talk to you."

"Hello," Robert said.

"Was there anything about the deal you had with Spencer that you didn't mention?" I asked.

"Like what?"

"Like why they would go to so much trouble to make it look like you'd married a woman who then stole all you had."

There was silence for a moment. I could hear birds in the background, so I knew I hadn't lost the connection.

Finally, Robert's dejected voice said, "They wanted it known to everyone when my new wife took off with all my money."

I hadn't heard about Robert's situation when it happened. Not that I was highly informed of what everyone did in Marathon. But everywhere I turned down here, Thom Smythe's name was being shoved in my face.

"There has to be something else," I said. "Some reason they're making this Smythe guy more public."

"They offered to make it look like I died," Robert said. "But since I had no family, I opted for the simpler plan—get ripped off and then just fall off the edge of the Earth. Which is exactly what happened."

"I still don't get it," I said, knowing there was more he wasn't telling. "You said you met her through a dating site. How'd that turn into faking your death?"

He paused, then let out a sigh. "I screwed up. I got into a deal with some unsavory people who wanted more out of me. Somehow Katya and Mike knew about my financial problems, and she pretended to be looking for the same things in life as me. For all I

know, they could have been working with the South Americans."

"When did she reveal she was catfishing you?"

"The day after I told her about the financial bind I was in," Robert replied.

"Put Savannah back on."

After a second, Savannah asked, "What's wrong?"

"I think they plan to fake Smythe's death, not just his marriage."

"Why? And more importantly, how?"

"I don't know," I replied. "Maybe Smythe's in a lot deeper than Robert was with creditors. Maybe the mob's looking for him. He and Popova were just interviewed on the Miami news channel, and they both gave their names."

"I'm worried," she said. "You don't have any idea what these people are capable of and now you're planning to get hip-deep in it. What happened to trying to get them to relocate the two of us?"

I knew she was concerned. For the most part, I'd put my old life behind me, content to skipper *Ambrosia* and leave most of the heavy lifting to the younger guys. I didn't think this problem was all that dangerous, but what I thought was secondary to what my wife thought. And she'd be more comfortable if she were involved, even if only in a small way.

We could have Coral introduce us as a couple, drop a little hint that we were in financial trouble, and see what happened. After that, I'd make sure any future meetings would be just me. Just to be on the safe side.

"Pack a bag," I told her. "Have Rusty drive you down here. I'm staying at La Concha, room 510. I'll contact Chyrel and have her add to Stretch Buchannan's fake background that he was recently married."

"What about Alberto?"

202

"He'll be fine there with Jimmy and Naomi," I replied. "And tell Robert to stay there on the island."

I showered and put on clean clothes—jeans and a T-shirt, then headed down to the lobby and out onto Duval Street. The attire I had in my go-bag wouldn't be suitable for what I wanted, so I headed north.

Within a block, I passed a Salt Life store. I probably had half a dozen T-shirts from that company—not exactly what I had in mind. Just a few doors down, I found Earthbound Trading Company, and went inside.

Fifteen minutes later, I left the store with a bag containing two pairs of pants that were both comfortable and stylish, along with a couple of dress shirts, and a new pair of deck shoes.

Stretch Buchannan's fake background had a lot of online news stories about arrests for everything from attempted murder to drug smuggling, but he'd never been convicted of anything.

I paused in the lobby and sent a text to Chyrel asking her to add Savannah to my cover ID and say that we'd been married last year.

She replied instantly. *What will her name be?*

The best covers contained elements of truth, which made remembering facts easier.

I typed back, *Savannah Richmond, of Beaufort, SC. But make her a little darker. Maybe she used her father's fishing fleet to smuggle drugs or something.*

On it, she replied. *Deuce asked if you need anyone down there to help?*

I don't think so, I replied. *Send Savannah's bio when you have it worked out.*

She sent one of those yellow laughing faces and I shoved my phone in my pocket, wondering what Chyrel thought was funny. I went to the desk and asked if the room I was in was available for

another day, or if they had another room.

"My business here isn't moving forward as quickly as I'd hoped," I explained.

It was a woman at the desk this time. She checked the computer and said, "The room you're in is available until eleven o'clock on Monday, Mr. Buchannan. Would you like me to extend it?"

"Yes, please," I replied. "Just keep it on the Amex Black."

"Yes, sir," she said, as her fingers danced on the keyboard. "Will there be anything else?"

"My wife will be joining me in a couple of hours—Savannah Buchannan. Please give her a key card when she arrives."

"Of course, sir," the woman said with a smile. "Have a great day. Oh, and we've been asked to let guests know there will be an engagement party tonight by the pool, if you and your wife would like to attend. It's an open bar."

"Oh really? Who's the happy couple?"

"One of our guests, Thom Smythe, and his fiancée, Katya Popova."

I thanked her and headed toward the elevator, thinking. If the desk was telling everyone at the hotel about the party and specifically mentioning their names, I could only assume they wanted his fall from grace, and possibly his death, to be front page news. But if they *were* going to fake the man's death, they had a problem. Making a person disappear was one thing, but it took quite a while before that person could be declared legally dead.

Unless they found his body, I thought, as the elevator door opened, and two couples got out.

I stepped in and pushed the button for the fifth floor. Two women came running toward the elevator, so I reached out and held the door.

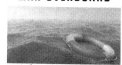

"Thanks," a woman with short, dark hair said. "Fourth floor please."

"Don't mention it," I replied and pushed the button for her.

"I can't believe she'd do that," the other woman said to her friend in a conspiratorial tone.

She looked a bit younger than the brunette, with long, straight, blond hair to her waist.

The brunette nodded, whispering. "Strip one night, have an engagement party the next, and get married the day after that."

"You're talking about Thom and Katya?" I asked.

"You know them?" the blonde asked.

"We're from the same area," I replied as the elevator stopped, and the door whisked open.

The brunette smiled. "Well, maybe we'll see *you* at the party."

"Wouldn't miss it for the world," I said, as the two women exited, smiling and whispering to one another.

When I got to the room, I stretched out on the bed and waited. It was something I wasn't naturally very good at but twenty years in the Marine Corps taught patience. We'd always been in a hurry to get to wherever we were going, only to sit and wait once we got there. On *Ambrosia* or back home on the island, I could do something else while I waited. But I was in a hotel. A nice hotel that didn't have anything that needed fixing. At least, not that I'd seen so far.

With other pieces needing to fall into place and no ability to hurry them along, I just closed my eyes and relaxed. I must have dozed off, but snapped instantly alert when my phone chirped, telling me I had a new email. It was from Deuce and contained two attachments. The first one I opened was background information on Popovich.

She was a Czechian national, born in Prague in 1990, making her thirty-two years old. Her family had immigrated to the U.S. when she was fourteen and she'd become a citizen at twenty-one. She never went to college and had worked in New York as a fashion model and actress, mostly in commercials, until 2015. In 2017, she'd been arrested in New York for prostitution. The charges didn't stick, thanks to a sharp lawyer hired by the escort company she worked for. She was arrested again a year later in Miami. Same charge and same result. Then she'd met and married Mike Spencer, who was nearly thirty years her senior—almost double her age.

The second file contained more information on Spencer, things that he'd paid a lot of money to fancy lawyers to get expunged. Things that a normal background investigation probably wouldn't uncover. But Deuce wasn't any normal background investigator.

Spencer had done time in Leavenworth Federal Prison while he'd been in the Army. He'd been convicted of manslaughter in 1980 and sentenced to twenty-five years. The Army'd released him in '92, when he'd served only half the sentence. There were also two arrest reports from Miami PD—one for tax evasion, which he'd bought his way out of, and the other for fraud, which he was acquitted of. When a judge orders a case expunged, it's deleted from the prosecutor's files, both the hard copies and electronic files, and it's those public files most people search when checking someone's background. Arrest reports usually still exist in the files of the apprehending authority, even if a judge orders the court's and state's files deleted.

"Hard for a leopard to change its spots," I said aloud, as a knock came to the door.

Out of habit, I grabbed my Sig 9mm semi-auto from the side pouch of my go bag. I press-checked the chamber, ensuring there was a round in it, then clipped the holster to my belt, adjusting my

MAN OVERBOARD

T-shirt to cover it.

Looking through the peep hole, I couldn't believe my eyes. Popova and Smythe stood outside my door, smiling.

I opened it wide, appearing confused. "Oh, I thought you were my wife."

Popovich's eyes came up to mine and she smiled as Smythe extended a hand. "I'm Thom Smythe," he said, as I shook his hand. "And this is my fiancée, Katya. We're having a big party tonight, down by the pool, and we're inviting everyone at the hotel."

"Yes, the desk clerk told me. Congratulations. Would you like to come in?"

"We can only stay a moment," the woman said, stepping past the surprised man and into my room.

"What is your name?" Popovich asked.

"Oh, I'm sorry. Buchannan. Stretch Buchannan."

"It is good name for you," she said, smiling at Smythe.

Smythe had been surprised by her accepting my invitation to come in, so I read it as unusual. But he immediately followed her in.

"Hate to barge in on you like this," he said. "But we don't know anyone in town, so we're just inviting everyone we meet."

"Not a problem," I said, waving toward the couch. "Have a seat. When's the big day?"

Either I'd slept longer than I thought, or the news story had been prerecorded. Most likely both, since it was now afternoon, and I was pretty sure they did the underwater concert in the morning.

"We are not wasting time," Popovich said, taking a seat and crossing her legs.

She wore a dress that was more suitable for clubbing than hanging around in a hotel in the afternoon, inviting strangers to a party. The side was slit, exposing ample thigh, and she sat straight on the edge of the sofa, her back arched in perfect posture, which also permitted an ample view of her cleavage. She still had the looks of a model or actress, that was for sure.

But when I looked into her ice-blue eyes, I saw something less innocent there. She'd turned to prostitution and had probably made very good money, renting her body out to wealthy clients.

"Each of us is given only so many minutes," I said. "I don't believe in wasting time, either. In fact, I only just checked in myself. My accountant set up a meeting with a local land management..." I paused, letting it hang there. "But you don't want to hear about all that. Long story short, I dropped what I was doing in Palm Beach and flew down here. So, how long have the two of you known each other?"

Smythe feigned looking at a watch he wasn't wearing and put a fake smile on his face. "We only just met this past week," he said with a laugh. "And we'll be married tomorrow morning at seven o'clock out on Whitehead pier, just as the sun rises."

It sounded almost as if he'd rehearsed it and had been saying it over and over.

I smiled back at Popovich. "A new day, a new beginning." Then I let the smile fade, as I looked out the glass door. "Sometimes, I'd love to be able to start completely over, myself."

CHAPTER TWENTY-SEVEN

Whatever was going to happen, it wasn't going to be long. As soon as the couple left, I called Chyrel to see how she was doing.

"I'd be five minutes ahead of where I am now, if you hadn't called me," she replied, fingers clicking on a keyboard. "Remember, I still have a cookout to prepare for, on top of helping to run the school."

"And I know those things are all in the best of hands," I said. "It's just that if Savannah has to prepare, she'll need some time. And this party is in seven hours."

"Don't worry," she said. "Savannah and I have been working on something for a while already. Relax, Jesse. We got this."

The call went dead.

They'd been working on it for a while? Working on what?

As if in answer, my phone chirped and when I looked at it, there was a notification of an email from Chyrel. I opened it and read her quick note; *They're still wips.* Meaning the attached file and the link were works in progress.

I opened the file, found a bio on Savvy Montrose, born in Port Royal, South Carolina, and laughed out loud.

"Keep enough truth in the cover to make it easy," I said, echoing

Deuce.

Savannah's maiden name was Richmond, and I knew Montrose was a suburb of the Virginia capital and she had once had an uncle who lived there. I also knew Port Royal was a town very close to her hometown of Beaufort. In fact, Beaufort was *on* Port Royal Island.

I read the rest of the bio, seeing where some recent changes were made, and grinned. When I tapped the link in the original email, I started laughing again.

When Savannah arrived an hour later, Rusty was with her.

"You didn't need to walk Savvy all the way to the door," I said to my friend. "Key West is weird, but not very dangerous."

He tossed a small bag on the bed nearest the door. "I'm stayin'."

"I tried to tell him it wasn't necessary," Savannah said, placing a much larger bag on the bed next to mine. "But he wouldn't hear of it."

"I been cooped up too long," Rusty growled. "Sid's taking care of everything and all I do is run the bar. It's boring as hell, seeing the same faces day in and day out."

I looked at him in surprise. "Um, you've done nothing else for nearly forty years. Why's it different now?"

"It just is," he muttered. "Now, you gonna let me stay here, or do I have to get a separate room?"

"The hotel's booked solid," I said. "What's eatin' you, brother?"

He sat down on the foot of the bed and looked around, stopping to stare out the sliding glass door. "Heck of a view."

I simply stared at him with a blank expression, waiting. It was something I've learned could be a useful tool.

"I don't know," he said. "A man gets an urge to do something now and then."

As far as I knew, Rusty's going off to join the Marine Corps was the only time any of his Thurman ancestors had left the island chain for any extended period since the island was settled. Some people were born with an unquenchable wanderlust, and others were content to put down roots. The Thurman family's roots were imbedded deep in the ancient limestone shelf that made up the islands.

"Your family has been on that same piece of property for over a hundred years," I said. "You've been to Europe, Japan, Cuba, and half a dozen other countries—the first in your family to do so since Captain Augustus left Boston two hundred years ago. What's going on?"

He shrugged. "I just feel trapped, okay? I'm over sixty and my life's as boring as watching the tides."

Savannah sat next to him. "Your life's not boring. You have a beautiful wife, friends, family, people who love you. The ocean's at your back door, where you like to fish and dive with good friends." She gave him a playful slap on the shoulder. "You're a successful businessman and a popular man about town. Hardly boring."

He looked up at me. "You got all that, bro. And next week you're gonna skipper a nuclear-powered research ship and probly go around the world."

I grinned at him. "So, you're looking for a little action this late in life? Some excitement? Is that it?"

"I don't know," he said, rising and moving toward the balcony, where he stood and looked out over the island and the sea beyond.

"Yeah, I guess you could call it that," he said quietly. "Don't get me wrong— I love Julie more than anything on this earth, but when her momma died, any dreams I had for doing anything else died with her."

Rusty had raised a daughter all alone, never asking nor seeming to need any assistance.

Before Julie was born prematurely, Rusty was looking forward to a month's leave to be there. It was to have been a thirty-day ship-over leave, and along with that, the reenlistment papers included sergeant stripes and choice of duty station. His wife had agreed, but only if they could go to Hawaii. When Juliet died in childbirth, Rusty had rescinded the paperwork and applied for terminal leave instead, using up part of his leave time accrued, and taking the rest in cash.

"This will likely be as boring as sitting in the water at low tide watching paint dry," I said. "All we're going to do is try to get these people to do for us what they did for Robert. Only when I make the money transfer, Chyrel will be ready, and she'll suck their account dry."

"Sounds like fun," he said. "So, is this my bed?"

"If you start snoring," Savannah warned, "I'll have Jesse toss you out on the balcony."

"Maybe there is something you can do," I said, and started pacing.

"What?" Rusty asked.

"Hush now," Savannah said. "He's coming up with a plan."

I grinned at her. "What'd I tell you about plans?"

"They don't survive first contact," she replied. "But you're onto something. I can tell."

"Stand up a sec," I told Rusty. "How much weight have you lost?"

Rusty jumped from the bed. "Down to one-ninety," he said. "Lost a whole damned Back Street Boy—a hundred and forty

pounds."

At only five-six, Rusty still carried a little weight, but even when he'd been over three hundred pounds, he'd been quick on his feet.

"The clothes won't do," I said, heading toward the door. "Let's go fix that."

"Wait," he said. "What the hell's wrong with my clothes? You ain't even looked at what I brought."

"I've seen everything you wear," I replied. "For what I have in mind, you're gonna need something else."

"Do you need me?" Savannah asked.

"Definitely," I replied. "Neither one of us is much of a fashionista."

"Oh, like I am?" she muttered, as they both followed me down the hall toward the elevator.

"For this, you have the perfect eye," I told her, grinning like a Cheshire cat.

"What is it you got in mind?" Rusty asked.

"Making *you* look like a lawyer," I replied. "With Savvy's help, of course."

"That's the second time you've done that," she said.

"What?" I asked, innocently.

"Called me Savvy. What gives?"

I pushed the button for the elevator, still grinning. "Oh, Rusty, for the duration, I'm Stretch Buchannan and this is my new wife, the former Savvy Montrose, from Port Royal, South Carolina. And you're my lawyer, James Thurman."

CHAPTER TWENTY-EIGHT

By the time they'd knocked on every door on every floor it was midafternoon as Thom and Katya returned to his penthouse suite on the sixth floor.

Due to the previous night's show, the mood it had put his pretend fiancée in, the booze he'd drunk, a night of amazing sex followed by a long drive and a morning dive, Thom had felt exhausted when they'd gotten back before noon.

Katya had been incredible and still full of energy and passion. He wasn't sure when it'd happened but at some point, he'd fallen for her, another man's wife.

But she hadn't been finished, and when they'd gotten back to the hotel, she'd dragged him room-to-room, smiling and glowing over their coming nuptials. All to make him even better known in Key West.

He ached to be with her as he opened the door to his suite once again. She was like a drug he'd become addicted to. He was already faking his own death, breaking contracts, and creating a fraudulent ID. There weren't many lines left that he wouldn't cross for her.

"I am telling you I am sure about this," Katya said over her shoulder as they entered the room. "I am very good at what I do."

She went straight to the glass sliding door and stood looking

out at the view. The thin material of her beach cover barely hid anything from his eyes as she silhouetted herself in the bright sunlight.

"You're talking about the tall guy in 510?" Thom asked.

"Stretch Buchannan," she replied. "Look him up on your phone."

"Why?"

She turned and glared at him. "Part of my job is to find... possible targets." She turned back to the view. "I could smell the money *and* his desperation."

"What makes you think he wants to disappear?" Thom asked, typing with his thumbs on his phone.

"I don't," she replied, turning back to the view. From the top floor, it was magnificent. She could see all the way to the ocean. "But providing new identities is only one of the things that Mike can do."

"Speaking of Mike," Thom said, moving beside her and looking out over the hotel's courtyard and the rest of southern Key West, "you said he wanted to do the transfer tonight."

"His contact at the hospital told him they have a possible look-alike. But we would have to move fast."

"When?"

"We will come back here at midnight," she replied, turning toward him and smiling seductively. "I will make sure everyone knows why. You will be able to watch the transfers take place on the computer and see the money appear in your new account. Then you can change the password and it is done."

"But that's really only the start," Thom said.

"It will all happen quickly after that," she said, smoothing the material of his coat over his chest. "I will not show up in the morning for the wedding, and you will discover what I have done.

216

MAN OVERBOARD

You will become angry and start drinking. Then you will drive to... the pull-off boat ramp thingy. It is just past Big Coppitt Key. Mike and another man will meet you there to put the body in the car with your wallet and watch. Later, the police will find your wrecked car, completely burned up with an unrecognizable body inside. And they will find the wallet and watch."

"Where will you be?" he asked.

"I have a wig," she said. "I will sneak out tonight and go back to Miami."

"The original plan was for you to pretend to be my wife for a couple of weeks."

She smiled knowingly. "Some parts of the plan are...fluid."

He put his hands on her hips, feeling an almost electrical spark. "So, uh, maybe you could sneak out of the hotel," he suggested, his hands slipping around her waist as she stepped into his embrace until their hips met. "Maybe instead of going back to Miami, you might catch the first flight to the Caymans."

She arched her back, slowly moving her hands up to his shoulders while pressing her thighs against his. "That will be fun," she said with a sigh, moving her face closer as she pushed her body against him. "Is that where you plan to stay?"

"Just a stop-off," he replied, breathing heavily against her neck as her left hand slipped down, found him, and began rubbing. "The South Pacific is where I'm headed...once I get the money."

She lightly kissed his neck. "I've dreamed of going there since I was little."

"Come with me," he said, as his hands roamed down her back. "I mean, you technically owe me two weeks, right?"

She pushed him away, nodding her head. "We could do that," she said breathlessly. "But we will need more money."

"More—?"

"If I leave Mike, he will kill me," she said, turning her back. "I cannot stay here. If we are to do this, it has to be permanent, and you must take me far away."

He stepped up behind her slipping his arms around her waist. "Yes, permanent. We'll go away together."

"I will have to work fast with Stretch tonight," she said, pressing herself back against him. "If I can find this man's weakness, I can come up with a way to separate him from his money very quickly." She broke free and turned to face him. "Did you find anything?"

Thom held up his phone and scrolled through several photos. "He definitely has money," he said, feeling uncomfortable about helping her, but wanting nothing more than to please her and be with her.

"What kind of money?" she asked.

"Big boats, big house, fancy cars, antique airplanes." Then he switched to another page. "And a lengthy arrest record. Mostly drug-related. He's about to go to trial and it doesn't look good. He's looking at twenty years, at best." Thom swiped the screen again. "And he'll be leaving behind his brand-new wife."

"The wife," she said, taking his phone in her hands, and reading the story. "Savvy Montrose? Horrible name."

Katya had been right. This guy had everything to lose and nothing to gain by sticking around for the trial. His lawyer had put up two million for bail. His best option—his only option—would be to run. Run far and fast. And that meant a new ID.

"Do you know how to get in touch with Mike's ID guy?" Thom asked.

She looked up from the phone. "Why?"

Thom pulled a roll of bills from his pocket. "Think he'd accept a

huge bonus for a rush job and his silence?"

"Sergei will do anything for money," she replied. "He is my brother."

Thom smiled and pulled her close again. "Contact Sergei. There's enough of their pictures and mugshots floating around he can use. Get him to make new IDs for the Buchannans. You can give them whatever new names you like. If he can do a fast turnaround, I'd bet everything I have that Mr. Stretch Buchannan would bite."

"It is very fast," she said.

"Tell him there's a hundred grand if he can get them to us before midnight," he said, slipping behind Katya again and pushing her against the glass. The idea of masterminding a quick bonus excited him. "New names and driver's licenses," he moaned as he flattened his body against her back, pressing her harder against the glass. "New passports, credit cards, everything."

She pushed back against him, moaning seductively. "With everything going on tonight," she said, looking down at several people lounging around the pool below them, "this might be our last time alone for days."

She tossed the phone on the big, king-sized bed, arching her back and pulling his hands up to her breasts as Thom smashed them against the glass and looked down at the people below.

CHAPTER TWENTY-NINE

Savannah stepped back and smiled. "You needed a trim anyway." Rusty rubbed his face, feeling the outline of the neatly trimmed beard. Savannah was good. The new shape gave him more of a square-jawed look and sharpened his features. His old beard had just been big and bushy.

"She's right," I said, holding up the new suit coat. "Try this on and have a look in the mirror."

Rusty slid the jacket on and moved over to the full-length mirror on the closet door.

"You look every bit the sharp-tongued Southern lawyer," Savannah said, then turned toward me. "Chyrel's idea was brilliant. That is, if they do any research on you."

"But lawyers got a smooth way of talkin'," Rusty said. "And they know about the law and stuff."

"Your part's gonna be super simple," I said. "Hang out in the periphery and make yourself as invisible as you can. When you see us talking to Smythe and Popovich, come and deliver the bad news."

"That's it?" he asked. "Just walk up and say, 'Oh, by the way, the prosecutor has an eyewitness and DNA and is offerin' up a deal?"

"The deal is ten years," I reminded him. "Just keep it fluid. I'll act surprised to see you, introduce you to the happy couple, and

then you pull me aside to give me the news. That part has to be loud enough for them to hear. Then you leave, drive home, or just come back up here."

"Think it'll work?"

I pulled "Savvy" close and smiled. "A man facing ten years without his new trophy wife will do just about anything to get out of it."

She pushed me away and slugged my shoulder. "You know I don't like that."

I laughed. "Probably why Chyrel wrote it into the outline and news story the way she did. Look, you can easily pass for ten years younger. What's the problem?"

"Like having a much younger woman for a wife makes her a trophy?"

"I am ten years older than you," I said, "but no, that's not how I see our marriage."

"So?"

"Stretch is a hotshot importer and exporter with tons of cash. To a man like him, a wife twenty years younger would be the very *definition* of—like it or not—a trophy wife."

She shoved me onto the bed. "Pedestal wife, maybe. Yeah, I think that's a little better. Or pedestal goddess."

"So, what happens after that?" Rusty asked.

I got up from the bed and shrugged. "Maybe nothing. She might not be paying attention when you drop the hint. Or maybe she's ordering a drink or something and doesn't hear it."

"A lot of mights and maybes," Rusty mumbled.

"She might be dumber than a box of rocks and not pick up on it," I added. "But I met her, and I don't think that's the case. We'll just have to play it loose."

"She just might see a golden ring dangling in front of her," Savannah said with a knowing grin.

"It's what she does," I agreed. "So, yeah, her mind should be prepared for identifying possible new victims. She and her husband are probably always on the lookout for desperate men who are wealthy and want to get disappeared."

"Disappeared is a past tense form of the verb disappear," Savannah said, pacing the floor. "You can't use it for future tense. Want to disappear or want to get relocated or something like that works. But not 'get disappeared.'"

Rusty looked at her. "You a grammar Nazi now?"

"It's how she gets when she's tense," I said.

"I am not!" she sputtered. "And I don't!"

"Get a grip, Savvy," I said, falling into the Stretch persona. "Just remember where ya come from."

She wheeled and then started laughing. "I'm sorry. This all sounds like it'll work. But yeah, I've got butterflies."

"Use that," I said. "Your new husband is about to be locked up for ten years and lose everything. Why wouldn't you be nervous and fidgety?"

"Yeah, *yeah*," Rusty agreed. "And me bein' the lawyer of a big shot smug druggler, about to lose a case that'll put my client in the clink for probably the rest of his life, I'd be pretty damned nervous, myself."

"That means," Savannah said, taking the crook of my elbow in her hands and looking at the three of us in the mirror, "the only one who has to pretend to be *large and in charge* is you, Stretch."

Reflected in the mirror, I could see out the glass sliding door behind us. Orange and pink light spread across the sky as the sun neared the horizon, painting the high, thin clouds with a delicate

brush. I looked at my watch. It was 2040 and only twenty minutes of daylight remained.

Daylight, I mused.

Since retiring from the Corps, my life had more or less revolved around the daily arc of the sun across the sky. It came with the territory. Sunrise, sunset, the rise and fall of the tides—they'd all conspired once to lure me away from the troubles of the mainland. Then the trouble quickly sucked me back in when I learned that paradise was a myth. And now, I was just weeks away from taking command of a ship that would travel to all the oceans, all around the globe. A ship that didn't have to stop for fuel and could handle the extremes the seas could throw at her with relative ease. The idea of more great adventures yet to come was inviting.

As was the spectacle of the sunset behind us.

"It's almost showtime," I said, and turned.

"Showtime?" Rusty asked.

I picked up three glasses from the tray next to the minibar, two fingers and a thumb inside the glasses, then grabbed three little mini bottles of Pusser's rum from the small shelf with my other hand.

"Sunset, brother," I said, heading toward the balcony. "Time to reflect."

The three of us stepped out onto the small, closed-in area and I put the glasses and bottles on the table as Rusty moved the chairs, so we were all looking west-northwest toward the setting sun.

"I don't think it's wise to be drinking," Savannah said.

"Well, that's crap," Rusty said, picking up one of the bottles and twisting the cap off. "Key West, Duval Street...Saturday night, rock and roll. We'd look out of place if we weren't half sunk."

I grinned over at him, pouring one of the mini bottles into a glass and raising it in salute. "To Russ."

"Sergeant Livingston," Rusty said, raising his.

A long time ago, he and I had been in a helo together on a training mission in Okinawa. Our platoon sergeant, Russ Livingston, who was Deuce's dad, stood up and gave the order, "Line of departure! Lock and load!" which meant for us to load our weapons and get ready, the landing zone was coming up. But what I'd heard, over the buffeting wind at the door and the giant helicopter's engine and rotor noise, was "Saturday night, rock and roll!"

I'd told Rusty about it later and it had since become our code phrase for "It's time to go."

As we watched the sun slipping toward the horizon, I thought back to the thousands of other sunsets I'd experienced all over the world. No two were ever the same. And though a good many had been watched with the same people, even the day's events made each of us just a little different, and the sun, wind, and sea never showed the same faces.

Below, I could see the hotel staff getting things ready for the party, bringing out more tables, and setting up a small buffet with snacks and finger food while guests lounged around the pool.

"There's no way this'll work," Rusty said, putting his glass down. "I mean, they'd only get tomorrow morning to do whatever it is you want 'em to do. Don't forget, you gotta be up at the school tomorrow afternoon."

I *had* forgotten. "That might not happen," I said.

"Word got around," he said. "The kids are lookin' forward to meetin' both of ya."

"First casualty of any battle," I said, as the sun finally touched the horizon.

"Is always the battle plan," Rusty agreed.

225

"I don't want to leave Chyrel in the lurch," I said, thinking. "So, we're moving to Plan L, or R, or 597, or whatever this makes it. So, if and when it ever comes up, we're going up island at noon for this proposed land deal tomorrow. That'll add more urgency, but we'll still be close."

We were all quiet as the last little bit of the sun was about to slip below the horizon. When I opened my eyes, I saw it.

Just as the last light of the sun winked out, there was a green flash. It lasted only a microsecond, but I knew I'd seen it. I turned to Savannah and we both smiled.

"There it was!" Rusty said, pointing. "Did you see it?"

"Yeah, we saw it," I replied, as the golden hour yielded to twilight. I raised my glass to Savannah. "To forever."

She clinked her glass to mine. "And one more sunset."

CHAPTER THIRTY

Savannah and I left the room first, taking the elevator down to the lobby, then walking out to the courtyard. It was a little before 2200, about twenty minutes after the 2130 start. That would allow us to do a little watching from the sidelines.

Rusty would wait until 2200 before he came down. So, until then, I wanted to avoid Smythe and Popovich seeing us but still be able to identify and stay close to them, keeping their whereabouts known until Rusty arrived.

We moved around the outside of the courtyard, beyond the pool, scanning the faces of several dozen people milling about in the low lighting provided by outdoor accent lights and the pool itself. After watching people come and go for twenty minutes, we'd moved around to the other side of the pool.

"There they are," Savannah said, taking my arm and turning me away from the bar area. "They're at the far side of the bar, talking to two other couples."

Though I had no way of knowing whether either of them would remember me, I knew they'd never seen Savannah, so keeping out of sight was strategic until I knew Rusty was in place. Unless Popovich had picked up on the breadcrumbs I'd dropped and done some research, it was unlikely either of them would recognize my wife. If

they did, I'd know they'd taken the bait.

"They're coming toward us," Savannah whispered.

Fish on! I thought, grinning a little.

"Rusty's just coming out of the elevator," I said. "Play it cool. If they looked me up on the Internet, they might know what you look like."

Savannah wore white, high-waisted slacks and heels, which made her long legs look even longer. She had on a pale blue top with a floral print design that she'd picked up while we shopped for Rusty's suit. The woman could wear anything off the rack and make it look like a designer label.

"Thank you for coming," Popovich said. "Stretch, right?"

I turned to face her. "Ah, the happy couple." Then I turned to Savannah. "Savvy, this is Mr. Thom Smythe and his fiancée, Katya Popova."

"Congratulations to both of you," Savannah said. "We haven't been married long, ourselves."

"Oh?" Popovich said, arching a perfectly shaped and trimmed eyebrow. "How long have you been married?"

"Ten months, next week," I replied, smiling and pulling Savannah toward me as Rusty came up from behind the couple.

I feigned a surprised expression, suddenly replacing my fake smile as Rusty approached and said, "Mr. Buchannan, sorry to bother you, but this can't wait."

I glanced at Smythe, then at Savannah. "Will you excuse me for just a second?"

Rusty and I stepped away from Savannah and the other couple. I could see them out of the corner of my eye as I kept my voice low. "Talk quietly for a few seconds," I whispered, but made it look as if I were admonishing him. "And make your actions seem like you're

explaining something important."

Rusty usually talked with his hands stuffed in his pockets or while polishing a beer mug. "This is really nuts," he said, shaking his hands pleadingly. Then he started ticking off his fingers. "I mean, it's nuts in a bunch of different ways. First, I don't know squat about being a lawyer and second, if I have to say a word directly to these people, I just know I'm gonna blow it."

"DNA?" I said, a bit too loud. Then I lowered my voice. "You're doing fine. Keep counting off on your fingers."

He continued mumbling, as he ticked off two more fingers.

"Ten years?" I nearly shouted. "What the hell kinda deal is that?"

Rusty took my elbow and pulled me behind a cluster of palms. "I ain't cut out for this, bro," he whispered very urgently. "I'm 'bout to piss my pants here."

I grinned at him, out of sight of the others. "It shows. And it should. You did great. Now, make yourself invisible. I'll let you know shortly if it worked."

He turned and headed for the lobby as I gathered as much concern as I could show, and then walked around the palms.

"What's wrong?" Savannah asked nervously.

It wasn't an act.

"I'll, um, tell you about it later," I said, mustering a forced smile for the "happy couple." "Just a little bad news from my lawyer."

"About the land deal you mentioned?" Popovich asked, either offering me a way out if she'd overheard me and Rusty talking, or just a dumb guess if she hadn't.

"Land...um, yeah," I said, feigning confusion. "He gave me some bad news about a deal I have closing tomorrow." Then I turned to Savannah. "It looks like we'll have to go up to Marathon tomorrow

before noon."

"If I may," Popovich said in a low voice. "I think I might be able to help you."

I could practically feel the tug on the line and hear the zing of the reel as she took the bait I'd offered.

"Thanks," I said, waving her off as she opened her small clutch purse. "It's nothing to worry about, just a relocation of the meet and a hefty increase in price."

She handed me what I recognized as a pair of passports. "Look inside."

I opened the top one, flipped a page and saw my own picture. But the name and information next to it weren't mine. When I opened the other one, it showed an image of Savannah along with a fake name.

Brad and Ursula Stone, of Albuquerque, New Mexico.

"What the—?" I muttered. "I don't understand."

She then handed me a pair of official-looking New Mexico driver's licenses. "If you can move fast," she whispered. "I can make you vanish."

"Make me...us...vanish?" I said, still acting confused.

"I am sure you must have considered it," Popovich said. "I know about your trial. I can make you cease to exist right now." Then she smiled at Savannah. "And I can launder and relocate your wealth, as well."

Smythe's face registered shock as he looked past us at something and then started to move slightly away from Popovich.

"What's she talking about?" Savannah asked, stepping in front of me as Smythe continued behind her, as if diving in slow motion.

Just as the nerves on the back of my neck tingled a warning, a shot rang out from behind me.

MAN OVERBOARD

People screamed.

Savannah's left shoulder jerked backward, and she turned her head to look at where the shot had come from.

A red stain bloomed in the white part of her blouse below her left shoulder. She stepped back, off-balance.

I grabbed her around the waist and wheeled, pulling her down to the ground under me as I searched the crowd for the gunman.

A commotion near the door caught my eye as Rusty stepped in front of a figure who was running toward the door. He planted his feet and clotheslined the guy, sending him crashing to the deck on his shoulders and the back of his head.

"Savvy!" I yelled, looking down at her.

As if a bomb had detonated, everyone, including Smythe and Popovich, scattered chaotically in all directions, eager to get away from ground zero, where I knelt, clutching my wife as she bled from what all my senses told me was a gunshot wound to the chest.

CHAPTER THIRTY-ONE

It seemed like forever but was probably only a few seconds before I heard sirens outside. When a security guard took over for Rusty, he dropped down beside me on the floor.

"How is she?" he asked.

"If you get this Neanderthal off me," Savannah said, "I'll show you how *she* is."

I looked at Rusty, desperately trying to hold myself together. "Did you get him?"

He grinned down at Savannah. "I got him, all right. I think I broke his freakin' neck and his neck 'bout dislocated my shoulder. He's in custody."

"Are you going to let me up, Jesse?" Savannah asked. "I don't think it's bad."

"No," I said. "No, you don't move. Wait for the corpsma... EMT guys to get here."

"Are you okay?" Rusty said, putting a hand on my shoulder.

The answer to that should have been obvious. Some guys got barbed by a stingray and learned from that one experience to not run headlong into the water. Some, like me, took a little longer. My not taking things seriously was what got Alex killed.

I was so sure this ID fraud thing would be a simple case. Lure the

bad guys into making a computer transfer and then have Chyrel suck the money back, along with everything else.

I'd failed to weigh the risk of putting not just myself in jeopardy, but my wife and best friend, as well.

I'd failed to look outside the box at other dangers, the actions of people I had no knowledge of, much less any control over.

I'd failed to get Robert Grant's money back, even if it was just a portion of it.

I'd failed to prevent Thom Smythe from losing everything he had.

I'd failed.

A cop in body armor came through the door, weapon drawn. He spoke to the security man, who pointed at us. Then he holstered his sidearm and came quickly over, as two EMTs waited outside.

"Everything's secure, Officer," Rusty said, rising to his feet. "The guy on the floor over there was the only gunman. I dropped him as he was trying to run away."

The cop knelt beside us and looked into Savannah's eyes. "Do you know why someone would want to shoot you, ma'am?"

"He was either nuts," I said, "or he was aiming at someone else, and my wife got in the way."

He looked up at me. "Any idea who that might have been?"

"No idea," I said, as Coral came rushing over, a man running along with her.

"What happened?" Coral asked, kneeling beside the cop and taking Savannah's hand. "Are you okay?"

"These are friends of mine, Archie," the man with Coral said to the policeman.

I suddenly recognized him. Bob Trebor, AKA Michael Grabowski.

MAN OVERBOARD

The two EMTs came in and moved everyone away from Savannah, quickly cutting her top open and bandaging her wounds. She'd been shot in the upper shoulder. I breathed a huge sigh of relief when I saw the wound. It had spread downward from her shoulder, before soaking into the loose-fitting blouse, making it look like she'd been shot in the heart.

When they'd finished, one of the EMTs ran outside

"We need to move you onto a stretcher for transport," the other one said, as his partner wheeled one in.

"I can walk," she protested.

"All GSW victims have to be transported," the second EMT said.

"You've been shot, Savvy," I said, then gathered my wits and turned to face the policeman. I took a small wallet from my cargo pocket and handed it to him. "My name's Jesse McDermitt. I'm a special investigator for Homeland Security. There are two guests at this hotel, Thom Smythe and a woman calling herself Katya Popova. He was about to fall victim to identity fraud and the woman, whose real name is Katrina Popovich, along with her husband, Mike Spencer, are the alleged perpetrators." I showed him the fake credentials. "I was about to make a deal for these when the shooting happened."

He looked down at my ID, something I'd hardly ever used. And this one was real. While the Caribbean Counterterrorism Command had been dismantled many years ago, those on the team had remained under the government's thumb ever since. They never liked to let go of anything.

"You'll want to go with your wife?" the cop asked, writing everything down. "We can straighten this all out later."

"Yes," I replied, as he handed back my wallet and the fake IDs. I took a card from the wallet and handed it to him. "You can reach me

at this number any time. I'll be with my wife until she's released."

The EMTs lifted the stretcher, letting the wheeled legs fold back down, and I started to follow after them.

"Agent McDermitt," the officer said, trotting to catch up. "Were you investigating these claims with your wife?"

She lifted her head and looked at me, nodding.

"Yes, I was," I replied. "If you round those two up, I have another victim all set to testify. But be warned. These are some very wealthy turd fondlers."

He grinned. "We'll start canvassing the hotel, sir."

I reached for the handle and pulled myself up into the ambulance, looking back. Rusty was standing with the cop at the lobby entrance.

"Start at the top, Officer," I said. "The penthouse suite. Coral over there can give you the descriptions." I looked at Rusty. "You coming?"

He ran and I extended a hand to haul him up. The driver closed the door and we started moving a few seconds later. Rusty and I quickly found places to sit.

The EMT started to work on Savannah, getting blood pressure and pulse readings, then connecting an IV.

"My name's Marco," the man said, smiling at her. "You were lucky. The bullet barely missed your collar bone and went through the meaty part of your shoulder—the upper trapezius. It's gonna be sore for a few days and you'll have to wear an immobilizer for maybe a couple of weeks, but it'll heal fine."

"Don't tell *him* that, Marco," she whispered, looking at me. "I can probably milk this for a month."

CHAPTER THIRTY-TWO

The ride to Lower Keys Medical Center took only a few minutes, but it felt like hours, as Marco carefully cleaned and rebandaged my wife's wounds, as his partner drove.

The bleeding had mostly stopped, leaving an ugly purple hole, puckered with coagulated blood. For the most part, Savannah kept her face turned away from it, facing me.

"Stop worrying," she said. "It hurts some, but I'll be okay."

"I shouldn't have let—"

"If you finish that sentence," she interrupted, "this guy will be bandaging you up, too. I'm here because I wanted to be."

The medic snickered as we made the last turn before the hospital.

I remembered that it was on this very street that I'd seen Savannah for the first time in nearly a decade. It was just after her sister had died, and she'd come down to claim the body. It was also the first time I'd met the daughter I never knew. Only I didn't know Flo was mine at the time.

The ambulance rocked and bounced as it turned under the portico of the emergency entrance. The back door opened as soon as we stopped, and Marco released the clamps holding the stretcher in place.

Two orderlies pulled Savannah out slightly, waiting for Marco to gather the IV bag and make sure she was ready to be moved.

Rusty and I climbed out and stood aside as they dropped the wheeled legs and began moving Savannah toward the door,

I held her hand, still feeling guilty for having gotten her into this situation.

At the door, a man in a suit stopped us. "Agent McDermitt?" he asked, putting a hand on my shoulder.

The EMTs accompanying Savannah and the orderlies stopped and Marco turned around. "Your wife's gonna be fine," he promised. "You can't go into the treatment room anyway. The desk will let you know when you can see her."

"I'm okay, Jesse," Savannah said, giving my hand a squeeze.

I released it and the two men wheeled her inside as I turned to the suit. "Who's asking?"

He produced a badge and ID. "I'm Lieutenant Morgan with the Monroe County Sheriff's Office. I have a few questions for you."

He looked familiar, shorter than me, pudgy around the middle, with a balding head of graying hair—the double-whammy of age. Then it hit me. He was the same investigator who'd handled the shootout at Key West Bight that ended up with several men dead, including GT Bradley, a former pro football player turned drug dealer. He'd come all the way from Pittsburgh looking for Grabowski.

"Have we met before?" the lieutenant asked.

I knew he'd remember it sooner or later. "It was raining," I said. "There'd been a shooting over at Key West Bight."

He snapped his fingers. "That's right. You and several other feds were involved. I need to ask you a few questions about what happened tonight."

"My wife's been shot, Lieutenant," I said. "Can we keep this short?"

"I've been informed by Key West PD that three people were taken into custody at La Concha," he said, as another ambulance started to pull in. "The shooter, who has yet to be identified, and is probably in that ambulance pulling in now, plus a couple was also taken in for questioning—a man and woman identified as Thomas Smythe and Katya Popova."

"Good. I'm glad they caught them. Her real name is Katrina Popovich. They were the subject of my investigation. At least she was. She and her husband, Mike Spencer, were running an identity fraud racket out of Miami."

"When does identity fraud fall under the jurisdiction of the Department of Homeland Security?"

I had to think fast. "A source informed us that the proceeds of these swindles might be going to an organization that's sympathetic toward terrorist cells operating in the Middle East." It was a convenient untruth, and I knew he'd figure it out sooner or later. "But you know how these tips are sometimes," I said, muddying the waters. "We were just conducting a preliminary investigation to get more information when we learned Smythe was about to fall victim."

"Uh-huh," he said, making a note in a small book. "And the tipster?"

"Confidential for now," I replied. "But when he testifies, it'll be revealed he was one of Popovich and Spencer's past victims. To the tune of several million dollars."

A phone jangled in his jacket pocket, and he pulled it out, checked the screen, and scrolled slowly.

Finally, he put the phone away as the second ambulance crew pulled the gunman from the back. His eyes were closed.

"That man has just been fingerprint IDed as Manuel Fuego,"

Morgan said. "He's a known enforcer in a Colombian drug cartel."

"Who could a Colombian hitman have been targeting at La Concha?" I asked rhetorically. "He definitely wasn't after my wife."

"Your Thomas Smythe is already talking," he replied, looking down at his phone again. "Apparently, he was involved in legit business dealings with people in that country and had decided he was going to cut his losses. Certain Colombians don't like it when people back out of a deal—the ones with ties to the *Nueva Generación* cartel in Jalisco for instance."

The gurney was wheeled past us, and I saw the man up close for the first time. He wasn't a man at all, just a boy about fifteen.

"The New Generation cartel?" I asked.

"Young, daring, and ruthless," Morgan replied.

"This identity fraud scam," I began, reaching into my pocket. I handed the phony passports and licenses to him. "Apparently, they look for wealthy men who are desperate to start over. I was posing as a Miami businessman and drug dealer, about to go on trial for manslaughter, and facing ten to twenty years."

Morgan looked at the IDs then handed them back. "Good forgeries," he said, then turned to Rusty. "What was your involvement in this?"

"I stopped the shooter as he was trying to run out the door," Rusty replied. "Name's Rusty Thurman."

"Yes, I know," the lieutenant said. "You have the same address as Agent McDermitt, here. Were you involved in his investigation?"

"I live on an island where there are no roads, much less mail delivery," I said. "I've used Rusty's address since the turn of the century."

"I was pretending to be his lawyer," Rusty said. "And not doing a very good job of it."

CHAPTER TWENTY-THREE

Several hours after the shooting, just after midnight, the questions had ended, and Savannah was released. Rusty'd said he was going to drive back straight from the hotel, so we could get some rest. Morgan drove the three of us to La Concha, so he could get his truck.

Though it was late, there were still a lot of people up and around and the hotel lobby was bustling. Key West bars don't even get into full swing on a Saturday night until it was Sunday morning. We'd received more than a few odd looks as we'd passed through the lobby. I'd been shirtless and Savannah had worn my new dress shirt, which was quite big on her.

Coral had found us at the elevator, and I'd asked if she and Bob could get away the following afternoon to come up to Grassy Key for a cookout.

By the time we'd gotten to our room, we'd both fallen asleep, exhausted. The next morning, we'd left Key West early, with Savannah napping uncomfortably most of the way. We arrived back at the Rusty Anchor before 0900 and Jimmy and Rusty came out to greet us as I helped Savannah climb down from the truck.

"We were all worried," Jimmy said, smiling at Savannah. "How do you feel?"

"It's still pretty numb from the local anesthetic they used," she replied. "Three stitches in front and four in the back. The ER doctor gave me some pills for the pain and told me not to use my arm for at least a week."

"Is my boat here?" I asked Jimmy, anxious to get Savannah home and in bed.

"Yeah," he replied. "I came down in the Grady."

"Good. I want to get her home and comfortable."

"The cookout starts in just a few hours," she protested. "We have to be there to—"

"No, we don't," I said, cutting her off. "You need to rest."

Her eyes flashed for just a moment. "Everything doesn't stop just because I got hurt, Jesse. We're going and that's that."

"Mom!" Alberto shouted as he came running from the backyard, Finn trotting along with him. He stopped a few feet away when he saw the sling. "Are you okay? What happened to your arm?"

Savannah knelt down and held her good arm out. Alberto quickly moved toward her and hugged her neck.

"A man shot me," she said, point blank. "He was trying to shoot someone else, but I got in the way."

Alberto looked up at me, accusingly. "He was trying to shoot you?"

"No," she replied. "Somebody altogether different. It had nothing to do with your dad or his work."

That was a lie. Savannah had never intentionally lied to the boy.

I went down to one knee and hugged them both. Then I took Alberto by his shoulders and held him at arm's length. "That's not exactly true, son," I began, then went on to tell him how we'd tried to get Robert's money back for him and put the swindlers in jail.

"Are we still going to the cookout?" he asked, after satisfying

himself with a few more questions and apparently putting the conversation behind him.

I could see he was still worried about Savannah and was about to tell him no, that we were going home, when the door opened and Robert stepped out, drying his hands on a towel.

"I'm very sorry," he said to Savannah. "Had I known this would happen, I never would have told any of you my sad story."

"Nonsense," she replied. "What happened to me wasn't anything to do with you." Then she looked down at Alberto and smiled. "And yes, we're most definitely going to the cookout."

A few regulars came out and crowded around Robert and Savannah, all talking excitedly.

Jimmy pulled me aside and said, "Ever since he heard about what happened, it's like he's a totally different person. He really wants to talk to you about teaching at the school."

"Why me?" I asked. "I have almost nothing to do with the school."

"Perception is reality, man. Isn't that what you say? Your last name's on the door."

"Okay then, why would he want to work for me?" I asked, still a bit puzzled. "I failed him, and we didn't get his money back."

Robert broke away from the group and approached us. "I'm glad she wasn't hurt too badly," he said. "I'd never be able to live with myself, otherwise."

"Jimmy says you want to work at the school?" I asked.

"I know I don't deserve to ask, after what happened. But I spent part of the day there yesterday, and Chyrel told me all about how the school works. I'd like to help if I can."

"What about your money?" I asked.

"Being penniless and homeless is kind of freeing in a way," he

replied with a smile, then shrugged. "I made it once and can do it again. But you know what? I don't think I want to. I talked to a few of the kids at the school. Most of them are from fractured homes, some were living on the street. They have a lot less than me and are more deserving of the effort. Being penniless means I'm worth nothing to the people I owed and since being here, I've learned a thing or two about what it really means to be a part of the community. I can give of my time to teach kids to sail."

My eyes drifted over to *Salty Dog*. She was a beautiful boat and she'd carried me, and later, me, Savannah, and Flo, all over the Caribbean. She'd held the three of us in close proximity to one another, allowing us to slowly come together as a family. She'd also allowed us adequate space to be alone at times.

Salty Dog set the limits and terms, keeping all three of us busy while the rest of the world went through self-imposed isolation. She'd shown us beautiful stretches of white sand, completely devoid of even a single footprint. She'd taken us to where mountains rose right up out of the sea. And she'd let us experience long, healthy, barrier reefs teeming with life, that were too far from the civilized world for any dive boat to reach.

We'd become a single entity during long passages over deep blue waters and now *Salty Dog* would bring others together. Kids from the slums and ghettos that Florida didn't want the tourists to see. She'd use her steadfastness against the elements as mute testimony to what her young handlers could aspire to.

"Feel like going for a sail?" I asked Robert, who turned, following my gaze.

Just then, a large gray van pulled into the lot, led by Chyrel, driving one of Tank's cars. He'd owned four, none of which was newer than fifty years old. This one was a light blue 1968 Camaro SS.

MAN OVERBOARD

A bunch of teens and adolescent kids climbed out of the van and followed Chyrel toward us.

"I hope it doesn't hurt too much," Chyrel said, hugging Savannah lightly. Then she turned to me before the kids got within earshot. "The gunman had been sent to give Smythe a message, not kill him. His target was Popovich, or Popova as it were. To hurt him and force him to continue the deal."

"Whaddya ya know," Rusty said. "Even the cartel fell for all the stories and media hype. They actually thought he cared about her."

"Are these the kids from the school?" Savannah asked, as we were quickly encircled.

Chyrel introduced all nine of them, including the two girls we'd met on the dock, a meeting that now seemed like it had happened a month ago.

Then she turned toward me and Savannah. "This is Jesse and Savannah McDermitt."

The kids clapped their hands; some even whooped. Savannah nestled against my side, slipping her good arm around my waist. "It's not far to the school," she said. "I'm okay. Really. And being on the water will probably help us both come to grips with what happened."

I looked at my watch. People would start arriving at Chyrel's house in a couple of hours. She lived right next to the school, and both had docks in twelve feet of water. It wasn't far as the gull flies—maybe two miles—but we'd have to go the long way around, under the Seven-Mile Bridge and then dodge around the shallow banks north of Key Vaca.

Easy enough with a good crew.

Or a large, eager crew.

I looked back at the kids. "Who wants to sail with me, Savannah,

and Robert to deliver *Salty Dog* to the school?"

They all shouted and clapped hands.

The next two hours were full of instructions and tours, as we split the nine kids into groups of three for bridge, deck, and galley operations. All of them worked together to cast off lines and raise the sails.

A stiff, twenty-knot wind blew dead out of the east, and we were still in the canal when I ordered the mainsail hoisted. After Savannah showed Robert which blocks were which, he got the kids lined up and quickly hoisted the mainsail old-school style. The halyard was around one of the electric winches, but the power was turned off.

The main snapped and tugged as she came up, then filled quickly and the boat began to heel. I compensated on the wheel, keeping us pointed directly into the channel, then put the engine in neutral and shut it off.

"Engines off," I said. "We're under wind power."

"Really?" a kid of about fifteen asked. "We're not slowing down."

"*Salty Dog* can go a lot faster under sail than she can on the engine," I told him, looking up at the tell-tales sewn into the lightweight fabric of the sail. "The engine's only for getting to and from the dock or anchorage."

I was about to ask Robert to trim the main when he, too, looked up and took care of it without being told. I sensed that the school was not only going to get a fine sailing vessel, but a decent instructor as well.

He went forward, anticipating my command, checking the starboard jib sheet as he went to make sure it was outside everything else, all the way back to the aft winch.

MAN OVERBOARD

When he went aft, I called out, "Unfurl the headsail!"

Robert selected three kids at random and showed them what to do. In minutes, using only manpower, we had the two sails trimmed and were making a good six knots on a beam reach.

Savannah stood beside me at the helm, holding onto a Bimini brace with her good right arm. Her hair blew across her shoulder as she gazed seaward.

She was going to be okay. But only by a few inches. Had the bullet struck a little lower, she could have died. I'd been reckless allowing her to take part in what I was doing and had almost gotten her killed. Sure, she'd insisted on it, but in the end I was responsible.

"Code D?" she asked, turning toward me with a smile.

"Huh?" I looked off to the west at East Sister Rock. "Yeah. Another half mile."

"The wind's right," she said. "We can show these kids everything in a quick, short sail."

Robert leaned in under the Bimini. "Wing and wing for the downwind run to the bridge, Captain?"

"No," I replied. "In the far forward hatch, you'll find a Code Zero and a Code D. Break 'em both out. We'll put up every sail in her inventory within the next four miles."

"On it," he said, moving along the side deck and picking out several of the kids to help.

When he had the bags up on deck and the halyard clipped to the Code D, he nodded.

"Hoist the spinnaker!" I shouted.

Robert repeated it to the two girls—Andrea and Kris—who were standing by at the mast. They quickly raised the furled spinnaker to the top of the mast and tied it off; the giant yellow sail filled with air as I turned downwind, clear of East Sister Rock.

The Code D had my charter logo stitched into the fabric—a big, laughing skull, complete with head bandana and sunglasses. Behind it, instead of crossed bones or swords, there were crossed fishhooks.

"Douse the main and jib!" I called out.

It was easy to pick out which kids besides Andrea and Kris had sailed with Naomi and her friend. While they and the three boys didn't know the mechanics of it, they quickly figured it out, and the mainsail came down first as Robert began furling the foresail.

"Work those winches together," Robert said to the two teams. "No matter which way the boat points, keep the headsail pointed evenly downwind from both sides."

As we sailed downwind, Chyrel took half of the kids down into the cabin to show them the galley and the rest of the boat, while I explained the helm, chart plotter, and wind instruments to the other half.

"Remember what Robert said about keeping the big spinnaker pointed evenly downwind?" I asked as I turned slightly to port.

"It's not even now," one of the boys said. "And it's flapping. Should we crank it in on that side?"

I put my middle and index fingers on two of the buttons controlling the port and starboard winches for the spinnaker sheets. "No need," I said, pushing the buttons and swinging the sail back into an asymmetrical shape, slightly off the starboard side.

"You mean we didn't have to pull on all those ropes?" another boy asked.

"Lines," I corrected him. "Each line has its own name, so it doesn't get confused with another one. I just adjusted the port and starboard spinnaker sheets. You've got a bit of an idea now about what each one is and what it does. That's called 'learning the ropes.'"

"But they're not ropes," he said, with a hint of sarcasm.

"Exactly. If you don't pick up anything else today, you're a better sailor already."

"So, this boat's faster using sails than the engine," the older boy asked. "How fast can it go?"

"She's a displacement hull, so not very fast," Jimmy explained. "You take the square root of the waterline length— in the case of *Salty Dog* that's fifty-eight feet, six inches. The square root of that is about seven and a half. Then you multiply that by 1.34, giving her a maximum hull speed of just over ten knots, or eleven and a half miles per hour. To go any faster, she'd have to climb her own bow wave and that means planing, like in our fishing skiffs."

"That ain't very fast," the boy said, still a bit snarky.

"But she can maintain that speed indefinitely," I said. "As long as the wind blows.

"How far can this boat go?" a younger boy asked.

"At ten knots," I said, "about two hundred and forty miles a day or almost seventeen hundred miles in a week."

"That's from here to Ecuador on the Pacific coast of South America," Jimmy added.

"That's about right," I agreed, though I'd never plan on making that sail in just one week. Transiting the canal could often involve a long wait. "But *how far* depends more on how much food we have down in the galley," I continued. "And how many people are eating it. But Savannah and I, along with our daughter, sailed more than two months without stopping anywhere where there was a store. We trolled for fish while underway and caught lobster and speared fish in little coves at dozens of uninhabited islands."

"You'd have to stop for water, at least," the older boy said.

"What's your name?" I asked him.

"Shaquille," he replied. "From Opa Locka."

I pointed at a bench astern the helm. "Open up that bench seat," I told him.

He raised the seat and looked inside. "What's all that?"

The bench seat provided quick access, via a vertical ladder, to the engine room directly from the cockpit.

"That's the engine room access," I said. "You see the shiny silver and blue thing on the port side, just forward of the ladder?"

He moved around to the side for a better angle. "Yeah, the thing with small steel pipes running to it?"

"It's called a reverse osmosis unit," I replied. "That's just a fancy name for a water maker. It takes water from the ocean, filters the salt out of it, and pumps it into the boat's water tanks. *Salty Dog* can make fifty gallons a day of fresh drinking water and will only run out if the RO unit breaks down or the ocean dries up. And if *both* are taken care of properly, through regular maintenance and good ocean stewardship, that won't happen."

"Ocean stewardship?" he asked, lowering the seat and moving up beside me. "What's that?"

"Look around, man," Jimmy said. "Water covers more than seventy percent of our little rock, floating through infinite space. Through a symbiotic relationship—each ocean dweller having a part in the balance—the sea produces more than half the oxygen in the air we breathe. Seawater evaporates and comes down as rain, providing us with drinking water. Yet, there aren't many places in the vastness of all that water where you won't see man's impact on the ocean."

"A good steward of the sea," I said, "will always leave Mother Ocean better than they found her."

He looked at me and smiled, white teeth a sharp contrast to his

ebony skin. "That's pretty deep, man."

I chuckled. "Good pun."

He looked puzzled, then grinned, finally getting what he'd said.

Stepping aside, I offered Shaquille the helm and he readily accepted, taking the large destroyer wheel in both hands.

I pointed to the compass. "Keep us on this heading, or just pick something on the horizon ahead of us and steer toward it."

I looked around at the faces of the young people on my boat. "Look, I'm no scientist, but neither was Einstein when he was your age. I'm just a guy who enjoys being on the water. You don't have to be a scientist to see the impact of humans on the ocean, especially the reefs. If each of us were to just do that one simple thing—leave the ocean better than we found her—we could restore the balance. It doesn't matter who you are or where you come from. Good stewardship is the responsibility of all of us. It's not like we have another planet to go to when we destroy this one."

Shaquille looked out over the water. We were far enough from any land that they appeared as small specks on the horizon. "No place to go..." he muttered.

CHAPTER THIRTY-FOUR

The kids decided themselves to take the *Dog* to Chyrel's house, so they could show it off to all the people who were coming. We'd dropped and bagged the spinnaker when we made our turn to the north and went under the bridge, then raised the Code Zero, along with the small staysail and mizzen sail, for the two upwind legs. *Salty Dog* beat to windward a lot better than many boats her size. Each one of the kids got a turn at the wheel, got to furl, trim, and unfurl sails, and have a complete tour below deck during the four-mile sail.

With *Salty Dog* finally at the dock, Chyrel and Jimmy dragged a hose out and the kids busied themselves washing down the entire boat, even jumping in the water and using a soft brush on her hull. And with Robert and Jimmy to guide them, everything was stowed correctly and securely. Alberto even showed several of the kids how to make neat coils of the excess dock lines, instead of just letting them lie on the dock.

"You're sure this is what you want to do?" Savannah asked as we stood in the backyard, watching the youngsters work and play with enthusiasm.

"I think this is exactly what the old girl needs," I replied.

"Dat is a fine boat," Kyndall said, joining us on the lawn. "Uncle told me how it come to belong to yuh, and I tink dese chi'drens

gonna take good care of her."

"You know boats?" Savannah asked her.

"Me mama used to fish wit Uncle on his boat when she was little," Kyndall replied, her accent not as pronounced as Rufus's, but still with that melodic, sing-song sound of the islands. "Me bruddah run dat boat now and I and I work wit him many summers."

"Your mother worked with Rufus when he was a fisherman?" Savannah asked.

"No, ma'am. Mama is Jamaican for gran-mudduh."

I looked at her, a bit surprised. "Wait. Your grandmother fished on Rufus's boat when she was a girl?"

"Dat right," she replied. "Uncle fished until he was 'bout my age, if I remember di stories right. Den he staht cookin'."

"So, he's not your grandmother's brother?"

She laughed. "Mama's bruddah? No, Cap'n. He is Mama's uncle."

I had no idea how old Kyndall was, but she was at least thirty. Even if each generation gave birth to the next at the age of sixteen, that would make Rufus at least eighty years old.

"How old is Rufus?" I asked, a bit bewildered.

She only shrugged. "Not sure, but Uncle talks sometimes 'bout olden tings."

"You don't know how old he is?" Savannah asked. "What kind of olden things?"

"I and I don' tink even Uncle know jest how old him is," she replied. "I 'member hearin' him talk 'bout meetin' Marcus Garvey when he was a young mon. He say Marcus Garvey swept him up wit di whole Rastafari movement when it just stahted."

"That was in the thirties," I said, dumbfounded. "If he was a young man then, he'd be close to a hundred now."

"One 'undred, two 'undred—who knows?" Kyndall said with a

smile, then headed back over to where her uncle, or great-grand uncle, was working under a tent.

"A hundred?" Savannah asked, as we walked toward the makeshift kitchen. "That can't be. Look at him!"

Alberto was with Rufus when the old Jamaican took a small spoon and dipped it into a sauce he was preparing. He took a small taste of it, then squatted down to Alberto's level and let him try it, asking what he thought.

"Mmm," Alberto hummed with a grin. "I think it's just right."

Rufus rose easily and gracefully from his squatting position and patted Alberto on the back, smiling down at him. "Dat is what I and I tink, as well."

"Your niece has done a great job, don't you think?" Savannah asked.

"Yes, Miss Savannah," he replied. "She a hahd worka, dat girl is."

"The apple doesn't fall far from the tree," I added.

He smiled, showing his gapped teeth as white and perfect as any I'd ever seen. "Yuh are one to speak 'bout trees, Cap'n," he said. "Di mighty lion will soon root itself like di mahogany, spreading wide across di ground and deep into di rock."

Rufus often talked in riddles like that, and I was about to ask him what he meant when Chyrel joined us under the tent.

"Can I talk to you for a sec?" she asked.

I nodded and we went out into the yard.

"They screwed it up," she said, shaking her head.

I looked around. "Screwed what up?"

"Key West's finest let both Smythe and Popovich go, thinking they were both victims."

"You gotta be kidding," I said. "How'd that happen?"

"I don't think they've even figured it out yet. But they picked Smythe up an hour after the shooting, trying to board a plane to

Grand Cayman. She wasn't with him. On a hunch, I contacted a friend with Miami-Dade, and it turns out Mike Spencer has also disappeared."

A complete failure, top to bottom. I'd hoped that with Katya's arrest, and the help of the police in Miami, the two would be charged at the very least. Even if Robert didn't get his money back, he'd at least have that.

I looked over to the boat, where he was squirting down the kids on the foredeck, as they laughed and scrubbed the deck. He was more animated than I'd seen him all week. Being around young people would do that to a person.

A white Jeep Wrangler pulled into the driveway and parked. I recognized it instantly and called out to Savannah. When she looked my way, I pointed, already heading toward the driveway.

"Flo!" Savannah shouted and started to run.

She winced in pain after a few steps, then slowed to a walk.

"What are y'all doing here?" I asked, as she and David climbed out.

"You're hurt!" Flo said, gently hugging her mother.

"We have the week off from classes," David said. "So, we decided at the last minute to drive down and get some research help from Chyrel. She told us what was going on here today."

Savannah and I explained what'd happened down in Key West and Flo gave me the stink eye more than once, though I already felt bad enough.

Over the next hour, more people arrived, and Chyrel made sure to introduce us to each one. The food was delicious and the weather perfect, or as perfect as it gets in the Keys in July.

I stood near the dock, gazing out at *Salty Dog*, her brightwork gleaming in the afternoon sun. She was fully capable of sailing

around the world, and I'd sailed her over ten thousand miles, circumnavigating the Caribbean in both directions. She was a magnificent vessel and still had many thousands of miles yet to put under her keel.

"That's quite the donation," a man said, joining me at the foot of the dock. "A true blue-water cruiser."

I remembered his name was Gary.

"That she is, Gary," I said. "The cruiser part, anyway. I only paid about two hundred dollars for her and she's exactly the same today as she was then. Maybe with a couple of minor upgrades."

"I'm building a boat," he said, still admiring the *Dog's* lines. "Of course, it won't be anything like this, but I'm good with my hands. I own a construction business up in Palm Beach."

Gary Burch, of course, I thought. Jimmy had told me about him.

I turned to face him. "You went through this school, didn't you?"

When he met my gaze, I saw a younger version of myself in his eyes. He was tall and fit, his skin tanned dark by long days in the sun. In those eyes, I saw the same drive and determination that had carried me through many tough years.

"Yes, I did," Gary replied. "And it saved my life."

"Jimmy told me a little about you. You've done well."

"All thanks to coming here and picking up a rod and reel for the first time. I was with a guy named Dink. Do you know him?"

"Be careful around him on land," I said.

Gary laughed. "Yeah, but he's a great teacher. About more things than just fishing. My second day out with him, another guy joined us named Scott Grayson. He was a Marine, like you, but had once been an inner-city kid like me."

"I know Scott very well," I said.

"He kept me out of prison, and Dink gave me a new direction."

I wasn't aware so many of the people I knew were involved with the school. It was natural for Tank and Chyrel to help out; they lived right next door. And now Tank was gone, and Chyrel pretty much ran the school.

"Anyway," Gary said, extending his hand, "I just wanted to thank you for creating this school. Most of these kids were lost when they got here—just like I'd been."

We shook hands, and he turned to walk over to a group of kids sitting on the grass; they quickly made room for him in their little circle.

Looking over at the tents, I spotted Savannah helping Kyndall serve meals to some of the youngsters who were coming back for seconds. Limited to one arm, she was dipping a corn cob and putting it on one of the girls' plates. She laughed at something the girl said, then put down the tongs, leaned over the table and pulled the young woman in for a friendly hug.

On the far side of the yard, Shaquille had produced a Frisbee and was showing Alberto how to throw it. Finn made it easier for them by running after the disk and bringing it back to them.

Flo and David sat cross-legged on the grass with Jimmy and Robert, all laughing over something Jimmy had said.

Just then, Finn barked, drawing my attention. Alberto was showing Shaquille something he'd pulled out of his backpack. Even from across the yard, I recognized one of the headsets from *Ocean Hopper*. Except it was different. Roberto had Finn sit down in front of him, then fitted the headset over the Lab's big head, adjusting straps that the headsets on my plane didn't have. Finn looked over at me and I nearly laughed. Alberto had solved Finn's problem when flying in a noisy airplane.

I looked all around the yard and smiled. I don't know why, but I did.

Just being back on these boney little islands seemed to have a pleasing effect. All seemed right with the world.

Except for Mike Spencer and Katrina Popovich. I didn't like loose ends.

My phone chirped and vibrated in my pocket. When I pulled it out, I saw that it was Jack Armstrong.

"I heard what happened," he said when I answered. "How is she?"

"Still a little shook up," I lied. Savvy really was a badass. "Just a shoulder wound and she'll be fine in a couple of weeks."

"That's the reason I called," he said. "I don't think recuperating on a ship is a good thing. I'd like it if you remained at your home with her for a few more weeks."

"What about the sea trials?" I asked.

"I spoke with Nils Hansen before calling you," Jack said. "He's having regrets about retiring. He can manage the sea trials until both you and Savannah can return, one hundred percent recovered. Little Alberto and Finn as well, of course."

I looked over at Savannah, who smiled and waved, already at a hundred percent mentally. These islands seemed to have the same effect on her. I was a lucky man and I'd almost lost her.

"Good," I said, waving back across the yard at my wife and smiling at her. "The job's his permanently. *I'm* retiring."

THE END

Don't miss the next Jesse McDermitt Caribbean Adventure tale, *Cast Off*, coming in November 2022.

AFTERWORD

Sometimes, I get the idea for a book from a song. In this case, the song was *Hollow Man*, by the Boat Drunks. I always wondered what the circumstances were that led the guy in the song to arrive at the dock and charter the boat, then never show up. He seemed so lost and empty inside. The more I thought about it, the more I had to write about such a person.

Then I got to thinking about how easy my earlier books were to write and how fun the setting was—right there in Marathon, the heart of the Florida Keys. Sure, it's not the Caribbean and this is the Caribbean Adventure Series, but at least part of it does take place within that beautiful sea. They say you can never go home again, and it's been thirty years since I lived there, but each time I go back, it *does* feel like home. And I think Jesse feels that way, too.

My wife, our youngest daughter and I went on a cruise last March. Not on one of those behemoths you'll see at the dock in Key West or Paradise Island or Cancun, but a 366-foot, four-masted barquentine—a clipper ship—called *Star Flyer*, with the Star Clipper Cruise Line. We sailed the British Virgin Islands and Eastern Caribbean for a week, dropping anchor and going ashore in remote spots those big cruise ships only wish they could go. I was able to climb the mast and hoist sails while our daughter piloted the ship. It was an experience we'll not likely forget, and some of the islands we visited and people we met will be included in the next Jesse book, *Cast Off*, coming in early November.

Today is Easter and I'm writing this afterword eleven weeks before the release of this book. By the time you read these words, *Elusive Charity* will have been out for a couple of months. Thanks to all of you for making it, and hopefully this book, a success.

I want to first recognize a core group of friends who are the first to read my stories after me. These folks come from different walks of life and contribute so much to the authenticity of my stories. In no particular order, much appreciation is given to Jason Hebert, Katy McKnight, Kim DeWitt, Glenn Hibbert, Dana Vihlen, John Trainer, Charles Höfbauer, Alan Fader, and Drew Mutch.

I pushed to get this ready ahead of schedule, to give my editor more time with it, as she deals with a family illness. I'm hoping that when you read this, her struggle will be a distant memory. Thanks, Marsha Zinberg, for all you do. I hope to see you at the beach in September.

Thanks also to my final proofreader, Donna Rich, for her talent at spotting the one or two things that will make a better read that everyone else overlooked, or more likely that I messed up in the editorial rewrite.

Once I finish the second rewrites, the manuscript goes on to Nick Sullivan's studio to record the audiobook. Though it's not a part of his job description, he inevitably finds a few things that would sound better in the audiobook. If it sounds better, it will read better, so I always wait until Nick has finished before sending a manuscript to Aurora Publicity for formatting into whatever form of media you're getting this.

A huge thanks to my teams at Down Island Press and Aurora Publicity. I greatly appreciate your tireless efforts in getting my books to my readers in whatever way they want, through whatever channel they use, and in whatever corner of the world they live. Thanks to your efforts, my books have been read on six of the seven continents. Jimmy Buffett's supposed to be doing a show in Antarctica; maybe one of his fans will have one of my books to read before and after the show.

Throughout our twenty-one years of marriage, I've always known my biggest supporter was my wife. She stood with me for thirteen years as a trucker and now coming up on nine years as a storyteller. Greta is the rock on which our family's foundation is built. Without her in my life, I'd be the "hollow man" in the song.

Many thanks to our kids, Nikki, Laura, Richard, and Jordan, for understanding when I've forgotten something while lost in a story. Thanks also to our grandkids, Kira, Lexi, Jack, and Emily, as well.

Lastly, Nick Sullivan and I just started our third year at TalkWrite, and I'd like to invite you to follow us on YouTube where on the first Monday of every month, we do a live show together with other authors, narrators, and folks in the publishing industry.

Just go to YouTube, search my name, go to the channel, and subscribe. Don't forget to click the notification bell so you'll get a message just before the next show starts.

The Gaspar's Revenge Ship's Store is open.

There, you can purchase all kinds of swag related to my books. You can find it at

WWW.GASPARS-REVENGE.COM

If you'd like to receive my newsletter, please sign up on my website.

WWW.WAYNESTINNETT.COM.

Once a month, I'll bring you insights into my private life and writing habits, with updates on what I'm working on, special deals I hear about, and new books by other authors that I'm reading.

The Jerry Snyder Caribbean Mystery Series

Wayward Sons

The Charity Styles Caribbean Thriller Series

Merciless Charity
Ruthless Charity
Reckless Charity
Enduring Charity

Enduring Charity
Vigilant Charity
Lost Charity
Elusive Charity
Forced Charity

The Jesse McDermitt Caribbean Adventure Series

Fallen Out
Fallen Palm
Fallen Hunter
Fallen Pride
Fallen Mangrove
Fallen King
Fallen Honor
Fallen Tide
Fallen Angel
Fallen Hero
Rising Storm
Rising Fury

Rising Force
Rising Charity
Rising Water
Rising Spirit
Rising Thunder
Rising Warrior
Rising Moon
Rising Tide
Steady As She Goes
All Ahead Full
Man Overboard
Cast Off

Made in the USA
Columbia, SC
10 August 2022